DEATH OF JEZEBEL

DEATH OF JEZEBEL

CHRISTIANNA BRAND

With an Introduction by
Martin Edwards

Poisoned Pen
PRESS

Introduction © 2022, 2023 by Martin Edwards
Death of Jezebel © 1949 by The Estate of Christianna Brand
Cover and internal design © 2023 by Sourcebooks
Front cover image © NRM/Pictorial Collection/Science & Society Picture Library

Published by Poisoned Pen Press, an imprint of Sourcebooks,
in association with the British Library
P.O. Box 4410, Naperville, Illinois 60567-4410
(630) 961-3900
sourcebooks.com

Death of Jezebel was first published in the UK in 1949 by The Bodley Head, London.

Library of Congress Cataloging-in-Publication Data

Names: Brand, Christianna, author. | Edwards, Martin, writer of introduction.
Title: Death of Jezebel / Christianna Brand ; with an introduction by
    Martin Edwards.
Description: Naperville, Illinois : Poisoned Pen Press, [2023] | Series:
    British Library crime classics
Identifiers: LCCN 2022061973 (print) | LCCN 2022061974
(ebook) | (trade paperback) | (epub)
Subjects: LCSH: Cockrill, Inspector (Fictitious character)--Fiction. |
    Police--England--Kent--Fiction. | LCGFT: Detective and mystery fiction.
    | Novels.
Classification: LCC PR6023.E96 D43 2023 (print) | LCC PR6023.E96 (ebook)
    | DDC 823/.912--dc23/eng/2023
LC record available at https://lccn.loc.gov/2022061973
LC ebook record available at https://lccn.loc.gov/2022061974

Printed and bound in the United States of America.
SB 10 9 8 7 6 5 4 3 2 1

INTRODUCTION

Death of Jezebel is an ingenious "impossible crime" mystery by Christianna Brand which is widely admired by connoisseurs of crime fiction. Originally published in the UK in 1949, the book has been vanishingly rare for decades; those copies that could be found have usually been sold for eye-watering sums. Bloggers and other fans have long bemoaned the novel's limited availability, while the lucky few who have laid their hands on a copy have waxed lyrical about the brilliance of the plot. Thanks to the British Library, readers by the thousand now have the chance to own the book for themselves and to see what all the fuss was about.

Right at the start, in characteristically bold fashion, Brand presents us with a short cast of characters beginning with Johnny Wise "who died; and to avenge whose death two of the following also died—and one was a murderer." Since only seven other individuals are named, and the motive has been spelled out, you might think that it would not be too difficult to identify the culprit. Don't be over-confident, though—the plot is fiendishly complex.

In a brief prologue, dated 1940, we learn what happened to Johnny. Then we are plunged into events that take place after the Second World War. The setting is an exhibition at the Elysian Hall, which is "in process of conversion into a small township of model homes suitable for the Heroes of England." Edgar Port is masterminding a pageant featuring knights of old. But preparations are disrupted when an anonymous message turns up, warning that Perpetua Kirk is going to be murdered. Inspector Cockrill—visiting London to attend a conference—arrives on the scene, but a further note is addressed to him, telling him to "wait till the opening night of the exhibition. Isabel, Perpetua, Anderson, which of them will be the first to die?"

Tension mounts as the central characters find themselves living "through the long hours, crawling with half incredulous, wholly uneasy fear." On the day of the pageant, Cockrill takes up a favourable position in front of the stage, waiting "with bored impatience for the fun to begin. The English and their pageants! Nobody enjoyed them, nobody ever knew what they were intended to represent, but it was in the national character to produce and witness them." Here, as so often with vintage detective fiction, the twenty-first-century reader is allowed a peek at a vanished world.

An intriguing ingredient of the novel is that it features *two* of Brand's detectives. Inspector Charlesworth, who first appeared in her debut novel, *Death in High Heels*, is also involved in the investigation, and the contrast between the two policemen is amusingly handled. Charlesworth, we are told, is of the "Hendon" school; in other words, he is a product of Hendon Police College whose modern high-calibre training prompts scepticism about the methods of a veteran country policeman such as Cockrill. When they meet, he breezily reminds the older man about the murder puzzle Brand recorded in *Green for Danger*:

> *"It was you who made such a muck of that hospital case down in Kent!" Innocent of the slightest intention to wound, he shook the Inspector thoroughly by the hand. "Delighted to have you down here. Hang around?"*
> *"Thank you," said Cockie, austerely.*

Suffice it to say, however, that Cockrill gets the last laugh. Brand always delighted in playing with the tropes of Golden Age detective fiction, and never more so than in *Death in Jezebel*. Not only is this a "closed circle" mystery, with a small and well-defined pool of suspects, it also presents a variant on the locked-room puzzle. As Cockrill says:

> *"This is a projection 'sealed room' mystery. The scene of the murder was bounded on one side by a stage, under the observation of several thousand pairs of eyes; and on the other by a locked door, with somebody sitting on guard on the other side of it. The murderer must have been within those confines."*

For good measure, Brand juggles multiple false (but superficially plausible) solutions to the puzzle before finally revealing the truth.

Mary Christianna Milne was born in Malaya in 1907. At that time the country, which is referenced in *Death of Jezebel*, was a British protectorate where her father, Alexander Brand Milne, was working as a "visiting agent" on the tea plantations. When she was two, her mother died and she was taken back to England to be looked after by her aunt, who had five children. The young girl was especially close to her cousin Ted, who in later life became well-known as Edward Ardizzone, the artist and illustrator. She was educated at a Franciscan convent in Somerset and also spent part of her youth in India.

The crime-fiction researcher Tony Medawar has written a short biography by way of an introduction to *The Spotted Cat and Other Mysteries* from Inspector Cockrill's casebook, a collection published by a small American press, Crippen & Landru, in 2002. Medawar describes how on learning that her father had lost all his money, Brand gave up her education and drifted from job to job; experience as a dance hostess prompted her to write a light romantic tale, "Dance Hostess," which appeared in *The Star* in 1939 and was soon followed by other stories, often featuring a plot twist at the end, and then *Death in High Heels* in 1941.

Her work was so highly regarded that she was elected to membership of the Detection Club as part of a post-war cohort of talented younger writers and Ardizzone's draughtsmanship skills were employed in designing a bookplate for the volumes held in the Detection Club's library (now dispersed, with individual copies bearing the bookplate much sought-after by collectors when they come on to the market). However, after *Tour de Force*, a "holiday mystery" featuring

Cockrill, appeared in 1955, she published no more crime novels for the next couple of decades.

In the meantime, she was far from idle, producing short stories as well as a wide range of other books. These included the Nurse Matilda stories for children, illustrated by Edward Ardizzone, titles published under various pen-names (Mary Roland, China Thompson, Mary Ann Ashe, and Annabel Jones) and a nonfiction study of the Sandyford murder case, *Heaven Knows Who*. Towards the end of her life she returned to the genre, and *The Rose in Darkness*, published in 1979, offered a reminder of her gift for intricate plotting. At that point in time, however, "mere ingenuity" had fallen out of critical favour, and the novel made little impression. Recent years have seen a welcome resurgence of interest in Golden Age writers and in Golden Age storytelling techniques. Christianna Brand's crime fiction exhibits a rare mastery of the craft.

—Martin Edwards
www.martinedwardsbooks.com

A NOTE FROM THE PUBLISHER

The original novels and short stories reprinted in the British Library Crime Classics series were written and published in a period ranging, for the most part, from the 1890s to the 1960s. There are many elements of these stories which continue to entertain modern readers; however, in some cases there are also uses of language, instances of stereotyping and some attitudes expressed by narrators or characters which may not be endorsed by the publishing standards of today. We acknowledge therefore that some elements in the works selected for reprinting may continue to make uncomfortable reading for some of our audience. With this series British Library Publishing and Poisoned Pen Press aim to offer a new readership a chance to read some of the rare books of the British Library's collections in an affordable paperback format, to enjoy their merits, and to look back into the world of the twentieth century as portrayed by its writers. It is not possible to separate these stories from the history of their writing and as such the novels and stories are presented as they were originally published with the inclusion of minor edits made for consistency of style and sense, and with pejorative terms of an extremely offensive nature partly obscured. We welcome feedback from our readers.

TO
GLAIBORN MCD. CARR
in America
with a big bunch of roses from England

THE CHARACTERS

JOHNNY WISE, who died: and to avenge whose death two of the following also died—and one was a murderer.

ISABEL DREW, a Jezebel.

EDGAR PORT, just a sugar daddy.

EARL ANDERSON, "a poor player."

BRIAN BRYAN, a knight in armour.

PERPETUA KIRK, a damsel in distress.

GEORGE EXMOUTH, a very young young man.

SUSAN BETCHLEY, a not-very-young young lady.

Showing the stage, the tower and balcony, the Assembly
Room, the doorway leading to the dressing rooms and
the positions of the eleven knights in armour.

1940

Johnny Wise rang up the Siamese Kitten. The Siamese Kitten said crossly that everybody had left long ago; the place was closed for the night. Mr. Earl Anderson's party?—never heard of the gentleman...

"He's an actor," said Johnny. "Dark, squat fellow—sort of raffish: *you* know the chap? Well, look here, he'll have been with Miss Isabel Drew."

Ah, that was different. Miss Drew had been here with a party, but had left a long time ago—two hours ago. Yes, there had been a young lady in the party. A very pretty young lady?—well, the gentleman would understand that all the young ladies who came to the Siamese Kitten were very pretty young ladies to the Siamese Kitten. Miss Perpetua Kirk—very well, if the gentleman said so: the Siamese Kitten did not know; and it evidently did not care either, for, suddenly tiring of the whole conversation, it rang off.

Johnny rang up the Kangaroo, and the Black Bear and the Unreluctant Dragon, but all these creatures were apparently asleep, for they did not reply. "They must have gone back to Isabel's flat," he thought. "Poor Peppi, she'll be so tired, and probably bored to tears listening to Isabel's eternal mono-logue about sex and how to make money... And she'll never get a taxi at this hour of the morning. I'll go round to Isabel's and perhaps have a drink, and bring Perpetua home." He got out his shabby old Chrysler and drove round to Isabel's door: and into his tender, gay and innocent young heart there never entered one single doubt that he would be welcome there.

Isabel was bored with the Johnny-Perpetua engagement. She thought that Peppi was a silly little fool, throwing herself away, with all those good looks, on a penniless irresponsible like Johnny Wise, from India or the Malay or where ever it was that he came from: and besides, Earl Anderson had fallen for her—Earl specialized in fresh young things, it made him feel such a roué. And Earl was in the money just now: and Isabel needed some round brown pennies, and Earl was always easy when he was good-tempered... Nothing had been said, no deliberate plan existed even in the still waters of Isabel's complex heart: but somehow this party at The Siamese Kitten arranged itself, with another man, to keep Isabel busy: and somehow it was boring there, despite so much to drink, and so they all rolled back to Isabel's flat: and somehow when the bottle at the flat got low, another one took its place: and Perpetua wasn't used to all that gin... So that when Johnny Wise arrived, guilelessly smiling, to take his beloved home, Isabel opened the door to him, and said irritably: "You can't—she isn't ready to go."

"Well, I'll come in and have a drink then, may I?" said Johnny.

"No, Johnny, you can't," said Isabel, beginning to close the door.

Johnny was astonished. "Well, tell Peppi I'm *here*, anyway."

"Perpetua doesn't want you, Johnny, she's busy: so for God's sake go home and mind your own business and let the poor kid have a night out if she wants to."

"What on earth are you talking about?" said Johnny. He pushed past her into the flat. "I'll ask her myself, and if she doesn't want to go home yet, well naturally she needn't. Where is she?"

Isabel set her tight little rosebud mouth. "Very well," she said. "Go ahead—help yourself!" and she flung open the door of a room. Perpetua was there with Earl.

Johnny Wise stood there in the doorway. He said in a sort of strangled groan: "Oh no! *No!*" as though he could not, would not believe what he saw: and turned and went blundering down the stairs and into the Chrysler and drove it out to the Great West Road and there found a long straight bit with a wall at the end of it: and turned the car and went back a little: and turned the car once more and headed it for the wall, and trod hard on the gas.

Chapter I

MRS. PORT SAT AT THE OPEN WINDOW OF THE NARROW little room that was costing her husband twenty guineas a week. Her thin grey hands pleated and repleated a fold in her kimono. "But I don't see why you should *want* to manage a pageant, Edgar: knights on horses and a girl in a tower— what's it all about? I don't understand." She gave a little sigh and then said apologetically: "But there are so many things I don't understand."

"It's just to keep me amused and busy, dear, till you can leave this place..."

"Shall we go back to Malaya, Edgar, when I'm able to leave here?"

Mr. Port's round face grew suddenly haggard: there was the same grey look about him as there was about the restless hands. "There isn't very much left to go back to, my dear. Everything that we knew has gone. The Japanese..."

"I don't remember any of it," she said vaguely, troubled and apologetic again.

He pulled himself together. "Well, don't try, dear. Don't worry about it. It'll all come back." But there were some things that would be so much better hidden away in the cobwebs of her mind for ever! The Japanese... He shut his own mind to it all; and said with his own old bouncing cheerfulness: "Meanwhile you must get well and perhaps you'll be able to come and see my pageant!"

"What happens to the girl in the tower?"

"Well, the girl in the tower—that's Isabel Drew, you know..."

"I don't remember any Isabel Drew," she said.

"Not back in Malaya—you met her here in London, soon after we came Home... She was a friend of Johnny's."

"Of Johnny's?" she said.

"Don't you remember Johnny?" he said, sadly.

She shook her poor grey head. "I don't remember anything, Edgar, dear."

He pulled himself up again. "Well, never mind. It'll all come back one day soon. Anyway, this girl Isabel Drew knows all the other promoters of the Exhibition, and when she knew that there was to be a pageant, she—she persuaded us all that I ought to play the part of pageant master; just for the fun of it, you know."

"But do you understand about pageants, Edgar? Are you used to that kind of thing?"

"Anyone can manage a *pageant!*" said Mr. Port, with the more bluff heartiness because he was not at all sure that this was so. "And Isabel convinced them all in a couple of words that there right in their midst they had just the man they were looking for. It's hard work but—well, it'll keep me occupied," he finished rather lamely: and as her face took on that old hurt look of querulous uncertainty he added, with an almost desperate pleading: "Don't question me any more: don't bother about it all any more... I only mentioned it because I thought it might amuse you. It's all nothing: all just a bit of nonsense, but I—I have my reasons..."

Susan Betchley, meeting them in the park that afternoon, would have said that Mr. Port had only one reason for associating himself with Isabel Drew's pageant—and that reason was Isabel Drew. She titupped along beside him on her high-heeled shoes, a little round, honey-coloured creature, softly and warmly curved as a whipped cream walnut. He dropped her hand rather furtively, Susan Betchley thought; his arms hung short and stiff on either side of his bow-windowed tummy, small plump hands twitching self-consciously. It was too late to retire gracefully: she waved her stumpy umbrella at them and advanced purposefully across the forbidden grass—a little like a stumpy umbrella herself with her stocky figure and well-carved head, and dull, but neatly fitting silk dress. "Hallo, Miss Drew! Fancy meeting *you!*"

"Oh, lor' here's that awful Betchley woman," said Isabel petulantly to Mr. Port. She assumed an unconvincing smile. "Hallo, Miss Bitchley: fancy meeting you too! You and Edgar know each other, don't you?"

Mr. Port and Miss Betchley disclaimed; he touched her firm brown hand briefly with his pudgy one, pink and moist in the hot July sunshine. "First time I've had the pleasure..."

"How peculiar!" said Isabel. "I thought you both came from Malay or wherever it was?"

Mr. Port and Miss Betchley began with one voice to

protest that Malaya was the noun and Malay the adjective: that one might as well say that they both came from the French... "Well, I mean you're Anglo-Indians or whatever it is, then," said Isabel, not impressed. "You both knew Johnny Wise, anyway."

Their eyes met, shifted a little, and they each looked away again: was it only that Isabel could talk so lightly of Johnny? But Johnny had been dead more than seven years... Mr. Port explained: "Johnny Wise wrote home and told all his friends so much about England: when we finally got home, we looked up Miss Drew. He—he thought so much of her!" He smiled indulgently upon Miss Drew.

"Miss Drew must be quite fed up with all Johnny's friends," said Miss Betchley with a little apologetic grimace. "I'm afraid I presumed on my friendship with Johnny Wise in the old days, to do just the same thing." She added to Isabel: "I'm still looking for a job! Not very easy to find, with no qualification whatsoever, and being a 'new girl' in everything at *my* great age! But we poor middle-ageing spinsters..." She grimaced again and gave a small, rather snorting, self-deprecatory laugh.

Isabel, who was also a spinster and several years nearer middle-age than Miss Betchley, responded with a pitying smile. Mr. Port said abruptly: "Perhaps we could find Miss Betchley something in the pageant, Isabel?"

"There's no room for any more women," said Isabel briefly.

He persisted. "What about—what about Wardrobe—Mistress, eh?"

"There isn't a wardrobe, Edgar: nothing but my dress and a dozen suits of armour."

"Well, I'm sure she could make herself useful in lots of

ways," insisted Mr. Port, with unparalleled firmness, where Isabel was concerned. He looked at the swarthy, somehow rather wistful face, and said buoyantly: "Would that suit you, eh? It would only last a few weeks, but it might just fill in time…"

And Brian Two-Times also got a job in Isabel's pageant. Brian Two-Times was sweet. Brian Bryan, his name was actually, and he was Dutch, or his mother had been Dutch or something—Isabel was never quite sure: anyway he came from the Malay. Well, all right, Sumatra then, wherever that might be…

"Sumatra is an island, quite separate from Malaya…"

"How you people do *fuss!*" said Isabel. She sat curled up on the off-white sofa in her cosy, slightly grubby little off-white flat. "Now, Brian, look—about getting you a job…"

"I don't want a job so much," said Brian laughing.

"Well darling, you can't just moodle about doing absolutely nothing: now, I know this isn't *much* of a job, but thousands of awfully nice people are quite keen to do it and it's only for a few weeks while the exhibition lasts…" Isabel was not finding it too easy to find a dozen knights to ride round her tower in the pageant. "For instance, Earl Anderson's doing it: well now, he's quite a well-known actor, at least not exactly well-known, but lots of people have heard of him, only he happens to be resting at the moment—such an idiotic word, I always think, because the last thing they ever do is rest, but rush round like lunatics sucking up to everybody and trying to get auditions…"

Brian Bryan was thirty-nine or forty: short with broad shoulders, a rather square, smiling face, and astonishing blue, blue eyes. He habitually wore a long mackintosh which flapped as he walked; and he was radiant with vitality and a sort of impatient charm. He did not appear much interested in Earl Anderson's efforts while resting, but said, indifferently: "I seem to know the name."

"Well, actually, I expect you know it because of Perpetua. She's been living with him, or anyway running round with him, which I suppose comes to the same thing—ever since Johnny Wise did himself in." She looked at him alertly, curled up, soft and round and golden on her shabby sofa. "I suppose you think it's odd of Perpetua, Brian?"

Brian shrugged his shoulders. "I don't think about it at all." His English was quite good, though he spoke with a strong foreign accent. He changed the subject to one more immediately concerning himself. "What does this Anderson in the show, that is therefore suitable for me to do?"

"Well, he's in the pageant, darling," said Isabel, brightening. "Riding round on a horse, it's too ridiculous, but after all it's four pounds a week for ten minutes' work, twice a day. And they're only old circus ponies trained to go round and round in a ring and do the Grand Chain or some such nonsense. You needn't be able to ride a *bit*. Earl can't, not for toffee."

Brian Two-Times had spent perhaps two-thirds of his working life in the saddle. He gave her a little mocking bow whose irony was completely lost on her. "That is a great relief."

"Well, I'll tell Sugar Daddy that he must fix you up as one of the knights. You know old Edgar Port's the pageant master?

I can't think why he wants to do it, because he seems to have pots of money."

"All for the luff of a lady?" suggested Brian, laughing.

"I wouldn't be surprised," said Isabel, laughing too. "Anyway, I introduced him to the manager of the whole show, who's an old job of mine, and they fixed it up between them: heaven knows what Edgar knows about running pageants, but I suppose he used to get up the fire-walking stunts or whatever they are, back home in the Malay."

"Malaya," said Brian Two-Times automatically. "And I assure you that Edgar Port did not get up the fire-walking stunts there. He was a great man in Malaya: very pompious indeed!" He blew out his cheeks and stuck out his tummy in a startlingly life-like impression of Mr. Port at his most pompious.

"Oh, well, I always forget that you knew him there."

"I did *not* know him there. How many times I have to tell you that my home is in Sumatra? As it happens, I knew Johnny Wise, yes: but Mr. Port I never set eyes on till you introduced us. He lived in British Malaya: I in Dutch Sumatra."

"Oh, well, you were all good old Anglo-Indians together!" said Isabel impatiently. She got up off the sofa, stretched herself with a great display of bosom and thigh, and, since Brian Two-Times remained impassive, suggested without resentment that they go down to Elysian Hall and see what was doing in the way of preparation for the Homes for Heroes Exhibition. "Charity Exmouth will be there, doing the decor or whatever they call it for the pageant, and I can show you what it's all about. Besides, she owes me twenty pounds commission for getting her the job and I want to squeeze some of it out of her..."

The enormous shell of the Elysian Hall was in process of conversion into a small township of model homes suitable for the Heroes of England—(who meanwhile crowded in with reluctant relatives, and by day tramped the streets pleading with agents and officials that anything would do, the wife wasn't particular, not any more...) Pseudo-Tudo cottages jostled staring white plastic, tortured into a series of Chinese boxes moulded from a single sheet: all-electric flatlets—a single cell, as it were, detached from the parent hive—sparkled with chastely camouflaged efficiency. There were whole rows of bathrooms complete with fittings, whole rows of fittings divorced from their bathrooms, whole rows and rows of baths alone, standing like disconsolate white poodles left out in the rain. In the galleries young women in tight, short skirts and with complicated hair-dos, learned off by heart a set patter about goods they had never previously heard of, and now that they knew something about them, would certainly never dream of buying for themselves. Agitated exhibitors leaped up and down crying in anguish, "Not sleeping nets, dear, *Slumber* nets, I told you agen and agen..." and the young ladies took the plums out of their mouths for a moment to exclaim crossly: "Oh, wot the 'ell does it *matter*, Mr. Engelbaum?" Elderly gentlemen who had seen better days, ceaselessly passed a raw boiling fowl in at one end of a complicated mass of machinery and produced it, roasted to a turn, at the other end. Gardeners were planting out the Clock of Flowers with drooping pansies and sturdy Batchelors' Buttons, a locust swarm of chattering little women, uniformly grey, swept up the dust of the aisles into clouds and waited for it to settle again. In the centre of the main hall, Charity

Exmouth stood wrapt in admiration before the pageant tower, with her hobbledehoy son prancing sycophantically at her side. "We call him Motherdear," said Isabel, as she and Brian Bryan approached the little group. "You'll soon know why. And why *will* she wear three-cornered hats?"

"She wants to look like a woman M.P.," suggested Brian.

"Nobody can possibly want to look like a woman M.P.," said Isabel. She advanced buoyantly. "Hallo, Charity. Hallo, George. Oh, hallo, Edgar, my pet."

Charity Exmouth permitted a rush of teeth to the front of her mouth and hurriedly retracted them. Mr. Port bounded with pleasure at the sight of his beloved, his little feet almost leaving the ground in the excess of his joy. The hobbledehoy looked loweringly at Isabel's remorseless charms, and thought that if only his mother had not kept him so desperately "young" he would long ago have learned to gaze upon such bournes of bliss and remain undisturbed. Not that he... For after all he was in love with Perpetua Kirk... But Perpetua was straight and narrow and uncushioned as a reed, and he could not keep his eyes from Isabel's curves. He relapsed into a dream of angry adolescent resentment: a slim, dark, nervous boy in the throes of his first great love.

A stage was built out into the vast hall: semicircular, cut off from the great room behind—the Assembly room it was called—by a flimsy wooden "castellated" wall. In the centre of this wall was a tower, a mere empty tube, standing on one end: and through the tower had been driven a high arch, leading from the Assembly room to the stage in front. Above the arch was a narrow window, tall enough to give access to a tiny balcony looking out over the hall. A rickety flight of steps inside the tower led to the rickety platform within this window. Isabel Drew, whose nightly task it would be to ascend these steps, hang about on the inside platform, and finally appear dramatically in a blaze of sudden floodlights on the balcony outside the window, had insured her rounded limbs severally and together, for the duration of the job: and, so devout was her passion for good hard cash, could almost find it in her heart to wish that—right at the end of the run, when she had squeezed all she could possibly get out of Sugar-Daddy Port and the Homes for Heroes Exhibition—the ladder might give way and break just one teeny, weeny, terribly painless little bone…

Mr. Port on the other hand was in an agony lest anything might happen to darling Isabel. "Are you sure, Mrs. Exmouth, that the ladder is safe? And that balcony? It looks terribly gimcrack."

"The whole thing's as solid as it can be," said Charity crossly: and added, glancing at Isabel's delectable bulges: "That is for anybody of normal weight." Charity herself was of the meagre quality, too often associated with her name. She gestured at the tin ivy, of an arsenic greenery, that coiled itself up the tower and about the little balcony. "*Life*-like, don't you think? George positively thought it was the real thing: didn't you, George?"

"I said that the real thing often looked just as phoney," mumbled George.

"But do I *want* all this frightful ivy?" said Isabel, clinging with pretty petulance to Mr. Port's arm.

Edgar explained tenderly. It was all the fault of that naughty little, soft little, cooing little voice of hers. They simply must have it stronger than it had come up at the original run-through of her speech: microphones and things had had to be hidden up on the tower quite near her, but then the trouble was that they would magnify a lot of other sounds—he didn't quite understand the mechanics of it all…

"The whole thing's arranged and fixed up now, so we must have the ivy and that's the end of it," said Charity, settling the tricorne hat with determination upon her head, and preparing to give battle. "There's a switch hidden in the ivy up on the right-hand side of the arch, as you face the stage, and one of the knights will have to just reach up and switch it on when Isabel appears…"

"Oh, that reminds me," said Isabel. "Talking about knights, here's another one. His name's Brian Bryan—Brian Two-Times, I call him." She looked upon him with a fond and proprietary air, delighted with the excellence of her wit.

A handsome, rather swarthy young woman was now dragged forward from her self-imposed obscurity and introduced to Brian Two-Times: Miss Bitch-sorry-*Betch*ley: an old friend of that boy Johnny Wise who had killed himself—and so was Brian. Surely they must have all met, out there in the Malay or wherever it was? Brown eyes met blue, blue eyes rather quickly looked down at the floor. Isabel prattled gaily on, and all unconscious of their doom, the little victims played. The kill had been selected. The killer at hand. The bystanders were gathering at the scene of execution: and Isabel with every careless word knocked yet another nail into the highly complicated structure of double murder…

Two people, wandering rather aimlessly through the arch-way leading under the tower and out on to the semicircle of the stage, arrived at just the right moment to complete the cast. Earl Anderson was a short, stocky man, with chrysanthemum-curling black hair—his innumerable devoted friends doubted the authenticity of both curl and colour—luminous large blue eyes, and an air of determined raffishness, much assisted by the affectation of horsey checked coats, slit up on either side of his behind. Perpetua Kirk was a thin, fair, pretty creature, with hair so thick and frizzy that it looked like a well-kept yew hedge—trimmed to a clipped page-boy bob. She drooped along at Earl's side, walking as though in a sort of stupid dream. Earl had said why not go down and take a look at this absurd Exhibition—the Exmouth woman wanted him to do something about a light switch or something, during the pageant... And one might as well go: everybody would be uninteresting and everything would be meaningless, but then so they would anywhere else. "There's your dear Isabel," she said, indicating the group below the footlights, looking up at the tower.

"So she is," said Earl. He called down, "Hallo, Jezebel! Hallo, Mrs. Exmouth! Hallo, Mr. Port." He supposed that was the new Dutch fellow that Isabel was always talking about.

"Hallo, Earl," said Isabel. "And don't call me Jezebel! It makes me cross. Hallo, Peppi."

Perpetua gave them her pretty, mirthless smile. Brian Bryan turned away his head from his share of it. He thought: she's absolutely empty; as empty as a sea-shell. It seemed impossible that Johnny had loved with his whole young heart this husk of a girl with her curved lips and unsmiling grey eyes. But he remembered Johnny's letters. Damn her! he thought: and knew that it was not just an expression—that he really meant it: that he wished her soul in hell.

Susan Betchley also wished Perpetua's soul in hell... After what happened to Johnny—still going round with that Anderson creature—daring to come here and meet—all of *them*. Perpetua met the stare of her resentful brown eyes with a mild surprise.

Perpetua, for whom Johnny Wise had killed himself: who to all intents and purposes had murdered him. And Isabel Drew and Earl Anderson, assistant murderers. And Edgar Port, and Susan Betchley and Brian Two-Times who had loved Johnny. And hobbledehoy George Exmouth who loved Perpetua. Two victims: and a murderer: and supporting cast. And not very long to go...

They stood grouped together, discussing the action of the pageant with Charity Exmouth (Charity would be far away in Edinburgh designing yet another ivy-covered decor by the time the murder was committed for which she now so innocently set the scene). She stood outlining the progress of the pageant with sweeps of her bony hands. "The trumpets will blare: it'll be terrific—floodlights will be focused on the archway, all the people will turn to see what's happening and come crowding to the space here below the stage. Then more trumpets, and the Knights come riding through on their chargers, velvet cloaks flying, silver standards held high! Pace round the stage, form up for the figures, finally into the Grand Chain, harness jingling as the horses break into a trot: the tableau beneath the tower, all the Knights looking up to the window where the Queen of England, Home and Beauty is to make her dramatic appearance! The lights shift slowly upward: a thunder of drums—and in her silver dress with her tall pointed hat and flowing veil, she steps out on to the balcony…" She broke off, exhausted by the wonder and beauty of it all.

"What is it meant to represent?" said Susan Betchley in her flat, too-downright way.

Nobody had the faintest idea what it was meant to represent. "Just—er—just a sort of general homage to England, Home and Beauty," said Mr. Port, waving his fat little hands. Whether darling Isabel was supposed to favour England, Home or Beauty, he had never quite decided. "After all they all meant the same thing to—well, to a great many of us," he said. His eyes met Brian Bryan's and Susan Betchley's, and he looked down at the toes of his shoes. No use trying to explain to people who had not been there and could never understand, what such words had meant to those who for three years had lived in "the Malay," under the tender rule of the Sons of Heaven…

"Now who shall be leading Knight?" said Charity Exmouth, bustling down to work. She gazed fondly upon her son. "George is going to take the part of one of the Knights— just for the fun of it: aren't you, George?"

"Yes, Motherdear," said George, who was taking the part because his mother insisted upon it and for no other reason.

"So who shall be leading Knight?" repeated Mrs. Exmouth.

"Brian Two-Times," said Isabel promptly.

While Mr. Port was pageant master, Isabel's word was law. "Very well then," said George's mother sourly. "And then Mr. Earl Anderson must be Second Knight, because I've already arranged with him about the amplifier switch: so George must be third. The Leader wears a white cloak and rides a white charger—all the other horses are black: Second wears a red cloak, and Third a blue. So we'd better rechristen them White Knight and Red Knight and Blue Knight. Mr. Bryan, White. Mr. Anderson, Red. George, Blue."

Everyone looked more than satisfied with this masterly rearrangement.

"So you will lead them in, White Knight," continued Charity, coyly addressing Brian Bryan in his new identity, "in single file through the arch. You pace round the stage once or twice and then all take your positions to form a hollow square, White Knight in the centre..."

"They can't," said Isabel. "It'll be an uneven number if you put one in the centre."

"We're only having eleven knights," said Charity reasonably.

"But we've got twelve suits of armour," said Isabel. Her tight little soul revolted at the idea of wasting money—even the Exhibition's money—on something that was not to be used.

"Well, it's too late to bother about that now. We'll just have to look upon one of them as reserve. I've worked out all the moves and they can't be changed," said Mrs. Exmouth firmly, giving the tricorne a further belligerent tilt. "Hollow square, White Knight in the centre. Set to partners: White here, Red *here*, Yellow and Green Knights over *there*..." She sketched one or two simple evolutions, and as no one appeared to follow one word of what she was saying, mapped them out with pin-men on scraps of paper torn from her notebook. "Now, Red there, Blue over *here*... No, what am I saying, Blue here, and Red stands still in the centre... No, no, I'm wrong myself, you've got me all muddled: it's Blue that stands still and does nothing and Red rides round to the left..." By the time they arrived at the Grand Chain the floor was littered with little scraps of paper.

Isabel was impatient to get to her part in the pageant. She ran up the rickety ladder and hung out of the window, calling down to them in her fluting voice. "Well, then, they come out of the Grand Chain, with Brian leading and Earl behind and George behind *him*, and then the eight others. The eight form up in a semicircle round the edge of the stage, looking out towards the audience. Don't you think they really ought to be looking up towards the Queen?"

"No," said Charity.

Isabel decided to let that go. "Well, I'm in the window, all in the shadows because the lights are focused on the stage: Earl's on my left hand, looking up at me, and George is on my right: and Brian Two-Times is facing into the archway, with his horse's behind to the audience, also looking up... The lights slowly rise till they floodlight the window and the balcony: and I appear in my silver dress and my tall pointed hat and break into my speech." Without invitation she broke into her speech... All about them in blinding dust, in ear-shattering din, the Homes for Heroes Exhibition underwent the slow and painful process of its birth. Give us the 'ammer... Fetch that plank... Tray one of our Slomber nets... You just pass the chicken in *here*... The little grey locusts swept and polished and waited for the dust to settle again, the exhibitors leaped and pleaded with the plum-mouthed young ladies in vain. Isabel declaimed. Perpetua Kirk, bored beyond endurance, moved over to Susan and said, with her own little air of polite indifference: "Are you taking some part in the pageant, Miss Bitchley? All Isabel's friends seem to be."

"I'm not a friend of Miss Drew's," said Susan abruptly. "And my name happens to be Betchley; with an 'e.'" She added, because Perpetua only looked at her vaguely, that she did *know* Isabel Drew but that that didn't make her a friend.

"Oh, doesn't it?" said Perpetua, blankly. What did it matter? One was only trying to be polite.

"Of course she did get me this job," acknowledged Susan, anxious to be fair. "I had to get something. I lost all I had in the F.M.S., and I find it difficult to get jobs in England—or, anyway, to keep them."

The F.M.S. was a part of Malaya. Where Johnny had come from. "Oh, yes?" said Perpetua, brushing away the memory as though a cobweb had drifted across her mind.

"I'm supposed to be the Wardrobe Mistress," said Miss Betchley, fiercely self-derogatory. "I look after twelve suits of pretence armour and Isabel Drew's bits of rubbish. And I have to be on guard at the door into the Assembly room, to see that nobody goes in while the pageant's in progress."

"Why shouldn't they?" said Perpetua, for something to say.

"For the simple reason that the door's straight opposite the archway, and the audience could see through the arch right into the room. Of course we're hanging a bead curtain across the inside of the archway, but it's best to be on the safe side..."

Well, what do *I* care? thought Perpetua. She wished she had never started this stupid conversation, but her habit of good manners was always letting her in for this kind of thing. That was what a convent training did for you. You might not learn hockey or lacrosse but they turned you out with an instinct to say or to do the right, the kindly thing: to be polite. Other things died—for Perpetua all other things had died one moonlight night seven years ago: but the habit was upon her still. She gave Miss Betchley her vague, sweet, meaningless smile, and walked away by herself, staring unseeingly at the half-built houses, the skeleton "stands," the mouthing, gesticulating men and girls going through their patter. Why should the woman be so offensive? I only asked politely if she was doing some job here... But the brown eyes had looked at her with something like hate. I suppose it's because of Johnny, she thought. They're all old friends of Johnny's. They all look at me as if they could kill me... As if they could kill her because one night long ago, poor foolish, flattered, uncertain child that she had been, she had allowed Isabel and Earl to make her tight; and so had been "easy" for Earl... Because from that time forward there had been no life in her soul: because she had gone on, utterly indifferent, in the way that she was led: trying at first and at last not even trying, to blot out the memory of Johnny's face as she had seen it for that brief moment before he had turned and gone away for ever into the endless night... She did not care for their hate: it could not touch her, nothing could touch her any more—not Earl's devotion, blowing hot and cold, not Isabel's avid excitement over her reactions, tapering away into indifference; not the disgust or the sympathy or the understanding or the obtuseness of their friends... Johnny is dead and at peace, she thought: and I am dead, but not at peace. That's the only difference. We both committed suicide that night. She thrust her hands into the pockets of her light summer coat, walking with downbent head through the echoing aisles.

The last person one could possibly have wanted to meet just at that juncture was Charity Exmouth's gangling son George;

and yet here he was now, drooping along behind her, catching her up, diffidently beginning to speak: a thin boy with hands and feet that seemed much bigger than they were because they were always so hopelessly in his own way; with a pale, thin face and hungry dark brown eyes. A hobbledehoy. She said with patient politeness that she was just going home…

He wondered if he dared ask if he might see her to her door, but could not pluck up courage to put the request into words. Instead he left her with ungracious precipitancy, hung about until she emerged in her vague, blind way from the big front door of the hall, and when she got on to a bus, followed her and, unseen, went up on top. Perpetua leaving the bus and picking her way through the Bayswater streets to her bed-sitting room, had an uneasy feeling that she was being followed, and now and again glanced behind her; but her knight errant kept well in the rear, and she saw nothing. Nevertheless, it made her jumpy, and on edge, and the cobweb of her depression was with her still. Johnny is dead, because of me: and if the hate of his friends could kill, I should die a dozen deaths… It all meant nothing, one didn't care about that or anything; but still—it was a chill feeling to be all alone with on a sunny July evening: and with that shadow, dodging about, keeping quite still, moving on again, just a little way behind her…

At her door, she plunged her hand into her bag to find her key; and brought out a scrap of paper that had not been there an hour before. A small square of paper, covered on one side with a series of squirls and angles, and criss-crossed lines, with pin-men on pin-horses, pacing a semicircular space. On the other side was written in straggly printed characters: PERPETUA KIRK—YOU ARE GOING TO BE MURDERED.

Chapter II

EARL ANDERSON DROVE ISABEL HOME IN HIS FLASHY
little red car. "I can't find Peppi—she seems to have wandered
off somewhere. She's so vague!"

"She wants someone to look after her," said Isabel, beginning at once to check over in her mind all the people who
might do to "look after" Perpetua Kirk, and how she, Isabel,
might somehow benefit by the arrangement.

"She's got me," said Earl, shortly.

Isabel laughed. "A lot of use you are to her! You're always
fooling around with other people, and after all she s got her
future to think of. She's in and out of jobs all the time—look
at her, now, just vaguely waiting for something new to turn
up, and only a few pounds left to get by on. It's time she left
off trailing round with you and got married."

"What am I supposed to do, meantime?" said Earl sulkily.

"You don't care tuppence about her," said Isabel, clinging
to the door handle as the car dry-skidded a corner. "It's just
a habit with both of you. You ought to give her a shove and

send her out into the world to look for someone else. Dash it all, she's getting on a bit: she must be twenty-seven, if she's a day. And still not married."

"You're *thirty*-seven if you're a day," said Earl, more or less good humouredly. "And still not married."

"That's different," said Isabel shortly, with a certain truth. "Anyway, she meets masses of men."

"Sitting around in pubs: they all just assume that she's yours, and not fair game. It isn't right, you're spoiling her chances, and she'll never do anything until you drive her out to make new friends for herself. She's got no mind of her own."

"Thanks to you," said Earl.

"Oh, well, hell to that—we've had this out over and over again… You were in it much worse than I was, Earl, why pick on me?"

"I was having a bit of a petting party with the girl: not even anything very serious. It was you who let the chap come barging into the room."

"Well, I was half-seas over myself, and he got on my nerves, standing there insisting on seeing her. How was I to know that he was such a little Puritan? Anyway, I expect he was tight actually: he'd been sitting up waiting for Peppi and putting it away a bit, you bet, and didn't know what he was doing… The silly kid just went out and packed himself up not knowing what he was doing…"

"He knew what he was doing all right," said Earl. "I saw his face." He threaded the little car deftly through the night traffic, staring ahead of him. "I've done what I could to make up for it all, Jezebel: I've stuck to Peppi all these years, and got jolly little out of it, I can tell you. Not that I've only done it out of—well, sort of decency. In my own way I'm very fond of her."

"Your own way," said Isabel. "What's that?"

He looked down apologetically at his hands, rather heavy, rather hairy hands, beginning to grow old, beginning to grow a little puffy, a little mottled after all the years of drink and bad hours and lack of exercise and air: but delicately cared for, clean and well manicured. "I know I go off with other women and all that: I get into a show and it's boring out on tour and these damn women run after one…" He could not for the life of him help assuming his air of doggy raffishness, squaring his padded shoulders a little, twisting up his mouth in the well-known slightly bored, slightly cynical smile. But he dropped the pose again at once to say: "But when I get back to London, it's always Peppi that I run around with: and—well, when you talk about someone looking after her, Isabel, I—I know it sounds silly, but I—I feel that it ought to be me." He said suddenly with an odd air of challenge: "I've been thinking of—just running her round to a registry office and marrying her."

Isabel's round, pale goldeny eyes were suddenly wide with mischief and excitement. She said shrilly: "Marry her! You can't, Earl. You're married already."

"Who knows that except me—and you?" said Earl.

Earl Anderson lived in a rather twee mews flat, over his own garage. It was cheap and nasty, he told his friends, but (a) one lived where one could, and (b) it *was* rather heaven to be able to walk down the somewhat ladder-like stairs and get into the car without even putting one's nose out into the cold. He had done up the place with lots of gay blue paint and he had a pretty fancy in genuine Chippendale at two or three guineas a piece. The bathroom curtains were of oil-silk with red-legged seagulls all over them; turned upside-down, the seagulls looked like fighter aeroplanes, emitting bursts of red flame, so the curtains were hung that way. Perpetua thought this rather silly, because few people recognized the aeroplane motif, and merely wondered why old Earl hung his curtains upside-down. Perpetua herself lived a couple of streets away from Earl, in the uninteresting bed-sitting room to which she had moved, in her aimless fashion, after Johnny's death. No paint and silly seagulls for Perpetua. Her body demanded a certain standard of comfort and she conceded it: but her mind was blank alike to beauty and ugliness.

Between the door of his beloved's chaste bed-sitt. and the door of his mama's highly decor-ed little house near the Marble Arch, Motherdear on his way home was obliged to pass not only Earl Anderson's mews, but the shabby entrance to Isabel's block of flats hard by. It was awkward that just as he was about to hurry past, Earl's little red car should have tootled up and stopped at the bottom of the steps. He drew back into the shadows, not wishing to advertise his unsolic-ited act of chivalry in seeing Peppi home; and, innocent of any intent to eavesdrop, waited an opportunity to pass on.

Isabel's cooing little voice might not fill the Elysian Hall, but it carried golden-clear on the still night air. And Motherdear was not so hobbledehoy that he did not recog-nize blackmail when he heard it, however sweetly phrased.

Isabel, all unconscious of her audience, went, comfortably smiling, up to bed. Earl was not good for much, but he had "expectations": one day he would be well-to-do, and if this marriage went through… She saw a comforting solution to those grey years ahead when the honey should have turned to gall and wormwood in men's mouths; and she hummed a tune to herself, as she flung her handbag on to the sofa, and, yawning like a little cat, stepped out of her clothes leaving each garment ringed on the carpet where it dropped. Everything was honestly always for the best, in this best of all possible worlds: one had only to be patient and keep one's eyes open for opportunities—and trust to one's unfailing good luck. A scrap of paper seemed to have fallen out of her bag, and she picked it up and unfolded it as she trotted off, nude and golden, to the bathroom. A lot of Charity Exmouth's little pin-men: and on the other side… "Good Lord, how childish!" said Isabel, screwing the paper into a ball and tossing it into the huh-ha.

For who could possibly be intending to murder her?

Earl Anderson drove his car into the garage, and switched off the engine and went rather wearily up the narrow stairs. Damn Isabel, blast her, for the heartless little cat that she was! In the face of her probable interference, his new-born plan for marriage with Perpetua grew suddenly to be of terrible importance to him. In a rare glimpse of reality, he saw himself for a moment, as he really was—an ageing second-rater, in a profession where youth and youth's good looks counted for much—watching with painful anxiety the receding hair-line, the advancing waistline that with other men were no more than a rueful joke. His carefully cultivated reputation as a roué and man-about-town seemed all of a sudden shoddy and rather mean: "easy" middle-aged actresses, "easy" impressionable young girls... A devil with his money when he had any, but all too often a scrounger, cadging drinks off other men in memory of better days: a war-record of E.N.S.A. squabbles and grumbles, of grudging work, of indifferent performances electrified only now and again into enthusiasm by the presence of someone who "might be useful"... A bit of a bounder, that was the ugly truth of it: a bit of a bounder, a phoney, incessantly acting the part that he had built-in for himself to play. Even that business about his uncle and the inheritance: he had boasted about it so often that he himself had almost come to believe in the old boy! For a moment he wondered whether Isabel was really counting on that mirage of future wealth: but no, no, Jezebel was too old a hand at the game herself. And yet... His telephone had long ago been cut off for non-payment of bills, but he went out to a call box and rang through to her. Isabel, however, was half in, half out of a bath, and only told him to go to bed and not fuss, and oh, by the way, someone was writing her silly little notes and threatening to murder her: wasn't it sweeeeet? He put down the receiver, dug for another two pennies and dialled Peppi's number. "Hallo, darling: I hope you weren't asleep?"

Perpetua sounded rather strained. "No, I wasn't asleep. Actually, something rather horrid has happened." She told him about the frightening little note.

Earl reassured her. "Isabel's had one too; somebody down at the Exhibition's been playing a stupid joke. Don't worry your pretty little head about it any more." But since her mind seemed obsessed by the silly subject he said nothing of what so much obsessed his own. "Jezebel's put her's down the drain. You do the same and go off to sleep: good night, my sweet." He went back to the flat, switched on the electric fire and waited till its red glow ignited a screw of paper so that he could light a cigarette.

And knocking out the flame observed that the paper was covered on one side with pin-men and squirls and numbered criss-cross lines. On the other side was written EARL ANDERSON—YOU ARE GOING TO BE MURDERED... And this scrap of paper he had taken out of his own pocket: it must have been put there within the last hour or so. And Isabel had had one too: and Perpetua. And he and Isabel and Perpetua...

Do what one would, one had never wiped out the memory of that boy's white face—when he and Isabel and Perpetua had sent him to his death.

Chapter III

Inspector Cockrill had known Perpetua Kirk long ago in the old days, in North Kent: Inspector Cockrill knew everybody who was anybody in North Kent. She had been brought to his notice again over that unfortunate affair of the suicide, early on in the war, and he had come up to London and done a bit of quiet investigation on his own. Cockie detested London: a lot of hurrying, scurrying people and not one of them to nudge his neighbour and say: "There goes the Inspector—a fair old terror *he* is…"

But here he was in London and sitting on the edge of Perpetua Kirk's divan bed, rolling a cigarette between his nicotined fingers, peering at her with his hard little, bright brown eyes—a shabby country sparrow, confined for a while in a narrow town garden and not liking it one bit. "I happen to be up here for a few days, Peppi; and I got your message, and here I am. What's wrong?" His voice implied that there'd better be something worth all this trouble, or else! He puffed at the wispy cigarette, shielding it from the draught, in the cup of his thin brown hand.

"I saw in the papers that you were in London for this conference thing, Cockie: so I plucked up courage to ring you—I hope you don t mind."

"I've *told* you I don't mind," he said impatiently. "Now you tell me what's worrying you." But she looked very young and forlorn, sitting there crouched in the single armchair; she reminded him of her pretty mother—he hoped devoutly that she had not grown up such a fool. He squeezed out one of his wintry smiles for her. "There now, don't mind me—we all know I'm a curmudgeon! What's wrong, child?"

So Peppi told him: all about the pageant, all about the meeting at Elysium to discuss the arrangements, all about Isabel and Brian Two-Times, and Motherdear and Miss Bitchley—no, *Betchley,* and Mr. Port and Earl Anderson; all about the murder threats. "Do you think I'm just silly, Cockie? Or do you think there really is something to worry about?"

"I think it's fifty-fifty," said Cockrill, not mincing matters, watching the smoke from his cigarette curl up between his fingers. "I think it's very possibly a so-called joke—a cruel joke, though, intended to do more than just bewilder you all. On the other hand—if a person seriously contemplates murder, and especially murder for revenge, I'm never surprised when he lets his intended victim know in advance. A swift, unexpected death may not seem to him sufficient repayment: he wants to see his victim suffer. That's part of the revenge."

"Or of course he may want to be sort of—fair."

"Well, that's a beautifully British outlook," said Cockrill, dryly. "Not shoot a sitting bird, eh?" What sort of bird would poor little Peppi be? A plover, he thought, a little hen plover, lying inert with her soft feathers sleekly shining, and her pretty head lolling on her lifeless neck...

"If only I hadn't thrown the note away," said Perpetua apologetically. "But Earl said Isabel had put hers down the huh-ha and I must do the same and not be silly. Then of course he got one too..."

"And nobody else has acknowledged getting a similar note?"

Nobody had. "Just Isabel and Earl and me." She added, unhappily: "Of course, Cockie, you remember about Johnny?"

Brief, flaring headlines in the cheaper papers, filling the dud patches during the "phoney war": GIRL HE LOVED FAITHLESS! YOUNG SOLDIER KILLS HIMSELF! And comments by the Coroner: "This fine young officer went to his death because he found himself betrayed!" There had been a lot of sentimentality about a twin, too. Johnny had never been separated from his twin: but at the outbreak of war, he had torn himself away to come to England and fight. The family had disagreed—his father and his brothers and sister: they had said that the Japanese would one day come to Malaya, that their duty was to remain and meet the danger nearer home. But Johnny had not been able to wait; he had come on to England alone, and they had stayed behind, to be engulfed in the disaster they had too truly prophesied. They had remained and fought for their homeland: and Johnny, unable to withstand the enemy nearer his heart, had died by his own hand, GIRL HE LOVED FAITHLESS! YOUNG SOLDIER KILLS HIMSELF... Cockrill said, with unwonted tenderness: "The boy would probably have been killed anyway, my child. Dunkirk, or the Desert, or D-Day—they were all yet to come."

"He'd have died proud and happy," said Perpetua.

Inspector Cockrill doubted whether people in these disillusioned days died proudly and happily—even for their country: but women were always sentimentalists. He heaved himself up off the bed and brushed the cigarette ash off his shabby old mackintosh on to Peppi's carpet. "Let's go down to this Elysium of yours, and see if we can pick up anything useful there." In Kent, the very sight of Inspector Cockrill on the scene would have struck such terror into the heart of practical joker and murderer alike, that he would from that moment onward have stayed his hand. But this was London. He perched his wild hat rather crookedly on his magnificent head, and hurried off with small, rather shuffling steps at Perpetua's side: anyway, he was missing that infernal conference!

Eleven knights had finally been engaged and were now in the process of intensive training at the hands of Mr. Port, with Isabel leaning bossily out of her tower, directing affairs from above. The stage and Assembly room are permanent features built into Elysian Hall, occupying a narrow sector of the circular building; the archway through the castellated wall the only access to the stage from the Assembly room, the big doorway opposite the only access into the Assembly room, from the muddle of ill-lit dressing rooms beyond. Stalls had been improvised for the horses near the back doors leading to the outer yard; and at the door between dressing-rooms and Assembly room Miss Betchley kept patient vigil. The Assembly room was bare save for eleven empty hooks, and a single suit of armour, like a child's sleeping suit in painted tin, zipped and latched up the back for the easier apparelling of the knights: the helmet was hitched jauntily above it from a peg, from which also dangled a long velvet cloak of bottle green. On the stage, Brian Bryan sitting at ease in his saddle and with a white velvet cloak, led his followers through the gyrations of the Grand Chain, their absurd tin visors pushed up so that they might see where they were going. "In, out, in out in, *out*," chanted Isabel leaning over her balcony, oblivious of the fact that for at least fifty per cent. of the knights her instructions must of necessity be incorrect. They extricated themselves at last from the resultant chaos and came to rest in their places for her declamation, eight in a semicircle round the edge of the stage, facing out towards the audience, three looking inwards and upwards to the balcony. She took a step back into the window and reappeared in the blaze of upward-shifting light. "Oh, Knights of England…" Her voice died away into a wrathful whisper. Earl Anderson, red-cloaked, sitting his charger, fumbled desperately among the ivy leaves. Inspector Cockrill, standing in the body of the hall with Perpetua by his side, broke into a sardonic chuckle. "Never knew a pageant that didn't go just the same! The old faggots in Kent are always getting them up!"

Isabel hung angrily over the balcony. "What the hell are you doing with that loudspeaker, Earl?"

"I can't find the damn switch," said Earl, irritably. He shaded his eyes to look into the hall for Mr. Port. "I *told* you it was too high! My arm's not four feet long!"

The knights sat restlessly in their saddles, giggling among

themselves. "We'll have to have the switch moved down," said Isabel. "Charity will have to see to it."

George Exmouth looked up from his horse at the foot of the tower, to her right. "Mother's in Scotland. She's finished the job here."

Isabel burst into a muttered imprecation on Charity and all her works, which suddenly swelled to a roar as Earl found the switch and the amplifiers began to do their duty. The muffled giggles of the knights became downright laughter. She leaned over the ornamental railing to pour abuse upon the hapless Mr. Port, easiest victim for her wounded vanity. Workmen and demonstrators all over the hall silenced their chatter and patter to laugh at the tirade of personalities booming through the aisles. Suddenly conscious of what was happening, she disappeared through the window and, scrambling down the narrow stairs and out of her tower, appeared through the archway and came to the edge of the stage, staring down angrily to where Mr. Port stood laughing helplessly between Inspector Cockrill and Perpetua. "I'm so sorry, my dear, but you can't think how funny it sounded..." He stopped laughing at last and stood patting his aching tummy, and looked up at her in some alarm. "Now, Isabel, my dear, you're not going to mind a joke..."

"I don't see anything funny in it at all," said Isabel viciously. Her tone added that neither would Edgar, when she had had a few words with him alone. She flounced back through the arch and thundered on the door leading out of the Assembly room: they saw Miss Betchley's astonished face appear as she opened it from the other side, all unconscious of what had been going on in the hall. Isabel pushed past her and out to the dressing-rooms. "We simply must put a curtain across that arch," said Mr. Port. "The audience can see everything in the Assembly room."

Perpetua suggested that the knights would find difficulty in finding their way through.

"Beads," said Mr. Port succinctly. He added vaguely that they would look like an arras and be just the thing.

Up on the stage the horses stood patiently while their riders argued the problem of how Earl should be certain of reaching the amplifier switch. Motherdear's inherited eye for decor proved unexpectedly useful. "Could Mr. Anderson and I have our horses' forefeet mounted up on blocks? That would bring him in easy reach of the switch and at the same time give a nice effect of chargers rampant on either side of the arch: like the lion and the unicorn in the Royal thingamajig, you know…" His voice trailed off uncertainly.

"It would also give an impression of the Red Knight sliding slowly but helplessly backwards on to his charger's tail," said Earl.

"You can hold on to your standard," said Brian Bryan impatiently: the idea of a man who couldn't sit two minutes in a saddle unless it was positively and absolutely horizontal!

Mr. Port was longing only to get off and make it up with darling Isabel. "That will be perfect! It'll make a magnificent tableau and then at the critical moment Mr. Anderson can leave go of the standard for a second, and put on the switch. Your hand will be up near the switch anyway, Mr. Anderson, the audience won't even notice you just imperceptibly leaning forward to flick it on…" He clapped his hands in signal for them all to dismiss. Dancing with impatience, he allowed himself to be introduced to Inspector Cockrill and after a few civil platitudes dashed off back-stage. "Never *heard* of me, I suppose," said Cockie, wistfully.

"Of course, Cockie, you're used to having the Law behind you, and everybody in Kent being terrified of you, and you being the sort of centre of everything..."

"And you think I can't get anywhere on my own personality?" said Cockie grimly.

Earl had not seen Perpetua so nearly animated for years: something of her old gay girlhood seemed to have come back to her as she proudly presented the little man to the company behind the scenes, and dwelt upon the magnitude of his position and achievements down in Kent where he was really appreciated. The knights jostled through the tower archway from the stage, their long cloaks tumbling behind them and dismounted with more or less grace from their horses; or rode on through the outer door to the stables and there climbed down with the help of the single attendant groom. They all repaired to a pub outside the hall, for drinks: Earl very doggy and palsy-walsy with the barmaid, Brian Two-Times with the solemn black business man's hat beloved of the visiting foreigner, his too long mackintosh hung over his arm despite the cloudless sky, Susan Betchley standing her round with unfeminine insistence, George hanging on at the tail of the party, miserably convinced that it did not want him there, yet lacking the poise to take himself gracefully off. Sugar-Daddy Port was propped up in a corner with Isabel who was making magnificent capital out of her injuries. She consented to have Inspector Cockrill introduced to her, but soon returned to her purposeful squabbling. Cockrill decided that it was time for them to depart. "I'll see you to your door, Peppi." As they sat side by side on the top of the home-going bus, he took her thin hand. "There's nothing to suggest which of these people sent you the notes. You tell me these scraps of paper were littered about everywhere: and eight people had access to them—you three who got them, that Brian Twice or whatever they call him, Miss Betchley, Mr. Port, and young George Whatsisname, and his mama—who, however, wasn't here today. You never can tell: but I should think that the whole thing was just a rather ugly, very silly joke…"

He put his hand into his pocket to fish for his tobacco to roll himself another of his incessant cigarettes. There was something there that had not been there an hour ago. He said, coolly, unfolding the little scrap of paper: "Well, that lets out the mama, anyway, and reduces us down to seven." The same muddle of pin-men on one side; on the other the same straggly pencilled characters. It was quite a long note this time. It said: INSPECTOR COCKRILL, YOU THINK IT'S JUST A JOKE DON'T YOU? BUT WAIT TILL THE OPENING NIGHT OF THE EXHIBITION. ISABEL, PERPETUA, ANDERSON— WHICH OF THEM WILL BE THE FIRST TO DIE?

Chapter IV

IT WAS HORRIBLE TO HAVE TO GET THROUGH THE DAYS before the Exhibition opened: to live through the long hours, crawling with half incredulous, wholly uneasy fear. Isabel might make light of it, but she was frightened now: they were all frightened, gathering into little knots to discuss the fourth note, the note that had been found in Inspector Cockrill's pocket. Cockrill had given it more or less serious attention. It was all probably a "have" but there was a ring about it too grim for the threats to be entirely light-heartedly joking; nor when he looked round the little group of persons who could have planted the notes, were many of them really on terms for that kind of joking. Half apologetically, he took the scrap of paper along to Scotland Yard. The handwriting experts were full of mights and might-nots, but would say nothing definite. He left the paper with them, and returned to his conference, just keeping in touch now and again with Perpetua, a Perpetua woken now from her cold indifference to a new awareness of life—to an awareness of death, of the threat of approaching death…

They awaited the day.

A Thursday and a Friday crept by, and a long weekend; and then suddenly Monday and Tuesday had wings and it was Tuesday night and tomorrow was The Day: and Isabel Drew crouched in a huddle in her bed and gave herself up to sick fear. Supposing after all it isn't a joke! Suppose one of them is angry with me for something I've done—(so many little, mean little, cruel little, long-forgotten things that Isabel might have done!)—suppose they really mean that they'll kill me! In a couple of hours it would be midnight: it would be Tomorrow. It was terribly lonely. On an impulse she reached for the telephone; she would ring up Earl and tell him to come along round, and she would make him some tea, and they could at least talk about their common peril… But Earl had let them cut off his 'phone, the silly fool. She rang up Perpetua instead. "Hallo, Peppi."

"Hallo," said Perpetua's low voice.

"I thought a word between murderees might be comforting: tomorrow being D-day. I've tried Earl, but of course his damn 'phone's cut off. How *are* you? Scared?"

"I am rather," said Perpetua. "I went to bed early—but I couldn't sleep because of thinking about it. You see I—well, I don't quite know what to do about the exhibition: I mean, I needn't go down, really, *need* I? I haven't got a job there, nobody can force me to go. Just because I usually help Miss Betchley…"

"I think you're mad to even consider it. Why go and mix yourself up with that crowd? The rest of us are bound to be at the pageant, because we *have* got jobs there: why not stay home and be safe? After all, whatever happens is bound to happen down there."

"Unless the—the murderer has that all worked out: and he's purposely going to let everybody collect down there and then come and—and attack me all alone here at home."

"What nonsense you do talk," said Isabel crossly. But on thinking things over a little, it did occur to one that with Perpetua at Elysium, there was a three to one chance, while with Perpetua at home, the threat would be shared only by Earl and herself. She switched her powers of persuasion abruptly to persuading Peppi that perhaps, after all, it was her duty to go. "The Bitchley does count on you now to help behind the scenes: and tomorrow night, of all nights, she'll be in a flap…"

"Oh, yes, I shall go," said Perpetua. "It seems a bit sort of mingy to stay away. But it's rather petrifying, Isabel, isn't it? I mean people do do these things: one reads about them in the paper…" By tomorrow night, would *they* be "people in the paper"? Perpetua had been "in the paper" herself before now. (GIRL HE LOVED FAITHLESS, YOUNG SOLDIER KILLS HIMSELF.) She said wretchedly: "Of course probably it's all some silly idea of a joke: but supposing… Supposing…"

"A fine comfort you turned out to be," said Isabel crossly. "I might just as well have rung up Sugar-Daddy: at least he'd be worried about *me*. In fact now I come to think of it, I *shall* ring him: he can take me down tomorrow evening: it'll be company, anyhow…" She slammed down the receiver. Silly little fool! Just lily-livered, and anyway thinking only of herself. Friends aren't friends, thought Isabel resentfully.

Only acquaintances. When trouble comes, one hasn't got any friends. As for Sugar-Daddy—well, he more or less had to be a friend, these days, whether he liked it or not. An uneasy sort of relationship, but still... She lifted the receiver again.

Sugar-Daddy was delighted beyond measure at this sign of grace. Of course he would take her down in the car. They could stop off somewhere on the way perhaps, and have a drink: the bars would be open at half past five... On the other hand, he supposed he ought to be down there at least an hour before the balloon went up. A cup of tea then? And if Isabel wouldn't mind all that hanging about at Elysian Hall before the pageant began...?

But supposing after all that it was Edgar Port who was sending those notes? Supposing that all this time his devotion had been just a gag, just some sort of a trick to get her to put her trust in him...? Come to think of it, it had never really been a very convincing devotion: even in the early days, even before—before he had begun to be frightened of her getting in touch with Mrs. Port, even before he had begun that little series of "presents" that would sweeten her into saying that of *course* she would never give him away to his wife—even before that, it had seemed unconvincing: a sort of silly infatuation, a sort of deliberate fostering of that infatuation, as though in indulging it he were making a pet of himself, rather than of her. Supposing it had all been a ruse to win her confidence? Supposing, on the other hand, that once it had been sincere: but that now the little presents were becoming too much of a burden? That he really believed that in a fit of "conscience" she was in the least likely to approach his wife... She said abruptly that no, after all, she would go down

by herself: see him tomorrow, then, at a little before six…?
Once more she put down the receiver, and curled herself up
in her bed, and lay there, wakeful, while the hours chimed
balefully through the long night. Seven people: and she and
Perpetua and Earl had received the notes. Only four—and
Edgar Port was one of the four—who might have sent them.

The night passed; and the morning dragged by; and it
was five o'clock. She went through the ritual of her toilet in
a crawling fear. Tight satin brassiere, tight pink satin pants,
flowered silk frock, very light and caressing about her golden
curves. She combed her hair into its web of honey, widened
her eyes for the mascara, slashed the lipstick across her pout-
ing mouth… Lonely, lonely, lonely… How terribly alone one
was, among all one's friends… She stood herself a taxi down
to Elysian Hall. Here and there a few carpenters tinkered
desperately; but for the rest, the Exhibition was complete.
Lights blazed, loudspeakers blared, the rows of houses and
cottages and flats and bathrooms and baths stood ready and
polished within an inch of their chromium and enamel, on
view. The young ladies' mouths were rounded over their
plums, the exhibitors had retired behind the scenes. Tray
won of our Slomber nets… You place the chicken in *raw*…
The Clock of Flowers told the slightly incorrect time to the
wondering crowd, artificial waterfalls tinkled in gardens that
had not been there a day or two ago… At the turnstiles the
people shoved and jostled good-temperedly. Isabel, arriving at
the latest possible minute so as to spend no undue time upon
dangerous ground, displayed her little red "Demonstrator"
disc and was permitted to push a way through. She scurried up the long aisles between the Coldio refrigerators and

Ohsohot furnaces and Ultracomfy lavatory seats; the gentlemen on the Downibed stand chi-yacked her as she passed, the red-haired boy on Keepitot plate-racks called to her to skip away later for a drink... She shook her head at them one and all and made like a shot rabbit for the haven of her dingy little dressing room behind the stage. And yet—why there? Would she be safer there? Would she not be running right into danger there? But with the instinct of a wild animal for the shelter of the dark, she scuttled in among the shadowy stalls where the horses moved restlessly shuffling their listless hooves, and so to her room. If only the pageant would begin, she thought: nobody can do anything to me up there in the tower in front of them all. Outside, she heard Miss Betchley's voice marshalling the knights. "Now then, you boys, get a move on, we shall be starting in ten minutes... Mr. Brian, good you're nearly ready... Mr. Exmouth: *good!* Ah—Mr. Port! Yes, everything seems to be going quite smoothly; but have you seen Mr. Anderson anywhere? All the rest are here, except Mr. Anderson."

Evidently Earl had had the same idea as herself: the less time spent on the danger spot, the better. It was comforting—and yet horribly disturbing—to think that somebody else was frightened too: had also come to think of it as by no means just a joke. There came a nibbling of plump fingers at her door. Sugar-Daddy's voice called softly: "Are you there, my dear?"

She slid across the room and shot home the bolt. Better to see no one. Better just to keep to herself until it was necessary to cross the Assembly room and run up the inside ladder of her tower. There she would be impregnable. There she would be in view of five thousand people. There she must be safe. The ladder might have been tampered with, of course, the rickety platform made more rickety—but these were things that one could be prepared for, these were dangers one could recognize and understand... She pulled off her silk frock, stepped into the ankle-length silver gown, adjusted the tall pointed hat with the two false plaits hanging on either side of it and the chiffon veil flowing from its tip: and as she dressed, spared a thought for Perpetua and Earl, who also were threatened... Vague, gentle Perpetua, whose dead face had taken on a new look in these last days: but which had passed only from indifference to weariness and strain; and florid, show-off old Earl whom one had known for—was it twenty years?—and knew to be, beneath all that racketty act of his, only a rather simple, not very happy man... Still, he was cutting it a bit fine, only ten minutes more to go, and not here yet. Supposing, Isabel thought with a sudden clutch at her heart, he never did come to Elysium at all that night! And that Peppi stayed away also! After all—it was flying in the face of danger to be here at all: why on earth hadn't *she* thought of staying away herself, what on earth did this silly old pageant matter compared with the threat to her life...? And if Earl and Perpetua weren't there—there was only herself left. "ISABEL, PERPETUA, ANDERSON—WHICH OF THEM WILL BE THE FIRST TO DIE?"

And then she heard Perpetua's voice: and Perpetua was saying soothingly: "But Earl's *here*, Miss Betchley... He's changing into his armour."

Isabel pushed open her door abruptly and walked out swiftly into the Assembly room. Perpetua hurried after her as she began to thrust her way through the jostling knights.

"Oh, Isabel—I thought you'd like to know: I've got Inspector Cockrill down here with me. He's out in front." She was panting a little. "He took a bit of persuading: I thought I'd never get him here in time." She threw a glance over her shoulder. "I'm so *late*! Must go and help poor Betchley with these maddening knights." She slipped away.

The knights were pouring into the big room now, jockeying for their positions in the line. Brian sat quietly on his white horse, waiting to lead them through the arch. Isabel scurried through the throng, alert for the least sign of attack from any of the mail-clad figures; in their silly tin armour with their helmets and flowing velvet cloaks it was impossible to tell who anybody was: and now, if ever, was the moment to strike… Through the jostling crowd and into the haven of her dim, silent, tower. She paused inside the entrance, looking up the tall ladder, her hand at her heaving bosom in a gesture which for once had nothing in it of coquetry: and with one foot on the bottom rung, was suddenly electrified into immobility. Half-way up the ladder, was something that, to her excited imagination, shone with an evil glitter in the light from the open door.

Cockrill, left to himself, took up a favourable position in front of the stage and waited with bored impatience for the fun to begin. The English and their pageants! Nobody enjoyed them, nobody ever knew what they were intended to represent but it was in the national character to produce and witness them: and if one was anybody, it was expected of one that one should attend. In North Kent, Cockie assiduously attended all the local pageants, standing craning his neck in the crowd and always at a loss to know what in the world was going on. To come to London, where he was so pointedly nobody, and yet still have to go to see one seemed the very height of indignity. He concentrated all his attention on the hopeless task of rolling a tidy cigarette: and looked up swiftly as a blare of trumpets drew the attention of the crowd to the deserted stage. Lights sprang up among the ferns and hydrangeas tastefully banked up and about its base, footlights flooded the castellated wall and the archway through the tower: Mr. Port's "arras" across the archway screened the waiting knights in the Assembly room from the public gaze. The chattering of the crowd died down to a hum: something was about to happen on the stage, and whatever it was, was free! What had been a sea of variegated blobs, now became a sea of pink faces all turned towards the tower. The trumpets blared again, the footlights bathed the scene in radiance, dimming in contrast the fierce light of the vast auditorium below: and to strains of highly martial music, the bead curtain across the archway was pushed back, and the Knights of England, Home and Beauty came riding through.

The white charger walked at a stately pace: the silver armour gleamed, the silver standard held the white banner high, the long cloak flowed out over the horse's hindquarters in folds of glossy velvet. Slowly down the centre of the stage till, through the upthrust visor, Cockrill could see the blue eyes of the rider gazing down at him: then it turned abruptly and swung off to the right. The train of ten black horses followed, swinging off to right and left, meeting again beneath the tower, dispersing to their stations for the "hollow square," the White Knight in the centre: and so on into the movements that Charity had plotted out with her little pin-men all those weeks ago. The velvet cloaks billowed, the tinny spurs jangled, the knights sat squarely in their saddles, their mailed right hands glued to their standards to hold themselves steady, their left clutching the heavily decorated reins. The Grand Chain was coming, and in the Grand Chain the horses had actually to be urged to a highly dangerous gallop! Corner to corner... Set to partners... And finally, slowly stepping but gathering pace until the whole was conducted at a fine jingle-jangling, saddle-creaking, cloak-flowing, bucketing canter, into the twirling, in-and-out gyrations of the Grand Chain. The crowd applauded, the music changed again with a warning note, the pace slowed down, and the knights took up their final positions in the Tableau of Homage to heaven only knew what: eight in a semicircle round the curved edge of the stage, staring out through their upthrust visors at the crowd; one on either side of the tower, blue cloak to the left, red cloak to the right, their horses' forefeet posed patiently on their wooden blocks; the white horse backed to the audience, facing into the arch, its rider's white cloak flowing in its soft velvet folds across its rump and half-way down its gently swishing tail. The floodlights shifted, gradually ascending to the darkened window of the tower: and slowly, sickeningly, Isabel's body toppled over the low railing of the balcony and landed with a horrible, soft, slightly scrunching thud on the floor below.

Chapter V

THROUGH THE COLD HUSH THAT FOLLOWED THE THUD of Isabel's fall, the single scream of a woman in the crowd pierced the eardrums like the whistle of an engine. In the interminable moment that Cockrill stood, paralysed with horror and astonishment, the whole scene seemed to dwindle to the dimensions of a toy: a little brightly lit garish stage with its tinselly castellated wall and its miniature tower, toy soldiers motionless on toy horses, arranged by a child's hand into their careful pattern—the half-circle round the edge of the stage, the two rampant, one on either side of the tower. Even the white horse, rearing up on its haunches in the centre of the arch seemed caught for a moment into immobility. But the stillness broke: the toys were clockwork toys—the little round, painted heads of the riders turned on their pivots and were fixed again, staring: the white horse reared and bucked but would not step backwards on to the little heap of silver at its hind hooves—and suddenly took the bit between its teeth and bolted through the bead curtain hanging across the archway, and disappeared from view: and the red knight brought his horse's feet down from their wooden block and jerkily dismounted and jerkily moved forward on his clock-work legs to the body; and jerkily knelt beside it. The long red velvet cloak flowing about him hid the silver from Inspector Cockrill's view. He began to force his way through the forward surging crowd, using his elbows, shoving his way desperately along. "Let me through! I'm a police officer! Let me *through!*" As he heaved himself up through the banked flowers at its base, the Red Knight rose unsteadily to his feet, stood for a moment staring down at the body, and then turned and staggered off abruptly through the arch: Cockrill called out, but he did not seem to hear. His hand in the absurd gloves of knitted silver string was held against the forehead of his helmet, as a man in pain puts the back of his hand to his brow. By the time Cockrill had gained the floor of the stage, he was gone: but Brian Bryan and Miss Betchley came through the arch, Brian still in his armour but with his helmet under his arm. He looked rather dazed, staring about him almost blindly until his eyes lighted on the body lying at the foot of the tower: and he stood suddenly very still. Miss Betchley said: "For God's sake what's happened?" And also looked at the body. She whispered: "Earl Anderson said she was dead."

Brian Two-Times took off his white cloak, slowly: and silently laid it over the dreadful form.

Cockrill did not know quite what his position might be: but until the London police arrived on the scene, he supposed he had better take over. He went and stood over the covered body. "Don't touch her. Leave her alone." But, after all, the girl might not be dead. He glanced up at the balcony above him: fifteen feet or so—not very far to fall. He lifted the cloak away from her face. "Are you sure she's dead?"

"Earl Anderson said she is dead," said Brian: the foreign accent came out very strong. He rubbed his palm across his face wearily, from the forehead down. He repeated: "Anderson said: 'She is dead'!"

"Dead!" said Susan Betchley. Her old-young face was haggard and grey beneath its summer tan; but her brown eyes blazed with something that was not entirely grief or horror: her voice was as deep and throaty as a man's.

Cockrill pulled back the cloak, leaving the lower half of the body still covered. It lay face-downwards, the legs bent, the arms at ugly, crooked angles. He knelt and gingerly turned it as it lay.

Isabel was dead all right. Her face was honey-coloured no longer, but a dreadful, dusky purple, her tongue protruded from between blue lips and there was a trickle of saliva still dribbling from a corner of her mouth. He turned his head from the stare of the terrible, half-closed eyes. The crowding knights shuddered and moved back.

Two policemen in uniform and a plain-clothes man had by this time struggled forward and up to the stage. Cockrill got up and faced them, one hand still holding back the velvet so that they could see the face and neck. The spangled chiffon veil was wound tightly round the plump throat. With his unoccupied hand he fished in his breast pocket for identification papers. "My name is Cockrill, Detective Inspector, Kent police. I—just happened to be on the spot." His voice trailed off uncertainly. He asked: "Whose show is this?"

The plain-clothes man said: "I'm Stammers, sir: Inspector,

local police. I'm in charge at the Exhibition." He looked down at the body. "Looks as though she'd strangled herself. Caught her veil in a hook…"

No. That slow, thrusting, toppling fall had been unimpeded by any veil caught in any hook. He let the velvet fall again, to cover the terrible face, and drew the inspector a little aside. "This is all no business of mine: but I think you'll find the girl's been murdered. I advise you to ring up your station and get a lot more help. A *lot* more help!" He saw the polite incredulity on Stammers' face, and, slapping his shabby old felt hat on the back of his head, moved abruptly away. What a town!

"Inspector Cockrill!" said Stammers. "Good lord, yes: that business at the hospital down in Kent…"

"That is considered one of my less successful cases," said Cockie, coldly. But he felt better, all the same.

The crowd, stricken immobile by the shock of the fall, was beginning to stir itself into life again. Stammers gave brief orders to his men: like well-trained sheep-dogs they moved off in response, shepherding back the crowding knights now beginning to push their way through the bead curtains back into the Assembly room. "All remain 'ere, please. All remain on the stage, please…" Others went off to man the exits to the hall: Stammers sent messages to his superintendent… And suddenly here was Mr. Port among them on the stage, appearing at a trot, panting, through the archway. "Isabel! My God!—I saw her fall…" His feet faltered and were still: the down-drop of the velvet from Cockrill's hand had not entirely covered the unseeing, up-rolled eyes. "Oh, God— this is horrible… Isabel!"

Cockrill left Stammers to his job and went through the arch and into the Assembly room. An empty square, an unfurnished shell, save for its single suit of armour lolling drunkenly against the wall, its helmet askew on the peg above it. He glanced into the empty tube of the tower: the platform halfway up was flooded with light from the arc-lamps outside. A steep ladder-like flight of steps led to the platform: there was nothing and nobody there. He hurried across the big room and through the doorway opposite the arch. "I suggest you let nobody through," he said to the constable who arrived there for duty at about the same time. "Don't touch locks and things: the fingerprint people may be interested." It was none of his business but... He ran on down the straight corridor leading from the door of the Assembly room between the empty dressing rooms, and out to the improvised stables between the rooms and the yard. "Anderson! Hey—Anderson! Are you there?" A little man, bowlegged and horsey-smelling, appeared at last. "Cor, sir! What 'appened? I was aht front lookin' on, and I see the young lady fall..."

"Who are *you*?" said Cockrill.

"Groom, sir; in charge of the 'orses. I thought I'd better get back, sir, case anything was needed. Clever's the name, sir: Bill Clever."

"Have you seen one of the knights? He came this way a couple of minutes ago: well, five minutes, perhaps—directly after the girl fell. Hey—*An*derson!"

But there was nobody there. Earl Anderson's horse had been left standing uncertainly on the stage when he blundered away, the armour he had worn now lay in its single ridiculous piece with the helmet under the scarlet cloak on the floor of one of the stalls. Cockrill returned to the stage. Inspector Stammers was in a well-controlled flurry of activity, and at Cockrill's suggestion he sent a man out to the nearest official car park, to the nearest constable on point duty. But there was no news of Earl Anderson. Nor was he anywhere to be found in the hall.

A Detective Inspector Charlesworth was on his way down from Scotland Yard. "Never heard of him," said Inspector Cockrill, with a gleam of pleasure.

Meanwhile, loudspeakers blared out instructions to the crowds. The police would be grateful if anyone who could give any information whatsoever which might help in the matter of the—er—accident—would report to the officer at such-and-such a gate... All entrances would be closed for an hour or so but anyone with a good reason to leave might apply at such-and-such a gate... The crowd, which would ordinarily have been content to linger on getting its money's worth until late in the evening, was naturally much incensed at being asked to stay on for an hour, and besieged the officers on the gates with demands that justice might be done. As to information, several ladies fainted while describing the horrible faces they had seen at the window of the tower immediately before Isabel fell, one old gentleman who lived on grass seemed convinced that if only Isabel had done the same all this might never have happened, a lady had had her handbag stolen and considered Elysian Hall a den of vice, murder, robbery, and with any luck rapine, and seventeen young men had heard shots ring out at varying times before Isabel had fallen... The truth was that skill and care had been directed to attract all attention away from the window so as to prepare for the Queen of Beauty's dramatic appearance there: the lights had been focused on the lower part of the stage, and nobody had been looking at the window at all, or seen anything whatsoever there. The police finally broadcast a message saying that everyone who cared to might now go home: and the taxpayers demanded indignantly what the Police Force thought they maintained it *for* if it didn't know better than to let everyone go when, for all they knew, there might be a murderer walking calmly out of the main entrance at this very minute. For nobody paid the slightest attention to any suggestion but that of deliberate and fearful murder. And rightly so.

Inspector Stammers meanwhile had been busy directing his reinforced troupe of sheep-dogs: had rounded up all those connected with the pageant—except for the missing Earl Anderson, and had chivvied them into an office set apart for them by the authority of Mr. Port, to await the arrival of Detective Inspector Charlesworth from Scotland Yard. Cockrill looked round upon them: Susan Betchley, grey-faced but smothering some odd inner excitement, Brian Bryan and George Exmouth and the eight other knights, still sweating in their absurd suits of armour with their helmets under their arms, Mr. Port, his chubby face puckered with anxiety… But… Cockrill said suddenly, and his voice was cold with a rising panic: "Where's Perpetua Kirk?"

Nobody knew.

Detective Inspector Charlesworth was of the "Hendon" school, a personable young man with a disarming smile and his hair brushed up into rather maddening little "moustaches" over his ears. Stammers made a lightening report and explained Inspector Cockrill. Mr. Charlesworth's favour in the eyes of the Inspector hung wavering in the balance.

"Cockrill, Cockrill…" said Charlesworth, thoughtfully biting upon his underlip. "Where have I…? Oh, yes! It was you who made such a muck of that hospital case down in Kent!" Innocent of the slightest intention to wound, he shook the Inspector thoroughly by the hand. "Delighted to have you down here. Hang around!"

"Thank you," said Cockie austerely.

Inspector Stammers outlined the case for an immediate search for Perpetua. "Well, get your chaps to see to it. Get in touch with her home, of course, and all that: in fact," said Charlesworth, frowning a little anxiously, "I think you'd better take over the search yourself. Inspector Cockrill, I'd like you to stay here, if you will." He perched himself on the edge of the black glass and chromium desk thought proper for a pageant master down at Elysian Hall, glanced round the scared rows of faces lining the little, glassed-in office, and said crisply: "Now!"

"The girl was murdered," said Inspector Cockrill. He waved a packet of cigarette papers in Charlesworth's direction. "Any objection if I smoke?"

"None in the world," said Charlesworth. "You say you think this girl was murdered?"

"I saw her fall," said Cockrill. His fingers fumbled in his pouch for tobacco. "She was—pitched over that railing. She didn't faint, or trip, or lean too far forward and topple over: the rail of the balcony was too high for that. She was, in some way or other heaved up and pushed over."

"And you were watching her? And you saw nobody?"

"I wasn't watching her," said Cockrill. "I was watching the stage—like everybody else. The window was hardly lit up at all yet, and the girl wore a full skirt which would have hidden anybody who, say, lifted her from the knees, and pitched her over, and then dodged back into the darkness of the tower."

"Yes, I see," said Charlesworth.

"And she didn't catch her veil in any nail," added Cockrill firmly: no nonsense about *that*.

Charlesworth eyed him rather doubtfully. The little man seemed somewhat biased in favour of the sensational. "What makes you so *fright*fully certain that she was murdered?"

"She was told a week before hand that she would be," said Cockie impatiently. (And so had Perpetua been told that she would be murdered: and Earl Anderson. And now Isabel was dead, and Anderson had walked off the stage and disappeared into the evening: and Perpetua—where was she? The pit of his stomach felt sick and cold.)

Charlesworth considered, his behind propped against the black desk, his long legs stretched out, ankles crossed before him. "Well, if she was murdered, at least the threats have narrowed the field down very considerably."

"Amply assisted by the scene," said Cockrill.

"The scene?"

Cockie's brown fingers played with his cigarette. "This is a projection of the 'sealed room' mystery. The scene of the murder was bounded on one side by a stage, under the observation of several thousand pairs of eyes; and on the other by a locked door, with somebody sitting on guard on the other side of it. The murderer must have been within these confines. And the place is as bare as a biscuit box, so that there is nowhere where he can possibly have hidden, or remain hidden. With the exception of two people all the people who were on the scene of the murder, are here now. With the exception of those two people everyone who could have sent the threatening notes is here now. Eight of these people—" he waved his hand towards the attendant knights— "could not have sent the notes. Therefore the suspects are automatically reduced to the six who could. Miss Kirk and this man Anderson are missing: for the rest we have Betchley, Mr. Port, Mr. Exmouth and Mr. Brian Bryan, coyly referred to by Miss Drew as Brian Twice."

"Brian Two-Times," said Brian, irritably.

"Yes. So really," said Charlesworth, getting up and starting towards the door, "we may as well let the eight knights go."

"When we have heard their evidence," suggested Cockie, sweetly. Charlesworth returned to his desk, a trifle flushed.

Susan Betchley looked up from the chair where she sat with her well-turned legs just a little ungracefully crossed. "Of course you can say that I didn't stay on the door."

"Of course," said Cockie.

"In which case, I could be the murderer."

"Of course," said Charlesworth, getting it in first.

"You are either the murderer or you aren't," said Cockrill. "If you are—we shall soon find out. If you aren't—then you are one factor of the 'sealed room.'" It all sounded nice and simple.

"In sealed room mysteries," said Charlesworth, interrupting this pleasant interchange with what was intended to be a dash of cold water, "the solution is never really anything to do with the room being sealed. The murderer has always gone into the room before it was sealed: and he gets away after it's *un*sealed."

"Miss Betchley will tell us who may have got in and out of the room under those conditions," said Cockie. "But of course that theory would entirely disregard the clue of the threatening notes." He sat back and crossed his bony knees, comfortably: two up to the old man!

Miss Betchley got down to business. "Nobody else ever went into the 'sealed room.' At twenty-five to six I went out on to the empty stage. There is no sort or kind of place there where a fly could hide. I went through the arch and stood in the doorway of the tower. I switched on the electric light and looked up towards the platform: there was definitely nothing and nobody in the tower. I came back through the empty Assembly room and from then on I never moved away from the big door leading into it. Nobody went in or out of that door except Mr. Port, Isabel Drew, Miss Kirk, and the eleven knights."

"Somebody might have climbed up on to the stage," suggested Mr. Port, diffidently.

Inspector Cockrill startled Mr. Charlesworth by suddenly asking permission to speak. "Of course, of *course*—go ahead. And say anything you want to, any time, Inspector: don't mind me."

Cockrill tucked away the permission obtained by these shock tactics with a small, grim smile of satisfaction. "I was merely going to say that it was impossible for anyone to have got up on to the stage without its being noticed by a hundred people in the crowd. I did it myself later on. The air was thick with running commentary, 'He's climbing up through the ferns…' 'He's nearly on to the stage…' 'Now he's got right up…'"

"Like the people behind one in the cheap seats at the cinema," said Charlesworth, pleasantly. Nobody seemed to share his familiarity with the cheap seats at the cinema, however: it was sticky going. Personally he thought the old boy was just having a beautiful pipe-dream with his "heaved over" and "pitched across the railing" and all the rest of it: getting past his job a bit, no doubt, and all those threatening notes had gone to his head.

A constable knocked at the door and handed in a folded note. The eyes of the eleven poor prisoners turned to it eagerly, shifted, glanced politely aside. Charlesworth read it through twice and then put it into his pocket. He said to the constable: "All right. Tell the police surgeon I'm glad to have this, and I'll wait for his final confirmation."

Meanwhile, said the note, Isabel Drew had died within one minute either way of hitting the ground. She had died of manual strangulation: no chiffon veil caught on nails— nothing like that. She had been in what amounted to a "sealed room" with eleven knights in phoney armour: and while the eleven knights sat their horses in full view of several thousand people, one of them had gone up into the tower and strangled her and thrown her down.

All about them, beyond the glass windows of the little office, the exhibition proceeded upon its course, the buzz and chatter heightened almost to a roar by the violent excitement of Isabel's terrible end. Never again would the young ladies with the Slomber Nets do so much business: if the exhibitors had had their way, a fresh young woman would have been sacrificed every night upon the tower as long as the exhibition remained open. Meanwhile, the buzz and chatter and clamour rolled on…

Within Susan Betchley there glowed a fire which would not be concealed: but she lowered her lids upon the blaze of it, and continued with her account of the evening, precisely and clearly. "The pageant was due to begin at six o'clock. At twenty-five to, I looked over the whole place, as I've told you. There was nobody behind the scenes yet, the dressing rooms were empty, the horses were in their stables with Bill Clever, the groom in charge: and nobody else. And there was nobody on the stage or in the tower or anywhere in the Assembly room—you can take my word for that. At about twenty-to the knights began to arrive. Most of them spoke to me before going into the Assembly room to collect their armour. They always used to rehearse in armour, of course, because of getting themselves and the horses used to it: they'd developed different habits, some of them changed in the Assembly room itself and then clanked back to the stalls to get their horses, some of them lugged their armour through and changed in the stalls. You couldn't tell which did what: and once they were in the armour, they were practically unrecognizable any way. I checked them all in: by ten-to everybody had arrived except Mr. Anderson. At least I thought he hadn't come yet. I was worried, and I spoke to Mr. Port about it. Mr. Port said not to worry: he went and knocked on Miss Drew's door and she called out to him, and then he went away towards the dressing rooms, and I didn't see him again. But a few moments later Miss Kirk turned up and she said that Earl Anderson was there all the time."

"Did anyone else see him to speak to?" asked Charlesworth of the company in general.

Nobody had. "But then of course he must have ridden on later with all the other knights," said Miss Betchley. "Because after all, he was there."

"Yes, now—tell us about that."

"Well, Mr. Bryan rode through first as he always does at rehearsals, and took up his place as the leader of the knights. I said a word to him. Wished him luck and so on. The others came jumbling through in ones and twos and sorted themselves out into their proper order: some of them mounted in the stalls and rode through, others led their horses and mounted in the Assembly room. By now it must have been seven or eight minutes to the hour. Miss Kirk was rather late."

"I kept her rather late," said Cockrill. "I couldn't see what she wanted to go mucking about behind the scenes for anyway, since it wasn't her job—and she was scared. But she said that she'd got into the habit of it, and Miss Betchley would be needing her—so off she went." Even to his own dry heart he would not acknowledge how bitterly he regretted now that he had ever let her go: pretty, frightened, unhappy Perpetua…

"Well, anyway, very soon afterwards, Miss Drew came out of her room and went quickly across the Assembly room. Miss Kirk followed her and said something to her, and then Miss Drew went into her tower, and Miss Kirk left the Assembly room and went down towards the dressing rooms: she generally went and checked up that all the knights were ready. There's a whole wilderness of dressing rooms and corridors back there."

"And you?"

"There were only one or two more knights to come: as soon as I'd checked them all in, I locked the door on them to keep them safely there, and sat down on my little stool outside it: and I just sat on there, whistling away to myself and never moved away."

"What did you whistle?" said Charlesworth, unexpectedly. (These University detectives with their fancy ways!)

Miss Betchley looked surprised. "I only *know* one tune: so I expect it was that. 'Sur le pont D'Avignon...'"

"And you never moved away at all?" said Cockrill, sticking pointedly to the matter in hand.

"I never budged."

"This is awfully important," said Charlesworth, earnestly. "If for any reason—any reason at all, quite unconnected with the murder, perhaps—you moved from that stool, it's your duty to say so. In fact, it may be very much to your advantage to say so."

"Because after the knights had ridden through on to the stage, I'm the only person who could have followed Isabel up to the tower and murdered her."

Charlesworth made her a little bow. "You have a singularly clear mind."

"Well, I have a singularly clear conscience too," said Susan Betchley, coolly. "And I tell you flat that I didn't budge an inch."

"And nobody went through after that? Not even Miss Kirk or Mr. Port?"

Miss Betchley shook her head firmly. "I—well, I was in and out of the Assembly room and the dressing rooms seeing to things," said Mr. Port, hurriedly. "And then I went and stood in the crowd. There was nothing more for me to do. Miss

Betchley had the whole thing well in hand, all the knights had arrived, Isabel—Miss Drew—was already in her dressing room changing. I wanted to see from out front what the effects were like: I wanted to listen to the comments of the people, and generally see how things went. Just for future reference you know..." He mopped his pink forehead. "I—I saw her fall."

Eleven knights. And Isabel. In what amounted to a "sealed room." And while the eleven knights sat their horses in full view of several thousand people, one of them had gone up into the tower and strangled her with his hands: and thrown her down.

Proceedings were interrupted by the arrival of Charlesworth's henchman, Sergeant Bedd: large, thick-set, grizzled, kindly, in his stove-pipe utility suit. He had come from a cursory search of Earl Anderson's flat. Nobody there. "And, funny thing, sir," said Sergeant Bedd, eyeing Charlesworth for permission to speak in front of the old boy in the comic mackintosh—obvious police of some kind, all the same—"what's more no bedroom slippers: if you see what I mean."

Charlesworth saw what he meant at once. "Done a bunk, eh? Oh, by the way, Sergeant, this is Inspector Cockrill, Kent police."

Sergeant Bedd's large face took on a look of mingled excitement and awe. "Good lord, sir: not Inspector *Cock*rill? Not that affair of the sanded paths down at Swansmere? And them decapitations at Pigeonsford?"

"*And* the anaesthetic deaths at Heron's Park hospital," said Inspector Cockrill, grimly.

"Ah, yes: you was unfortunate there, sir. These things do happen: you'll remember, Mr. Charlesworth, we had a bit of a slip-up ourselves in that yachting business down in Devonshire?"

An extraordinarily pleasant fellow, really, for a Londoner. And observant too. "You say Anderson's slippers are missing from his flat?"

"That's right, sir," said Bedd. "And his shaving tackle and toothbrush and things. Of course they may be poked away somewhere: I didn't take time to have a real good search. But I had the impression that the gent had done a bunk, sir. If that's what you expected?" He cocked his head to one side like an intelligent, elderly rough-haired terrier.

"We're getting the ports and stations and things watched," said Charlesworth to Cockrill. "So he can't get far. After all he was in the building less than an hour ago."

"*If* he was in the building," said Cockrill: two could play at the fancy stuff.

Left to their own devices in the office, the ten knights fell to a discussion of Isabel's death, bored or excited according to the parts they had decided to play—for most of them were out-of-work actors and incapable of being merely themselves. Mr. Port sat silent, wringing his pudgy hands. Miss Betchley moved over unobtrusively to Brian Two-Times, perched on the edge of his chair, drumming with his feet on the ground, his blue eyes afire. He said contemptuously: "Vonderful exhibition we have now of the English police force. Talk-talk-talk and nothing do. Terrific!"

"These people talk," she said: "but there are a lot of others doing things behind the scenes. Fingerprints as spoke to Miss Drew outside the exhibition, and then only in the ordinary way of business—the pageant, a drink in the pub and so forth. Is there anything anybody wants to add: or is that O.K.?"

The knights chorused in plushy voices made plushier by RADA that this was indeed so; and so were dismissed to their homes and eventually from the case. None of them had so much as been to Elysian Hall at the time that the "murder notes" had been planted on the intended victims; none of them had moved from the semicircle at the edge of the stage. There was no use cluttering up the case, thought Charlesworth, with impossible suspects. They had quite enough to go on with.

The police surgeon arrived with his little black bag. Charlesworth spoke to him outside the office door. "Hallo, doc? Have you finished mucking about with the lovely?"

"Yes, I've finished," said the doctor, swinging the black bag gaily in one hand. "And I must say, a nice little armful she must have been when she was alive!"

"She's a nice little handful now that she's dead," said Charlesworth. "Must you stick to this manual strangulation business? It makes things very awkward for *me*. You don't think she can have caught her veil in a hook or something after all? There seem to be some pretty stout nails up there, holding up all that ridiculous tin ivy."

"No I do not: the veil was twisted round her throat probably just in case of finger marks; but somebody had taken two hands to her, outside the veil. It wasn't the veil that killed her: and it wasn't the rope. By the way, you haven't seen her since we got down to the job, have you? We found some rummy bits and pieces when we started moving her about. Ropes and things. But she was strangled with two hands." He cheerfully departed: his not to reason how Isabel could have been manually strangled by one of eleven people at least fifteen feet away from her.

Cockrill, in a fever to see the rummy bits and pieces, was nevertheless consumed with anxiety about Perpetua. Charlesworth departed for another look at the body, with instructions to Sergeant Bedd to fill in the interval by taking down the statements of the suspects, one by one: Cockrill saw no obligation to follow him, or to remain and have his testimony taken by the sergeant. He trotted off unobtrusively and sought out Inspector Stammers. "Any news?"

Stammers shook his head. "Not a sausage. She hasn't been home, she hasn't rung up anywhere, she isn't with any of her friends that we can rake up... And she isn't in the building— not this part anyway, not as far as we can see."

"Alive or dead?" said Cockie, without expression.

"Neither. Of course this place is a nightmare of hiding places." He put a hand for a moment on the little man's shoulder. "Don't worry. We're doing our best."

"All right, all *right*." said Cockie crossly. "I'm not the doting grandfather, you know." He walked smartly away.

The man on duty at the Assembly room door seemed to take it for granted that he had a right of access, and he went in, and through the arch on to the stage. The body had been screened off from the avid curiosity of the exhibition sightseers, and Charlesworth was bending over it as Cockrill advanced. He glanced up briefly: "Any news of Miss Kirk?"

"None," said Cockrill.

"Nothing heard yet of Anderson either." He returned to the body. "Look what we've found!"

Isabel's twisted legs and arms had been mercifully straightened out. She looked very quiet and composed now, lying there covered by the cotton sheet, waiting more patiently than in life she had ever waited for anything, to be taken away to the cold loneliness of the mortuary. Cockrill bent over her, his hands on his knees. "What are these? Ropes?"

A length of rope, about five feet long, and another, the same length, of stout twine. Each was tied in a noose. "They found them under the skirt of her dress when they turned her over," said Charlesworth.

Cockie picked them up gingerly, and examined the ends, turning them over curiously in his brown fingers. "Most illuminating!"

"Yes," said Charlesworth, doubtfully. He glanced up at the balcony above their heads. "No nonsense about lassos and things, though. That must be fourteen or fifteen feet up—the archway's at least twelve, to allow for the knights riding through with their fixed standards and all that: and another three feet up to the balcony. Then the girl's neck would be another four or five feet above her feet, if you see what I mean. So all in all..." He appraised it carefully. "I think we could safely say twenty feet. So a rope five feet long made into a noose would not do much lassoing, and anyway why two lassos?"

"It's all very—confusing," said Cockie, with a light in his eye.

"But then, of course there's this: the knights on either side of the arch were sitting on horses which were sort of reared up on their hind legs. Say a man in that position is—what?—nine feet to the shoulder? He raises his arm, that's another goodish bit, and then perhaps throws the lasso *up* a little, and the rope's five feet..." He broke off for a moment. "Of course it's rather a new bit of rope: it would have shown up very white against all that ivy."

"The lights would not have moved up to the ivy perhaps," said Cockie. "Attention would have been concentrated on the knights."

"Yes." He grew quite excited. "I wonder! What do you think, Inspector? Could it have been done?"

"It might," said Cockie. "The girl died of manual strangulation, of course, but that's a detail. It might have been done, as you say—if the rope had had hands."

They each had an ugly little vision of a rope with hands: of the stout twine curling itself into stringy fingers, knotted and twisted, seeking out the warm, round, golden throat. "Well, all I can say, then," said Charlesworth, laying them back in their wrappings, slightly crestfallen, "is what on earth were the two ropes *for*? They must have been chucked down with the body I suppose." He cheered up a little. "Perhaps he just brought them along in case."

Cockrill doubted whether there had been much "in case" about this crime. He said: "Anything else?"

"Yes, this." Charlesworth fished out a small cellophane envelope: it contained a slip of paper, with some typewriting on it—but this time there were no pin-men. "It's a poem, if you'll believe me! Or shall we say a verse?"

"Let's hear it, either way," said Cockie, impatiently. "We're not the B.B.C. Third Programme."

Charlesworth recited it with relish. "I've learnt it off by heart already!

> *"Oh, Isabel, how beautiful thy face is!*
> *It brings out homage in unexpected places.*
> *And so the donor of this little gift*
> *Is who?—the Mystery Knight upon the left!"*

He looked at Cockrill alertly. "What do you make of that?"

"Most illuminating," said Cockie again.

"The knight upon her left would be Earl Anderson."

Cockie scratched his ear. "So much depends upon an *e* or a *y*."

Charlesworth recited the poem through to himself again. "H'm, yes. So it does, doesn't it?" He lifted the sheet away from the body and looked down, pitifully, at the dreadful face and the little crook'd, plump hands. "She looks like a dead canary, doesn't she, poor little thing? Lying on the bottom of its cage with its pathetic bent claws…" In the centre of her breast there gleamed among the silver, her only jewellery, a diamond brooch. "We found the paper tucked down the front of her bodice."

"What there is of it," said Cockie severely. He glanced at the cellophane envelope. "Is there a—pinhole in the paper?"

Charlesworth looked at him alertly. "Two pinholes. In fact they tore it badly taking it out of her bodice."

"Interesting," said Cockie.

If he found it so interesting, why couldn't the maddening little man say why? Charlesworth, all unconscious of the slightest antagonism, permitted himself a quizzical lift of the eyebrow. "You think it's important?"

"I think it may be vital," said Cockie.

Charlesworth grinned outright. "You think it tells us who the murderer is?"

"Yes," said Cockie, eyeing him steadily back. "I think that, read properly, it could tell us who the murderer is. And how, when he was more than fifteen feet away from her, he could have strangled Isabel Drew with both hands round her throat. It certainly tells us who the murderer isn't. And I think it might suggest new methods in the search for Earl Anderson." He bent down and absently pulled up the sheet again, to cover the dead girl's face. "I don't say it would necessarily be right," he said. "There are more ways than one in which this poor girl may have been killed—at random one can think of, let's see—one, two, three… But the ropes, and the sheet and the brooch, and above all the poem—they do suggest one of them: and especially if there was a pinhole in the paper. So I do think that it's—well—mildly important." He slammed his old felt hat sideways on his magnificent head and marched away. Young jackanapes!

A constable, galloping down the main corridor, met him half-way to the dressing rooms. "We think we've found her, sir. Mr. Stammers sent me for you." He started to run back down the echoing passages, and thrust open the door of a dark little room…

Stammers was there with a couple of men, employed in heaving aside the heavy stage scenery stacked against the further wall. "Look out… Be careful you don't drop it back on her... Look *out*, you fool!" In the cobwebby angle of the wall lay what looked like a large bundle, covered by a cloak of bottle green velvet.

The hiding place had been carefully chosen. You might look there a dozen times before you would notice the thin white hand protruding from beneath the dark cloth.

and—checking-up and all that. I don't think they're as casual as they seem." She added deliberately: "For my part, they can be as casual as they like."

He eyed her, her air of odd triumph. "*You* are not sorry, for one, to see Jezebel die?"

"Revenge is sweet," she said, her eyes on his.

He thought it over quietly. Then he said with an air of finality: "Yes."

She moved a little closer to him. "I thought I would tell you—if there's anything more I can do…"

He had an odd little movement of the head, drawing in his chin as though puzzled, considering deeply, jutting it out again. He said, mystified: "What then can you do?"

"For you, I mean," she said.

"For me? What can you do for me?"

"I told them about your being first in the line," she said.

He drew in his chin again. "Well—so I *woss* first in the line. You saw me, you spoke to me."

"Exactly."

"But it does not need your testimony. Everybody knows I woss there. And besides the girl was killed after this: by that time I woss on the stage."

"Oh, yes, I know you were on the stage." She raised her eyebrows a little and moved away. "I only wanted you to know," she said.

Sergeant Bedd, notebook in hand, took down the evidence of the eight knights, and Charlesworth sent them off to their homes. "We've got your names and addresses: and we've got your assurances, which I may as well remind you we can, and most definitely will, check, that you none of you ever so much

Chapter VI

Miss Betchley, Mr. Port, and Motherdear sat patiently on the shiny round chairs of Mr. Port's little office, waiting to be allowed to go home. Brian Two-Times paced up and down like a lion caged. "These English police! How true they are vonderful! Two hours now passes and nothing done. Whole thing is idyotic!" Even Miss Betchley was beginning to feel that if Brian Two-Times said just once more that the whole thing was idyotic she would go mad. "Stuck in here, prevented from going out, not knowing what is going *on*…" For the hundredth time he poked his head out of the door and appealed to the constable. The constable replied for the hundredth time that he was Only Obeying Orders.

Charlesworth arrived carrying Perpetua easily in his strong young arms, with Cockrill rather sourly bringing up the rear (muscle isn't everything!) "Put her down here," said Cockie, pulling forward the only armchair. He shoved aside the eager questioners. "She's all right. Only fainted. Muffled up in a damn great cloak and nearly stifled, poor girl." He dipped his brown fingers into the water jug and smartly patted her face. "Come along, child. Pull yourself together." As she rolled her weary head, laying it with a little gesture of exquisite relief and trust against his arm, he put the other arm about her shoulder and gave her a little shake. "She's been locked up in one of the dressing rooms, poked away behind a lot of lumber, poor little devil." He added to Brian Two-Times in a conversational tone of voice: "She says you put her there."

"I?" said Brian staring wildly about him. He looked absurdly handsome, still in his shining tin armour, his helmet, with the white cloak thrown over it, under one arm, the other hand clutching at his own bright hair. "What for *I* should put her there? What for *I* should lock her up?"

Perpetua rolled her head against Cockrill's arm. "It *was* him: it *was* him! He pushed me in and—and threw the cloth over my head, and tied it round, and then he sort of dragged me over and pushed me down into that awful corner, wherever it was. And he said—he said, 'I com back!' He doesn't say 'come back' he says 'com.' It *was* him! He lured me into that horrible place, and I've been locked up there all this time..." She shuddered and closed her eyes again: sick and dizzy with the very memory of her terror.

Brian looked as if he would blow up at any moment. "*I* lure her into som room? *I* tell her, 'I com back!' I have not seen her since—since she was speaking to Isabel Drew in the Assembly room: I was waiting on my horse, and I saw her then. I have not been since off my horse till the pageant is over."

"I went back to the corridor," she said, ignoring him. "I went along to the various dressing rooms to chivvy up any of the knights that still weren't ready. His voice called to me from one of the rooms…" She broke down, gulping wretchedly.

Charlesworth tenderly passed her a glass of water. Cockie said brusquely: "Come along now—pull yourself together."

"I'm sorry," she said. "Well, so his voice called out to me. He called out, 'Oh, Perpetua,' or 'Miss Kirk,' or whatever it was—'please come and help me with this armour: I'm stuck!' Well, of course I didn't hesitate for a moment: they were always getting stuck—I thought his visor had probably jammed: his voice did sound rather muffled—and that was the sort of job I was there for. So I just ran down the corridor and into the dressing room… Well, it wasn't one of the usual dressing rooms, I just had time to take that in—there was a lot of stuff stored there as far as I could see; but there he was, just as I expected to see him, in his armour, with his visor down. So I went up to him, to help him to unstick it, as I thought: and he—he caught me by the arm and threw the dark thing over me…"

"Ah!—so you did not then see my face?" said Brian.

"How could I see your face when you had your visor down? But you said: "I com back"! Do you think I don't know your voice?"

He looked at her, dumbfounded. He said at last: "My voice I suppose is easy to imitate. I say fonny things. But who then can *want* to imitate my voice?"

She ignored him again. There seemed a compulsion upon her to tell everything *now*, to get it all out of her system, as if she would go mad if she kept one detail of the whole terrifying experience for one moment longer bottled up in her breast. "I didn't hear him move away: I suppose I was so dazed by the whole thing and by being thrown down... And there was the cloth over my head. I tried to wriggle free but I couldn't. But I could hear one of the knights riding by, and then I think another: I tried to call out to them, but my voice was all muffled by the cloak. And I was afraid he was outside the door: I was afraid he would come back. Then everything was silent, and I could just hear somebody whistling very softly: and then there was a sort of muffled banging and then I—I heard his voice again... I didn't hear what he was saying, I didn't hear anything... But it was his voice..." She shrank back against Cockrill's shoulder. "I was so horrified by the very sound of it that I—I think I must have fainted. I can't remember anything more at all."

Cockrill thought Brian Two-Times would certainly go off his head with the impotence of his rage and bewilderment. "This is idyotic! I—why should I do this to her? I do not want to hurt her!" He looked like a wounded teddy-bear, desperately hurt and angry. His blue eyes blazed, his hair stood up in crisp curls as though electrified by his excitement. "Anybody can imitate my voice."

"And you say yourself that it was rather muffled," said Susan Betchley to Perpetua. She could not take her eyes from Brian Two-Times's anxious face.

Charlesworth was developing a slightly frantic air. "Supposing for the sake of argument that this was someone imitating Mr. Bryan's voice?"

"Then it could have been any of the knights," said Susan Betchley eagerly. "*Any* of them. By that time there would be a hopeless muddle in the Assembly room, Inspector: the place was crammed with knights—after all, eleven men on horses take up quite a bit of room. And the horses were restless, waiting to go on, and moved about and stamped and tossed their heads: most of the riders couldn't manage them at all— some of them used not to mount till the last moment, but stood at their horses' heads, holding the reins. The place was just packed tight with men and horses: you couldn't tell who *any*body was."

"Except by the colour of his cloak?"

Something pricked at Inspector Cockrill's subconscious, as though trying to prise out a winkle of relevant memory: something about colour, something about recognizing the knights… But it slithered back into its shell. Miss Betchley was hurrying on.

"Except by the colour of the cloaks, of course. Each rider knew which cloak to follow, and as the leaders went through the arch and made more space, they all sorted out and fell into their places. All the cloaks were different."

Charlesworth spun round on Peppi. "Did the knight in the dressing room wear a cloak?"

"He had one thrown over his shoulder," said Perpetua. She looked at Brian defiantly. "It was white, and yours is white."

For just one moment it was as though a balloon had been pricked and was slowly collapsing. But the puncture mended itself, the balloon reinflated. "This cloak perhaps was folded outside-in. All the linings of all the cloaks are white."

Brian Two-Times turned round on Motherdear, who had sat very quiet and miserable all this time, gazing with a sort of stupefied pity at Perpetua. "*You* do not say any-thing! And yet—there is only you and me. Earl Anderson has disappeared—but, if we count him in too, then is you and me and Anderson. Your cloak is blue, his woss red: but all have white linings."

"And of course the cloak thrown over Miss Kirk was bottle green," said Inspector Cockrill thoughtfully. If he added that that was most illuminating, thought Charlesworth, this would be the end!

Isabel's body had been removed at last: the fingerprinting and footprinting and photographing and measuring were done. "I think I'd like you to all come on to the stage," said Charlesworth. "I want Miss Betchley to reconstruct for me exactly what happened after Miss Drew fell."

Miss Betchley's little stool still stood outside the big door of the Assembly room. "I saw all the knights in: then I bolted the door from my side and sat down to wait. I heard the bugles blow and then the jingling as the knights rode off: I couldn't hear much after they all got on to the stage. After about— well, actually it was twelve minutes, wasn't it?—I heard the music change for Miss Drew's appearance, and then stop, and I knew she must be coming out to make her speech. And then suddenly I heard the faint sound of a scream…"

"A woman in the crowd," said Cockrill. "I remember."

"And then I heard the sound of a horse's hooves in the Assembly room, and then a sort of thud. And a bit more moving about. I—I was just going to open the door and find out what was going on, when Mr. Bryan came and opened it from the inside. He had his helmet off and his hand up to his forehead and he looked rather dazed. He said: 'Something fell over the balcony. My horse bolted.' He hardly seemed to know what he was talking about…" Brian made an impatient gesture, but Charlesworth waved her on, and she continued rapidly, not looking at either of them. "I said, 'What fell?' and I think he said could it have been Isabel, or it must have been Isabel or something like that. He seemed quite vague and stupid. I went into the Assembly room and bolted the door behind me on the inside. We crossed the room: and on our way we met Mr. Anderson—the Red Knight. I suppose we said: 'What's happened?' or something like that; he just said, 'She's dead,' and went on past us: he had his hand up to his face. We went on towards the arch. I didn't quite know whether we should go through or what, so instead I turned aside for a minute, and went into the tower, and looked to see if Miss Drew was there. She wasn't. I ran half-way up the ladder, so that I could see on to the platform, but there was nobody there. So then I knew that she must have fallen. Mr. Bryan was waiting for me, just leaning sort of helplessly against the side of the tower doorway. He pulled himself together and we went through on to the stage." She spoke very quickly but carefully: as though watching her step. She avoided Brian's eye.

But Brian Two-Times was not to be silenced any more. His eyes were brilliant, his throat a clear column above the rigid circular shining neck of his armour. He faced Susan Betchley with his alert, challenging, slightly quizzical glance. "What is this? Why this fonny talk? 'I woss just going to open the door...' 'Mr. Bryan com and open the door...'? You know quite well you are banging and rattling at the door, and I com and the inside is bolted and I pull back the bolt and let you in." He said to Charlesworth: "My horse is jomping with fright on the stage. I was well under the balcony, the body must have fallen right on his tail:

he is frightened, he bucks and jomps, he bolts forward. I
am used to riding; but I am in this silly armour, I am like a
sardine in a tin: I topple as he jomps forward through the
arch. I suppose I must have fallen off. When I remember, I
am sitting on the floor outside the Assembly room with a big
bomp on my head, and the horse is standing quietly, asking:
'What are you doing there, you fool?' There is hammering
on the door. I do not exactly know what I am doing, but if
there is hammering on a door you go and open. I went to
the door. It is bolted from inside. I open, and she comes in
saying, 'What is it?'" He tucked in his chin, looking at her
from beneath wrinkled brows. "Why does she say now, 'I
woss just going to open the door'? The door was bolted.
She *could* not open it."

Susan Betchley answered obliquely. "Well—who bolted
it?" she said.

He shrugged his shoulders extravagantly. "*I* did not!"

"But that door never used to be bolted from the inside,"
she said to Charlesworth.

"It seems to have been this time," he said. The whole thing
was absolutely hay-wire.

Inspector Cockrill looked thoughtfully at Miss Betchley.
"You say you bolted the door after you on the *in*side, when
you went into the Assembly room to investigate?"

"I thought it would be safer: something seemed to
have happened, and we didn't want unauthorized people
swarming in."

Cockie swung round on Mr. Port. "Then how did
you get in?"

What little colour there was, drained right away from the

flaccid cheeks. "I? Well, I was... I was out in the crowd watching, and I saw Isabel fall..."

"I suppose Anderson unbolted the door as he went out," said Charlesworth. "Mr. Port didn't come in till after that."

Cockrill gave him a glance that would have annihilated a less resilient spirit. "Thank you: I had worked that out for myself. I was just wondering if Mr. Port would have the same explanation."

Mr. Port rubbed his hands drearily together. He repeated dully: "I was out in the crowd, watching the pageant. I saw her fall. I ran round as quickly as I could to the back-stage regions, and along the corridors to the Assembly room. The door wasn't bolted then. I just pushed it and it opened and I went through and on to the stage."

"You didn't meet Anderson on his way out?"

"I didn't meet anyone," said Sugar-Daddy, drearily. "I didn't see anyone." And he rubbed his hands together again and said sadly: "Poor Isabel!"

And suddenly Miss Betchley's calm deserted her. Her brown eyes flashed, her brown hands clenched into tight fists, her brown jaw was aggressively out-thrust: there was something extraordinarily masculine about the strength of that jaw, the firm line of her handsome mouth, the hard clench of the lean brown hands. She said: "Poor Isabel? Poor Jezebel, more like! That's what Earl Anderson used to call her; and he was right. What good did she ever do, that you should pity her now, when she's met with her just deserts? What good did she do to *you*, Mr. Port, a man of your age, fooling around with a woman like her? What good did she do you, George Exmouth, flaunting her vulgar charms before you, and you a young boy with a—a decent heart and a clean mind...? What good did she do to you, Perpetua Kirk, leading you into the ways she did, thrusting you into the arms of that Anderson creature...? What good—what good did she do any of us? What good did she do to Johnny?" Her voice died away almost into tears: but she raised it again and said, loudly and fiercely, with a harsh and ugly intonation, and yet with something in it of great pain and great dignity: "She was rotten: vulgar and greedy, and heartless, and immoral... How can you say, 'Poor Isabel'? Jezebel, I say: and good riddance to her, however it was she died." She turned and walked apart from them a little: and stood very still with her back to them, her hands up over her face.

"Jezebel!" said Inspector Cockrill. He raised his head and stared up at the foolish narrow window and the little balcony. "And she went up into a high tower," he recited. "'And she painted her face and tired her head, and she looked out of the window...'" He paused, glancing about him brightly.

Sergeant Bedd's eyes shone. "And they threw her down— three eunuchs it was, sir, threw her down: and her blood was sprinkled upon the wall: and the horses trod on her, and the dogs came and licked her up, every bit: all but her skull and the palms of her hands and the soles of her feet..."

"Such peculiar bits to leave, I've always thought," said Charlesworth. "How does one eat a person up, all but the soles of their feet?"

"And of course the horse did not tread on her," said Brian.

"No," said Cockie. He thought about it. "They say they never will."

Sergeant Bedd's face fell a little.

"And there was no blood," he acknowledged. And added reluctantly: "And no dogs."

"And no eunuchs," said Charlesworth.

"Thank you," said Brian Bryan, in a very deep voice.

The exhibition crowds were thinning. It had been a wonderful day: but now the weary women, burdened with purchases they would bitterly regret when they got home, fought for buses in the light summer rain, with cross husbands, slung about with Ohsofine nutmeg graters and Ohsosharp lemon peelers and Ohsotroublesaving gadgets of every description, lumbering irritably after them. The young ladies in the galleries argued with the exhibitors about their commission, the demonstrators on the exhibition stands surreptitiously started to tidy away so as to get off sharp when the clock of flowers said ten o'clock: its margin of error was ten minutes either way and morning and evening they took the benefit of the doubt. On the stage the concealing screens had been removed. "You'd better all go home," said Charlesworth to his hungry and weary little group. "Thank you for being so patient. You've really all been model suspects!" He gave them a brief, harassed, apologetic smile. "I'll want to see you all again, no doubt: dozens of times. But I've got your addresses; we can't force you to remain there, but—please let us know if you make any change." He added apparently guilelessly that obviously it would look exceedingly peculiar, to say the least of it, if anyone failed in this duty. To Perpetua, he said: "I expect Inspector Cockrill will see you safely home." They drifted off and he was left in the big, dim hall, on the lonely stage. A "sealed room." A single entrance, bolted on the one side, bolted and guarded on the other. Two short lengths of rope: a silly little verse: a diamond brooch. A man missing who could not be the murderer since he had been sitting on his horse when the murder was done: and a frightened girl locked up, but unharmed, in a room. And finally, eleven men in impenetrable disguise in full view of thousands of people: and a woman ten feet above their heads, strangled by two hands and thrown down out of the cardboard tower.

He wandered through the arch and into the Assembly room. Twelve suits of zipped-up armour, hanging on twelve hooks; twelve coloured cloaks drooping from the pegs above them, aglow with their velvet sheen; twelve tin helmets with closed visors hooked up carelessly on the pegs above the cloaks. White, red, sky blue… Yellow, purple, orange, a deeper blue, a bottle green… A bottle green. He went and stood before the spare suit of armour, dangling on its hook with the bottle green cloak and the grinning tin helmet above: and poked it in the tin tummy with an irreverent finger. "You blessed old sardine tin!—if only you could talk!" he said.

Eyeless, toothless—the helmet grinned back at him.

Chapter VII

I￼F THE KENT POLICE BENEFITED IN ANY WAY BY THE
conference held in London that year, it was not by the devoted
attention of their representative, Detective Inspector Cockrill.
Cockie sat absently doodling: doodling pin-men on pin-
horses, filling them out with tiny suits of armour, flying standards, flowing cloaks... Doodling a lay-out of the stage and
Assembly room at Elysian Hall... Doodling a somewhat lop-
sided face, adding a bush of thick, springy fair hair, clipped to
a page-boy bob... I wonder she doesn't trim it into a peacock,
he thought. Or a tree in a tub. He rounded out the page boy
bob into a tub, and added a little tree sticking out of the top.
It wouldn't be any odder than what most of the girls did with
their hair these days...

And there he was, back to Perpetua again. He mumbled an
excuse to his colleagues and got up and went out. Perpetua,
after a bad night was at last asleep, but woken by his ring,
answered the telephone at once. "How *are* you, Peppi?"

"All right, Cockie, thank you," said Perpetua.

"But scared?"

"Well—a bit. I mean, Isabel's dead, isn't she? And perhaps Earl is too. So there's only me left. You can't help sitting and wondering a bit where the tiger will spring from." She gave a nervous little laugh.

"Haven't you got any boy-friends that would look after you?"

"Well—no," said Peppi. She explained apologetically: "I always used to go round with Earl, you see. And when he was away I—just wasn't interested. I wasn't interested anyway: but when he was here he used to take me about. Otherwise I just used to stay at home."

"Well, stay at home now," said Cockie. "I'll have to deal with it." He rang off abruptly and marched out of the telephone booth, clapping his hat at its usual wild angle on his fine head. Might as well set up as a wet-nurse and be done with it, he said irritably to himself. What on earth was there in this gentle, pretty, maddeningly vague young creature that impelled his pity and care? Thinking deeply, he stumped off, his shabby old mac hooked over his arm in the London sunshine; and changed his direction; and then changed it again; and changed yet again, and made for Kensington.

Brian Two-Times lived in a "service-room," a small bright attic with "use of bath," and breakfast brought up on a nice clean tray by a weary young woman who, however, thought him ever so lovely and would have climbed more than the four flights any day, to see him in his beautiful flowered silk dressing-gown, with his hair standing up in ducks' tails all over his head. Cockie was not susceptible to the ducks' tails and thought a dressing-gown at 11 a.m. little short of a sin.

He sat down in the Utility armchair, took out papers and tobacco and wondered where on earth he ought to begin.

"I've just been talking to Miss Kirk," he said at last.

Brian Two-Times shrugged off Miss Kirk. "This yong lady—a fine nonsense she is making! How can I have pushed her in this room? It's idyotic."

"I should very much like to be sure of that," said Cockie.

Brian got up impatiently from his chair. Hands thrust into the pockets of his dressing gown, he shifted like a caged animal about the tiny room. "I was sitting on my horse in the Assembly room during the whole time that this nonsense was supposed to be taking place. How can I sit on a horse and at the same time tie some young woman up in a bundle, half a dozen rooms away?"

"Somebody sat on a horse and at the same time *strangled* another young woman a considerable distance away!" Cockie reminded him, wryly.

"Well, neither of these miracle-workers woss me," said Brian impatiently. "Why should *I* want to kill Isabel Drew? Why should *I* want to injure Perpetua Kirk? I never met either of them till a few weeks ago."

"But you knew Johnny Wise: and both of these women were—concerned in his death."

Brian clutched wildly at his bright hair. "For heaven's sake! Johnny Wise! I knew this boy, yes: but that is all. Just to meet sometimes when I went over to the F.M.S. from Sumatra—to run around to parties with, and so on: nothing more. He was a nice boy: everybody loved him—there was about him something fresh and—one can only say—good. He was one of those 'golden boys.' I, with all the rest, loved him: but only as an acquaintance, only as a casual friend. When he came to England, he wrote back much of his Perpetua, and also of Isabel Drew who introduced them together. When I came here to England, I looked up this Isabel. I wanted to know more of how Johnny died." His blue eyes grew hard and angry. "It is true, it seems, that between them these women killed the boy: Isabel Drew and Perpetua Kirk."

Poor, vague, sweet Peppi, who on that night had died also—only that her body continued to live on. "She was very young," said Cockie. "Almost a child. They got her half-drunk between them, Isabel Drew and Anderson... I don't suppose she knew what she was doing: she said afterwards that the whole evening was a sort of blur, until she came to suddenly to find herself in Earl Anderson's arms, and the boy standing there at the door. But Anderson had taken a fancy to her, I suppose, and Isabel was on his side. So she let the boy go in. I remember Peppi Kirk in those days of her engagement. She was quite a gay little grig—not the great Mind of the age, you know, not Greta Garbo, but a good little, pretty little, happy-hearted creature, and very much in love with Johnny Wise. You wouldn't think it now, would you? She's been like a—like a dead leaf, ever since that night. She's walked through her life in a sort of stupor of remorse and grief. And now she's awake again—and what has she woken up to? She has no friends, no inner resources, no defences—and a very real threat of murder hangs over her day and night." He looked up suddenly, his brown hand curled over his cigarette. "That's why I want you to be a friend to her—to look after her."

Brian was moving about no longer. He stood more quietly than Cockrill had ever seen him, his golden head outlined cameo-clear against the dingy wall. He said: "Then you do not think that I am a murderer?"

"I don't see how you can be," said Cockie, dourly. "Which is much more important to us both than what I think."

Brian Two-Times gave him his flashing smile. "Well—it is true that I am not. And this girl, she will be safe with me. I look after her!" Apparently unable to waste one second longer before passing on to execution of this duty, he fished a suit out of the little wardrobe, rummaged through a drawer for a clean shirt, and with automatic neatness and despatch began to dress. As his head emerged through the neck of the shirt, he added: "But *you* now have to convince her that I do not push her into any room!"

"As you say, you were sitting on your horse," said Cockie.

"This she knows. But still she does not believe sense. How does she think I attacked her, when I am sitting on my horse?"

"Perhaps she thinks you were *not* sitting on your horse?" suggested Cockie comfortably.

The shirt sleeves waved wildly as Brian thrust through his arms. "Everybody can tell you that I am sitting on the horse."

"Everybody has," said Cockie.

"But you do not believe?"

"The question is—will Perpetua believe?"

"But what can she possibly think?" cried Brian, doing up his shirt with such exasperated haste that there seemed imminent danger of a stage of buttonlessness.

Cockie considered. "Well, as to what she may *think*. She may think, for instance, that you were not on the horse all the time. The knights were on and off the horses, they were sitting in their saddles, they were standing at their heads, they were mounting and dismounting. Perpetua may *think* that you rode in and took up your position: and then quietly dismounted, came back and did your work with her, and went in and remounted again. The horses are well trained: yours would have stood still."

Brian could not help laughing. "That is very simple, certainly. But the point is that I never got down from my horse. Part of my job woss to take up this position and to remain there. The knights all took their lead from me. Each knight followed the coloured cloak in front of him: but all followed the white cloak."

"Perpetua might *think*," said Cockie, twiddling his cigarette, "that that's what they did: followed the cloak!"

Brian was enchanted. His blue eyes danced. "You suggest that it woss not *me* upon the horse!"

"I suggest that it was not anybody upon the horse."

Brian's face changed. "I don't know what you mean."

"I'm only just saying what Perpetua might *think*," Cockie reminded him. He was intent upon the cigarette. "I was saying that she might think about that spare suit of armour: that you could have hoisted it up on to the horse, out in the stable: and given the horse a whack—it was a circus-trained creature, and it would go forward quite meekly, wouldn't it?—and take its place before the arch. You'd done it many times. You'd been training it for weeks."

"You mean that I sent an empty suit of armour in with this horse! But..." He spluttered, words for once failed him. He groped wildly in the air for anything with which to refute such an idea. "But—ah! Miss Betchley! I talked with her: *she* knows I woss on the horse."

"So she does," said Cockie, beaming. He quoted: "A word spoken in season: how good it is!"

Brian fanned himself in a parody of panic relieved. "You frightened me. I have seen something of the working of your police: if they get hold of this idyotic idea…"

"But of course," said Cockrill thoughtfully, "Miss Betchley spoke to you *before* the episode with Perpetua. Nothing really to prevent your getting down off the horse afterwards, in all that muddle: hoisting up the spare armour, slipping out and back again…"

But you couldn't catch Brian a second time. "Now you are being fonny! Even this ridiculous armour—it will not sit comfortably on a horse which jiggles about… It will not hold up the standard…"

"The standards are rigid in the saddle: it would be more a question of the standard holding up the armour!"

"But how then do I beg my armour nicely to hold on to the standard! 'And please to take the reins in your left hand. I am back in one minute.'" He laughed again. "This you do not believe."

"One just longs to fit in that spare armour somehow," admitted Cockie, laughing too.

"And afterwards—if I have assaulted this Peppi, then I am the murderer, is't not? Do I then assist my empty armour to dismount and give it my parting instructions to go up to the tower and murder Miss Drew?" He stood before the dressing table, bending his knees to bring his eyes level with the inadequate mirror: the gold hair crisped up beneath the bristles of the brush, forcing its way back into its little waves. Cockrill thought that if he went at his head any harder with those brushes he would do himself an injury. "Have a heart, boy! You'll knock your brains down your neck!"

"In England it is not good to have silly curls," said Brian, slogging away without respite. "Your Perpetua will not like it, she will refuse to have me for her protector, and now I have a good fancy to be protector to Perpetua." He put down the brushes abruptly and came over and stood in front of the Inspector, pulling down his waistcoat, settling his shoulders into his jacket, straightening his tie. "Now I am ready. But before we go, I like to tell you something. We have a good joke about the spare armour, yes: but, Inspector—I am not a murderer. I give you my word of honour that your little Perpetua is safe with me."

These foreigners with their speeches! All the same, Cockie took the outstretched hand in his own. "I know that, my boy," he said. At least now he would be free to attend to that blasted conference!

Mr. Port in the early weeks of rehearsals had recommended his "residential hotel" to Miss Betchley: it was not what one was used to, but nowadays you took what you could get. One of the things you could not get in the hotel was breakfast in bed: they met in the dining room at nine o'clock on the morning after the murder and, warm in the intimacy of experience shared, joined up together at one of the horrid little tables. Both had had bad nights, and both looked tired and grey, but anxiety gave an almost youthful look to Susan Betchley's handsome face, while it brought out the sagging wrinkles in Mr. Port's. He seemed eager to talk of what had happened. "Little do all these peaceful people, browsing away at their breakfast like a lot of cows, realize that the papers they're reading are all about *us*..."

"It's terrible for you, Mr. Port. Bad enough for the rest of us, but after all—well, I mean, Isabel Drew was a friend of yours, I know..."

He poured out more coffee for himself, from his little metal pot. "Yes, it's been a shock. A terrible shock. I've been lying awake all night, thinking about it—*think*ing about it... But... I suppose there's such a thing as being deliberately infatuated, Miss Betchley: do you think there is? I was—I sort of *play*ed at being infatuated with Isabel Drew. Those days—under the Japanese: I don't need to tell you anything about them, my dear, you know it all as well and as bitterly as I do; and you must know how, amidst much worse things—the fear and the anxiety and the physical hardships—one hungered for—well, for a little ordinary luxury, for fun, for cosiness, for—for tenderness and relaxation..." To Edgar Port, Isabel had meant fun and cosiness: had meant—God help him, poor old boy!—tenderness and relaxation. Isabel, reflected Susan Betchley, had had about as much tenderness as a wolf: but after the terrible years, after the further anxieties of a wife broken down by the strain and mentally sick, the ruin of home and property, the loss of friends, all gradually emerging in the ensuing months, it was not wonderful if he had lost himself temporarily in those honey-coloured charms. "But now that she's gone I can't feel it as a personal loss, somehow; I'm shocked, I'm horrified, but—I suppose I just didn't really love her, that's all. I—I *wanted* to have my head full of a pretty woman, I *wanted* to think of nothing but chocolates and flowers and whether Isabel would keep her promise to have dinner with me on such and such an evening—I wanted to think that I was in love…" He looked at her from under his baggy eyelids and said, simply: "One has a good deal to forget."

"Yes," said Miss Betchley. (So one laid one's naked heart at two dancing feet: one let oneself drown in the seas of a pair of blue eyes…)

"But now that she's gone, nothing seems very terrible to me but the way she died. And other things are—important." He moved back in his chair so that the waitress could place before him his wrinkled grey sausage and a writhe of lean bacon. "My wife is still in the nursing home, you know. But—she's better, she's due to come out very soon and…" His fork rattled against the china with the shaking of his hand. He burst out: "What will she think if she finds that I've been playing about all this time with this stupid, shoddy exhibition, that I've been playing around with that vulgar, shoddy woman…? I only took up the work at the exhibition to please Isabel: she wanted to be the Queen of the pageant, she badgered me into applying for the job, and I did it to please her, to be near her…" He said again: "It was ridiculous for a man in my position, but I *wanted* to be ridiculous, I *wanted* to fool around and do impulsive things. I had a great deal of pull—more than Isabel had any idea of—with the sponsors of the exhibition: I had money in it myself. But how will my wife understand that it was only to—well, that it was just the reaction…" He broke off pathetically and wiped his sweating brow. "It's enough to send her back to that place for ever. As I *told* Isabel…" He broke off again, more abruptly this time. Susan Betchley said slowly: "Yes—I remember now. You were quarrelling with Miss Drew, weren't you?"

He interrupted hastily, "Just about that silly rehearsal. It was all nothing."

"It went on for a long time."

"Not so long as you think," he said quickly. "We—we really made it up some days ago." He added firmly: "I have said that I was not really in love with Isabel: but I *was* 'infatuated' with her." He looked at her beadily, and added with deliberation: "*You* can understand that."

"Why me, particularly?" said Susan Betchley, suddenly deciding against any more toast.

He smiled at her: kindly, but meaningly—warily. "Oh, my dear—do you think I haven't seen you looking at him? People in love are very sensitive to other people's love, you know. All these weeks of rehearsals—I've watched it coming over you like a—a sort of golden cloud. Every time he turns his blue eyes on you, every time he uses one of his funny little expressions, every time he runs his hand through his yellow hair… Do you think I don't know that you're sick with love for him? That you can hardly keep your mouth from speaking his name, just to hear the sound of it: that you can hardly force your hands from touching his sleeve or the place that his sleeve has brushed against as he passed by…? My dear girl—I may have been playing at love, but I played a very good game: I know it all, down to the utmost guttering flicker of despair, up to the topmost pinnacles of hope…" He looked at her sitting there, with her swarthy face and her upright shoulders and her square brown hands. "You're in love with Brian Bryan," he said. "Even though you know that he's a murderer."

A fly buzzed across the scraping of marmalade in the cracked white saucer; otherwise there was absolute silence at the little table. She said at last, quietly: "You too? You're a friend?"

"I knew Johnny," he said.

"Yes," she said. "She murdered Johnny: she and that creature Earl Anderson. It's nothing to do with my loving or not loving Brian. They killed poor Johnny: and they deserved to die."

"You knew him very well?" said Mr. Port.

"Not so very well as all that: but I loved him—everybody loved him: he was just one of those people. We were much the same age; we used to play tennis and golf together a bit, and ride together—oh, there was nothing like that in it, I was just fond of him and he looked upon me almost as though I were one of his brothers. He was devoted to his family; and he had a twin that he loved more than anyone on earth. When he was away from them all, he used to like to be with me—he was a person who craved for affection and companionship all the time…" She stared out of the dingy window into the dingy square. She said again: "Yes—I'd protect anyone who killed Isabel Drew."

"We'll shake hands on that," said Mr. Port.

Detective Inspector Charlesworth arrived to call for Mr. Port. Mr. Port, like a man going off to execution, stepped into the little car. "I do hope, Inspector, that you're not going to be—tactless—with my wife."

"I shan't mention the case to her at all," said Charlesworth. "I merely want her to confirm what you tell me of your background in Malaya. You must see how difficult it all is for us, with all the records missing: we simply aren't able to check up on anything or anyone... Yes, I know all about your bank account, but... Yes, O.K., I know all about Miss Betchley confirming your identity... Now, look, Mr. Port..." By the time they arrived at Hampstead he was exasperated and cross. "Any more fuss, Mr. Port, and I shall turn back and leave this to an ordinary plain clothes man, which would be the usual procedure: I came myself because I know your wife's ill and I wanted to save you trouble..."

The nursing home was a tall, thin-lipped house with an air of prim starchiness: it looked, thought Charlesworth who was not often given to pretty fancies, as though for two pins it would turn upon the neighbouring houses and pop them willy-nilly into bed with unwanted hot-water bottles at their feet. The Matron came to them in the waiting room, and, having failed in her duty, was naturally highly incensed with poor Mr. Port. "In spite of my strict orders, there has been a mix-up and one of the daily papers, some sensational rag, has been taken into your wife's room." She stood over him menacingly. "A nice half hour we've had! Tears, fainting, hysterics—and now our memory has gone right back to where it was! I can assure you, Mr. Port, that this kind of thing causes a great deal of trouble in a nursing home."

Mr. Port stood staring back at her, almost unable to believe his ears. "You let her see a paper!"

"I cannot be personally responsible..."

"I gave you implicit instructions..."

"If gentlemen would refrain from getting themselves mixed up in sordid affairs of this kind..."

Charlesworth left them to it; he walked out of the room and calmly went upstairs. To a nurse he said: "Mrs. Port's expecting me," and since this was true, was ushered into a room where a woman sat in a chair by the window. The forced brightness of the atmosphere seemed to drain Mrs. Port of all the little life and colour that were natural to her; but she smiled at him very sweetly. "Good morning. Who are you?"

He gave her his own friendly smile. "My name's Charlesworth. Who are *you*?"

"I'm Mrs. Port," she said. "Haven't you come to see me? Such a lot of strange doctors do."

"No," he said. "And I'm not a doctor. But as I'm here, perhaps you'll let me stay and smoke a cigarette?" He sat down on the window-sill with his long legs crossed and smiled down at her. "What a silly little room this is," he said. "Aren't you longing to get well and get out of it?"

She looked back at him doubtfully. "It's safe in here."

He was frightened. He was not dealing with a normal person and he was afraid of saying anything that might react unfavourably upon her; he wished with all his heart he had not come: had not embarked, unpermitted, upon this conversation. He said: "The world's pretty safe now: the bad times are over." He wished he was quite so sure of it himself.

"Do *you* think it would be all right to leave?"

"Well, I think so," he said comfortably. "You'd like to be with your friends again? It must be lonely here."

"I've forgotten my friends," she said simply. "I've forgotten such a lot. Do you know that I just can't remember anything from the time I was a girl. I remember my wedding, and I remember something of the—the voyage: my husband took me out to—well, he took me away from my home, you know; they say we went to Malaya, but I remember nothing of that. I remember the voyage—not much, just the bits that one *would* remember, from so long ago. And I remember being on the ship again, coming home. They've kept me here all this time trying to help me to remember in between."

"I don't see why you should bother to," said Charlesworth, putting into words the only thought that came into his head. "You may have had a horrid time in between and so you've forgotten it. Why trouble to remember? I should just be happy in the present and the future, get as well as you can, and start all over again…" ("This is something-or-other therapy," he said to himself. "I'm probably doing marvels if I did but know." But once again he wished he was so sure.)

Mrs. Port looked at him gravely; he noticed with alarm that her fingers had begun to pleat and repleat a fold in her dressing-jacket. "Have you seen the papers this morning?" she said.

He topped a cigarette of its ash, knocking it carefully into the tray on her little table. "Well, I have. A girl called Isabel Drew seems to have been killed. I believe your husband knew her a little. So did I, as a matter of fact."

"What did my husband know of this woman?" He thought it was an effort for her to ask it; there was a nervous dignity in her manner, and the busy fingers worked more quickly, not ceasing in their unrewarding work.

"Very little, I think," he said carelessly. "The papers make a lot of that kind of thing: they go for what they think is 'sensational' and Isabel was that kind of person. She was always worrying people to get her jobs and get jobs for her friends, and Mr. Port was kind to her and to them all. I understand he had financial interests in the exhibition, and so he brought a little influence to bear: he even took a hand in it himself, just to amuse himself while you were stuck away here. He must be bored, not having many friends in England—and it was a harmless enough way to amuse himself—wasn't it?"

Her fingers slowed down. She said: "Well, I suppose it was, really."

"Then a thing like this happens, and the papers get hold of it and, of course, they make a fuss," said Charlesworth, reasonably explaining it all away. "It sounds ugly and sensational and horrid—but that doesn't mean that it was: after all, there was nothing on earth *wrong* with his playing about with this silly little pageant. The girl gets killed, and, of course, he's dragged into it, and questioned, like the rest: but that's all there is to it." He was not so sure: to salve his own conscience, he offered: "I have a few friends on various papers: if you like I'll do what I can to get them to tone this down a bit."

Her hands were quite still: lying, pale and quiet, in her lap. She said gratefully: "We'd be very thankful to you if you would," and he noted with relief that she included the errant husband in her own reaction. "It's been kind of you to explain it all to me. I'd heard of the pageant, of course, and I believe I've even met this Miss Drew, though I don't remember her. Her—her pictures are not very—reassuring."

"She was all right," said Charlesworth, easily. "She was kind and friendly in many ways: she wasn't too bad... There's nothing in all that to worry yourself about." He looked at her quiet face and quiet hands and feeling highly pleased with himself, heaved himself up from the window-sill and said good-bye. He had learned all he wanted: Mrs. Port could tell him nothing about the Malayan background, and that was that. He said: "I must trot off now. It was nice of you to let me sit with you for a minute, and smoke a cigarette. Get well soon, won't you?" He turned to the door.

And suddenly the matron was standing there, with Mr. Port, ashen and trembling, at her shoulder. "Detective Inspector! How did you get in here? What are you doing here? We thought you'd gone out to the car..."

"Detective Inspector?" cried Mrs. Port.

"A policeman! Mrs. Port—what has this man been saying to you? What have you told him? Mrs. *Port*... ! Mrs. Port!"

The sound of her screaming, the sound of hysterical laughter, followed him as he fled down the stairs and made his way out of the house and into the square.

And while Perpetua declared to Inspector Cockrill that she had no true knights to look after her, and Cockie stumped off, feeling like a benevolent old pimp to rustle up boy-friends for her comforting, one who would have given his hob-nailed young soul to save her an instant's heartache, nursed his despair alone and unremembered. Thank God, at least, that Mother was away in Scotland: he could not have endured the boring-in of that gimlet eye, the resolute understanding of that too fond maternal heart. In the shop-window little house with its nightmare of crippled white birchwood and imitation okapi skin, he sat with his head in his hands and tried to blot out from his memory the events of the previous night. And so came back to the scene he had witnessed, the words he had overheard on his way home outside Isabel's front door: to the plot between Earl and Isabel that would make Perpetua wife of a bigamist: to the story of the blot that had long ago sent Perpetua's lover to his death: and so, by slow insidious degrees, back to the hateful vision of his beloved held in Earl Anderson's arms. Sick with repulsion, he thrust it away from him: but adolescent imagination dwelt on it, toyed with it, built it up, adorned it, could not let it be… Sick with himself and his ugly visions, he dragged himself up, went to the bookshelves and pulled down volume after volume: the "right" kind of books, specially bound for his mama in the right kind of leather, elegantly tooled. Thackeray, Trollope, Dickens… Motherdear flicked through the pages of *Vanity Fair* where the hobbledehoy hero had got his girl in the end: of *The Small House at Allington*, where the hobbledehoy had failed: of *Little Dorrit* where poor John Chivery had wandered through the Marshalsea prison, composing a hundred epitaphs for himself. What would George Exmouth's epitaph be, if… He sat down at Charity's wrought-aluminium desk, and drew a sheet of her notepaper towards him. "Here lies in unsanctified ground the body of George Exmouth, aged only seventeen, who, to save the honour of his lady…" But it was dangerous to put this kind of thing on paper. He altered "his lady" to "a lady" and then tore the paper into tiny scraps and set fire to the bits with a match. You could not be certain that the police would not search the house.

Perpetua, a little reassured by Cockie's phone call, went to the door of her room and put out her head. "Oh, Mrs. Solly—I've had a rotten night and I think I'll go to bed. Will you guard my door for me?" The cleaner said cheerfully that that was right, rest was the best thing if you was tired, and, having been up all night with an ailing baby, not to mention the second one's cough and pore Alfred's nasty indigestion, more like a lump of lead on his chest it was, herself continued to dust and polish and scrub with unabated zeal. Perpetua glanced at the mat outside her door: the paper and a single envelope—but it was probably only a bill, and she left them both there and returned sleepily to her bed.

Detective Inspector Charlesworth rang up at noon. He was going to Earl Anderson's flat and it might be helpful if Miss Kirk would accompany him: she would know better than anyone if anything out of the way was missing… Perpetua had spent less time in Earl's flat than a great many people supposed, but she agreed to go. Charlesworth would call round in half an hour. No—sorry; no news at all of Mr. Anderson.

She wrapped her silk kimono about her and went to the door. The newspaper still lay on the mat and the bill; but with them now was a little round bunch of flowers and a folded note. The note was signed with a B. It said: "Perpetua, Inspector Cockrill now confirms that I cannot have lured you into that room. When this was done I was on my horse in the Assembly room and the spare armour as far as I am concerned still hanging on the wall. Please believe this. And why should I wish to harm you? Be no longer afraid. We all look after you." Underneath Cockie had written in his well-known indecipherable scrawl: "Dear Perpetua, you may trust this young man. He is O.K." She put her head out of the door again. "Who brought the flowers?"

The cleaner said that it had been ever such a lovely young

gentleman, foreign he was you could tell because he wore a mackintosh on such a hot day, and a black hat like Mr. Eden, and he had come rushing in and stood at her door and said: "She has not then woken up? Her paper is still on the mat," and had thrust the flowers into her hand and said, "Tell her I com back," and rushed off again. "Would the gentleman be in a hurry, Miss?"

"I don't expect so, really," said Peppi, with a little inward smile at the thought of Brian Two-Times dashing in and depositing flowers on her doorstep as though they had been a bomb and he must hurry off out of the way before it exploded. "He just—gives an appearance of always being in a hurry." And of course it was true that he could not have attacked her in that little room. For some obscure reason she felt suddenly much more light-hearted. "Be no longer afraid. We all look after you." It was very *kind* of Brian Two-Times.

Hugging her kimono about her, she put down the note and the flowers and ripped open the "bill." The envelope bore last night's post-mark, and it was not a bill. It was a typewritten note and it said: PERPETUA KIRK—YOU'RE NEXT.

Chapter VIII

CHARLESWORTH ARRIVING AT ELEVEN O'CLOCK WAS sympathetic but frankly excited. "We'll get him by the type-writing: there can only be a few machines that the people concerned can have had access to." He sent off the note to Scotland Yard, and himself proceeded with Perpetua and Sergeant Bedd, to Earl Anderson's flat. "Oh, and Inspector I've had a note from Inspector Cockrill, and he says that Brian Bryan is quite out of suspicion now, and I can trust him."

"*Does* he, indeed?" said Charlesworth, interested.

"And Mr. Bryan left me some flowers: wasn't it rather sweet of him?"

"Heavenly," said Charlesworth. He thought that this dim young creature who last night had looked as colourless and unsubstantial as a cobweb, had suddenly taken on a remarkable new lease of life.

A chauffeur was washing an ancient Rolls in the mews. "Good morning, Miss," he said to Perpetua, glancing up. She was looking very pretty this morning: seemed to do her good, having her paramours doing the vanishing trick. Actors indeed! Earl Anderson published his profession to all the world, considering, and no doubt rightly, that it set him a little apart from his fellows, and confidently believing that on account of it, the Mews accorded him its breathless interest. The Mews, since he was admittedly neither Stewart Grainger nor James Mason and had never been heard of in the *Radio Times*, simply did not believe that he was an actor at all: but since he frequently had females to see him in his flat, they accorded him their interest anyway. The chauffeur was only too ready to repeat such information as he could offer—already made glib from repetition to Charlesworth's myrmidons. At just before eleven, Mr. Anderson had walked down to the telephone booth at the corner and after a while had come back and taken the car and gone out again. They had been woken by the return of the car some time after one. The chauffeur did think that later on he had heard footsteps going off out of the mews: but he had been more than half asleep, and it could have been a dream. This final admission had been wrung from him by Sergeant Bedd on an earlier visit, and he repeated it reluctantly with that gentleman's eye upon him; but he privately believed that there was no question of any dream. He shoved his cap further back on to his head and phewed at the heat: standing here in the hot sun talking to the police, his gesture implied, was thirsty work. Charlesworth left him to supply the need for himself, and with Perpetua went into Earl's garage, past the little red car, and up into the flat. As he went he said to Peppi: "When did *you* last see him, or hear from him?"

Perpetua in her pretty flowered frock, toiled up the narrow

stairs at his heels. "On the afternoon of the day before the pageant. He used to ring me up most evenings if I didn't see him, but his 'phone was cut off. Isabel rang me that evening about ten, and she said that she was going to ring him, but of course his line was n.b.g., because he hadn't paid the rent: so she said she would ring Sugar-Daddy—Mr. Port, I mean— instead. I don't know if she did."

Charlesworth jerked his head towards Sergeant Bedd. "Check with Port's hotel." He waved a hand round the shoddy little flat. "Anything missing?"

The police had searched the whole place pretty thoroughly, but it was now restored to order. Perpetua glanced at the hall-stand, glanced into the bedroom and the bathroom. "Yes, his hat's gone: and his raincoat. It was drizzling a bit last night, wasn't it? And his dressing gown and slippers used to hang here: and there don't seem to be any pyjamas on his pillow. And his shaving things and his toothbrush and flannel and stuff…" She broke off and stood staring. "But why on earth has he taken the bathroom curtains?"

"The *cur*tains?"

"Yes, clear oilskin ones with seagulls on them with red beaks: only Earl said they looked like Spitfires and hung them upside down. But why on earth should he have taken them now? And where can he have gone?" She looked at Charlesworth rather desperately; but more puzzled he thought than alarmed; or, if alarmed, more for the sake of her friend himself than for anything that he might have meant to her.

He shrugged. "Of course it all may be nothing. He may have had an urgent call—apparently he did go out to the phone; he may have rushed off to visit his sick Mum or something, and has no idea there's all this hue and cry: being as his Mum's in the depths of the country, snowed up probably, or cut off by the floods, and they haven't seen a newspaper this three weeks come Michaelmas..."

"He hasn't got a Mum," said Perpetua. "She's dead. It's much more likely to be a girl friend: he was always whizzing off without a moment's notice, Casanovering. Yes, that's it! I bet you anything, Inspector, he's just chucked up everything and gone off to some love-nest."

"But why on earth should 'e take the bathroom curtains to a love-nest?" said Bedd. He had heard some rummy things, but this beat all.

"Maybe he had a fetish about seagulls," suggested Charlesworth.

Sergeant Bedd who had always vaguely understood that a fetish was them little round hats worn by the blacks in Africa, looked more mystified than ever.

Down at Elysian Hall, Mr. Port, Susan Betchley and Motherdear hung miserably about the stage. "Well, well, I always heard that the murderer returns to the scene of the crime," said Charlesworth cheerfully, arriving there after a scrappy lunch at the pub opposite. "None of you people seem able to keep away. I shall begin to think that this was a mass slaying: a slaying by a mass, I mean, not a mass of people getting slain." Inspector Cockrill, standing between Peppi and a much-subdued Brian Two-Times, observed to himself with sardonic satisfaction that his colleague was covering up, with a lot of rather frantic badinage, the fact that he did not know what on earth to do next. With any luck, Detective Inspector Charlesworth was going to "make a muck" of the Jezebel case! Until, of course, he, Cockie, the despised, the rejected, stepped in to put things straight for him...

"I called at your house," said Brian, to Perpetua. "I thought perhaps ass I am not a villain you might have had lonch with me."

"I had lunch with Inspector Cockrill, Brian, and he brought me on down here. But I got the flowers and they were simply heaven. And I'm sorry I was so stupid about— sort of suspecting you. It was because of the white cloak and the voice and things..."

"I look after you now, Peppi," said Brian comfortably.

Charlesworth took Mr. Port to one side. "I'm most frightfully sorry about your wife, Mr. Port. That blasted woman..."

"The damage is done, Inspector," said Mr. Port, quietly and bitterly. "She had to be put back to bed. God knows how long it will take now."

"I swear to you that she was perfectly O.K. with *me*. I didn't ask her anything, I didn't tell her anything, we just had a friendly talk..."

"A friendly talk about my affairs in Malaya and about Isabel Drew and the exhibition: what I've worked and striven and prayed and paid to keep away from her all this time..." He broke off, and went if possible whiter than he already was. "I mean—paid out these big sums to that nursing home to keep her there, away from the world... It's been an anxiety: her mind is so delicately balanced..." He added with bitter satisfaction: "Anyway, it may interest you to know that your visit to my wife today has just about sunk any hope you ever had of discovering anything about this crime."

Charlesworth let it go at that: no use making the little man angrier and more savage by ill-timed questions. He turned his entire attention back to the scene before him. Such fingerprints and footmarks as had been found had confirmed the stories of the suspects, as far as those went: Miss Betchley had certainly hammered and rattled at the Assembly room door, Brian Bryan had certainly admitted her from the inside: it was humanly impossible to have manipulated the inner bolt from outside the door. Earl Anderson in his blundering exit would have had on the chain mail gloves (of knitted silver tape) which all the knights wore with their armour, giving a highly romantic effect and one devastating to the tracing of fingerprints: but there was a mark of Mr. Port's pudgy palm as he had pushed the door open from outside and come hurrying through after Isabel's fall. There were no significant prints in the dressing room where Perpetua had been locked up: but there again, her assailant would have worn the silver gloves. Charlesworth addressed the little group. "I expect you'd all like to know whether there's any news of Earl Anderson. Well, there isn't. He left his flat night before last—the evening before the evening of the murder, that is, of course, and, except for his having been seen here in the pageant, he hasn't been heard of again. He seems to have taken a suitcase of things with him—or somebody has taken it to give us the impression of flight. The question more or less boils down to this: has Anderson been done away with himself—or is he the murderer?"

To this question, nobody appeared ready with a reply. Perpetua said: "But what motive could Earl have had to be a murderer? *He* had nothing on earth against Isabel Drew."

Motherdear stood unhappily wrangling with his own conscience: to speak or not to speak? Above the muted din of the exhibition, the voice of his love rose cool and clear: "Earl wouldn't have killed poor Isabel. Earl wasn't brutal like that, he wasn't cold and calculating and cruel…" And in the big empty room, the twelve suits of armour hung, watching them—watching *him*, poor muddled, unhappy, desperate George Exmouth, with their blind and steady gaze. He blurted out the ugly truth. "Earl Anderson was calculating and cruel: he was—going to ask you to marry him, Perpetua. And he was married already."

Perpetua's face flushed. "It isn't *true!*"

"It's true all right," he said. "I heard them planning it: him and Isabel Drew." *That* was the man who had held Perpetua in his arms! Would she defend him after that? But his heart was sick and heavy at the look of horror he had brought to her face. He said wretchedly: "But you needn't be unhappy any more, Perpetua. They're both dead now."

"Why do you say that?" said Charlesworth, quickly. "How do you know that Anderson's dead? If anything, this gives him a motive to kill—not to get himself killed!"

"Wishful thinking," suggested Cockie, eyeing the boy's face with uneasiness.

George Exmouth looked terrified. "I—I just thought…"

But Charlesworth had lost interest in Motherdear: who, after all, had simply sat his horse from beginning to end of the whole affair, apparently unobserving, observed of none.

He concentrated on the missing Anderson, now so handily supplied with Motive. "He packed a suitcase and spent the night before the murder somewhere other than his home: why I don't quite see, but possibly to build up a new metier for himself not too closely associated with the actual evening of the crime. He got down here very late, changed into his armour, probably in one of the dressing rooms or out in the stalls, since nobody saw him actually putting it on, and then hung about in the corridor waiting for Miss Kirk. He pushed her into the little room, tied her up in the cloak and locked her in."

"Do you mean to say that was Earl—imitating Brian?"

"Off course this fellow woss an actor," suggested Brian, shrugging.

"And why lock *me* up, anyway?"

Charlesworth had no idea. "Some vague notion of keeping you out of the way while he got up to his tricks: it was your job to sort of keep an eye on the knights, wasn't it?"

"Mine and Miss Betchley's."

"But he knew Miss Betchley would be busy on the door."

Mr. Port started to say something, but held his peace. "So he went on into the Assembly room," continued Charlesworth. "Left his horse standing—it was a circus-trained beast, it would have stood still—and slipped through the crowd and into the tower and... Well, went into the tower."

"But wouldn't Isabel have seen him coming?" said Peppi.

"What if she did? It was only old Earl, the childhood pal. And anyway, he may have been hidden up on the platform: it would be pretty dark, and she wasn't supposed to turn on the light because of its being seen through the window. She seems always to have gone up the ladder just by the light coming through the window itself and the door. And then…"

"And then," said Inspector Cockrill sweetly, "he strangled her and threw her down, in such a way that twelve minutes later when he had been cavorting about on a horse for some time, beneath the gaze of all, she should have the appearance of having only that moment been strangled and thrown down. A talented fellow."

Collusion then. But with whom? Everybody else had been on the stage: except of course for Susan Betchley and Mr. Port—oh, and Perpetua. Why or how any of them should have wanted to collude with Earl Anderson in the murder of Isabel, it was not easy to suggest: but supposing they had? Miss Betchley undertook to say that neither Mr. Port nor Perpetua had remained in the Assembly room. Supposing for the sake of argument they had either of them dressed up in the spare uniform, and gone in so disguised, unbeknown to her? But how then had they gone out again? There had been no one, in armour or otherwise, in the tower or Assembly room when she had burst in after Isabel's fall: the spare armour had dangled on its hook half-way down one wall, its helmet hanging on the peg above the hook. Supposing that, Anderson having murdered the girl and gone back to his horse, Miss Betchley had crept in, waited for the psychological moment and thrown the body down. But no: for Isabel would have been dead then long before she hit the ground, and the postmortem tale of bruises made within a few seconds of death was too definite for that. And anyway, Brian Bryan had found the door bolted from the inside, so that Miss

Betchley could not have gone through. And *any*way, why wait and throw her down?

And anyway, why the two nooses?

"Too much standing about here," suggested Brian Two-Times to Perpetua, weary with the self-communings of the stupid British police. "Better I take you to the Exhibitors' Club for some tea."

The Exhibitors' Club was a large, square room furnished with basket-work chairs in which it was impossible to do anything but lie down or sit bolt upright, and round glass-topped tables with—on the second day of the exhibition—a good deal of pale brown fluid already staining to leprous patches the violently pink paper between the wooden table and its covering glass. The Club owed its membership almost entirely to the fact that its sanitary arrangements were slightly more civilized than those of the rest of the exhibition. By three o'clock there was no cake left, tea-cake was also "off," buttered toast had never been on. "Come home and I'll make you a cup of tea in my room," said Perpetua, to prevent Brian Two-Times from rising up and laying about him in his impotent rage at all this apparently studied frustration. "I'm afraid the tea-cake is off there too, but at least I won't solemnly write down an order for it when I know all the time that it's crossed off the menu with nasty indelible pencil."

"Is this correct, that I shall go in England to a yong lady's flat?"

"It's even worse than a yong lady's flat, it's a bed-sitting-room," said Peppi, laughing. "But this is London, and 1947, and Cockie says I can trust you—I've got it in writing!" She tucked her hand into his arm. "Or are you afraid?"

"It is you who are no longer afraid, Perpetua, I am glad to see," said Brian Bryan: and his blue eyes shone.

Inspector Cockrill remained on the stage with Charlesworth. "In this matter of Anderson's being the murderer—aren't you overlooking that poem? And the diamond brooch?"

"They aren't necessarily concerned with the murder at all."

Cockie raised his eyebrows. "I should have thought that everything that happened within an hour or so of the murder might at least have commanded your interest."

"We don't know that anything happened within an hour of the murder. Isabel Drew may have had that brooch for years: she may have carried the poem around with her for years."

"Next to her heart?" said Cockie.

"Well, she *may*. Girls do these things."

"Not Jezebel," said Cockie.

"Well, all right, let's say that Anderson gave her the brooch then, within an hour of the murder: as you put it…"

"I don't suggest that Anderson gave it to her: I suggest that she received it. If it was to be handed to her, why the poem? Why the mystery? Say she *received* the poem: and the brooch."

Charlesworth shrugged. "Well, O.K. Then what? She puts the poem down her front, pins the brooch into her dress, and gets on with the job in hand. Up the tower, glances out of the window and registers gratitude in the general direction of the Knight upon her left…"

"By doing what?" said Cockrill: gently leading the child along through his class by the hand.

"Well, sort of leaning over a bit…"

"Wouldn't the audience have seen that?"

"No, because the balcony was in darkness. But the Knight was just beneath it, looking up."

"And then?"

"And then his arms suddenly grew about ten feet and he reached up and pulled her down and laid her on the ground at his feet and strangled her," said Charlesworth, hopelessly.

"Exactly," said Cockie.

Charlesworth stood staring at him. And suddenly was galvanized into action. "Everybody off the stage, please. Screens up, Bedd, please. Some rope—I want some rope: here, those bits of thick string there will do." He disappeared with it, and reappeared shortly afterwards at the window of the tower, reaching out, feeling among the green metal ivy-leaves. "Yes: there are hundreds of nails here." He called down to Cockie: "Why the second noose?"

"I suggested last night that it was all very confusing," said Cockie.

"Deliberate, you mean? Second one to put us off the scent of the first. Where would you hide a leaf, *in* the forest," gabbled Charlesworth gaily. He tied the string into a slip noose and hitched it lightly over three nails so that it hung down, half framing the narrow window. The second length of string, tied to the first to make a total of somewhere around ten feet, hung down one side of the arch, to the left of the window as he faced out. He disappeared and came back on to the stage.

Bedd stood staring at the two shining faces. "You mean to say that he lured her to look out: and then put up his hand, like, to the switch. And the noose come off the nails: and closed round her neck—and he give a tug, and brought her down? But, 'ere!" His brow was furrowed, he shook his grizzled head. "You're going too fast, Mr. Charlesworth, sir, begging your pardon. The doctor said she was strangled from behind with two hands, not a minute from when she hit the floor: and that's flat."

"You'll be flat, you old image, if you don't hold your tongue." He stood up on the horse's block and reached up and gave the string a jerk. It came away easily from its nails and lay coiled in a heap on the ground. "You lie down here with it, Bedd, and don't talk so much: you've just fallen fifteen feet." He said to Cockrill: "That's what you meant—isn't it?"

"It was what the poem and the brooch suggested," acknowledged Cockie. He ran over the poem once again. "Oh, Isabel, how beautiful thy face is! It brings out homage in unexpected places. And so the donor of this little gift, is who?—the Mystery Knight upon the left! Of course, as I said, there are two or three other ways."

Charlesworth could not be bothered with the two or three other ways. "Now: I'm the Red Knight on his horse, sitting up here like a stuck pig, having pulled the girl down. The White Knight's in a bit of trouble, but I'd taken all that into my calculations: they say a horse never steps on a body, and this one didn't either. He bolted forward, and that was the White Knight out of the way. I waited another second or two: and then I got down off my horse and came over and knelt down by poor, dear Isabel. My cloak flowed out about me and hid my hands…"

"Hoy, *sir*," said Sergeant Bedd in a gurgling voice; "you're straglig be!"

"Right bang there in front of the audience," said Charlesworth, in a tone of awe. He stood up and, fresh from the business of strangling Sergeant Bedd, dusted his hands together fastidiously.

"And me in the front row," said Inspector Cockrill. Awe was not the word for it.

"Unhooked the ropes, tucked them out of sight under her skirt and blundered, stupefied with sorrow, out through the arch!"

Sergeant Bedd staggered to his feet, holding his throat. Charlesworth finished dusting his hands; Inspector Cockrill drew deeply on a shabby cigarette. "Well—now all that's left is to discover what's happened to Anderson," said Charlesworth, girt for further action.

"And to make an arrest, sir?" said Sergeant Bedd, hopefully.

"And to make an arrest: I should think so, Inspector, wouldn't you?"

Cockie considered. "As you say, we must first find out what's *happened* to Anderson."

"Did anyone speak to him except Perpetua Kirk, last night?"

"Not that Perpetua Kirk did speak to him," said Cockie.

"Good lord, yes, she did."

"The evidence is that she told Miss Betchley he was there. That's all."

"Well, maybe she didn't speak to him: maybe she only saw him."

"*If* she even saw him," said Cockie, being difficult. "Miss Betchley was outside in the corridor, fussing. Peppi Kirk was at the Assembly room door. She said words to the effect that he was there all the time: he must be changing. Isn't it possible that she simply glanced at the peg where his armour should have been hanging, saw that it wasn't there, and assumed that he'd taken it out to the stables and was changing?"

Charlesworth felt that it was all rather splitting hairs, and that considering what Perpetua had later suffered, it did not very much matter whether she had or had not heard from Earl Anderson's own lips that he was now going to the stables or a dressing room to shuffle into his armour. But the old boy seemed to make a great Thing of it. He said at last: "Well, I'll tell you what—I must go back to the Yard now and thrash this thing out, so we'll take Miss Kirk in on the way and ask her. Besides, after that last note, we ought to warn her about the present development, and what she's got to watch out for." Cockrill folded his short legs into the front seat of the little car, and nursing his hat on his knees, was driven up to Bayswater.

"Jolly decent of you to give me that hint, sir," was the gratifying burden of young Charlesworth's song. "I daresay I'd have come round to it, but there's a hell of a lot to think about when one's on the case sort of—officially…" (All very well to potter around and build up neat theories in the intervals of some tin-pot conference…!)

Over the cup of tea and no tea-cake, Perpetua was confiding to her new gallant the story of the note that had arrived with the morning's post. "Who then, Perpetua, can have sent this letter?"

"I've no idea. The police have got it of course, and apparently it was posted last night: but anybody could have put it in a letter-box on the way home after the exhibition, or just before they came in. It was posted from the local box."

"Can they tell nothing from the writing of it?"

"Well, I suppose they'll check all the typewriters any of us could have had access to."

"We all have access to a thousand typewriters, Peppi. Any of us can go to a typewriter shop and try one or two machines. No need to write every time 'The quick brown fox jumps over the lazy dog'."

There was a postman's double knock, and at the same time Cockie and Bedd and Charlesworth arrived, Charlesworth carrying a brown paper parcel. "Have you been buying a dizzy new hat, Miss Kirk? Or who's sending you a fancy bouquet? We rescued this from the postman and brought it along to you."

Cockie could not help hoping that it was not a hat. Once there had been a hat: Francesca Hart's absurd little nonsense of a hat, found perched on the head of a dead woman... He hadn't made a muck of that case, anyway: or had he? He said, "Mr. Charlesworth has something to ask you, Peppi. And something to tell you."

"Yes, Mr. Charlesworth?" said Peppi, rather absently, longing to know what was in the parcel, since she had purchased no hat. Her fingers fiddled impotently with the cords.

Brian Bryan took it out of her hands. "I do it for you." Charlesworth asked about her having seen Anderson.

"No, I didn't *see* him. I just didn't see his armour." It was all exactly as that astute old devil had said.

Brian Bryan and Perpetua sat staring while Charlesworth outlined the method of the murder. "I thought I ought to explain this to you, and warn you, Miss Kirk," said Charlesworth solemnly. "You had that warning note today: and as long as Earl Anderson's at large, you re bound to be in danger."

"We can't really make an arrest, Peppi, you see," explained Cockrill, "until Earl Anderson's found." He thought Scotland Yard a trifle indiscreet, to say the least of it: but it was no business of his.

"Well, hardly," said Charlesworth.

"I know: that's just what I'm saying."

Brian and Peppi sat staring at them both. Brian had the cardboard box on his knees, and his neat fingers picked automatically at the strings; but he had forgotten it. "What are you gentlemen saying…?"

People were extraordinarily slow in the uptake, really. Charlesworth got to his feet and collected his hat. "We're just warning Miss Kirk: because of that second note she got this morning. Wherever he is, he's still got it in for her evidently; but don't worry, Miss Kirk, we shall be watching the place for him and you'll be safe enough. And as long as you realize that the murderer was Earl Anderson…"

"Earl *Anderson?*" said Cockie. "Who on earth said anything about Earl Anderson?"

"The murderer, you fool," said Charlesworth. "What else have we been talking about all this time? The murderer. The Red Knight. Earl Anderson."

Perpetua put out her hand—idly, almost blindly, not thinking of what she was doing, thinking only of Earl: and lifted the lid of the box, glancing incuriously at what it contained. A fold of tissue paper: and under that—pale and transparent, with tiny figures of fighter aeroplanes—or were they really seagulls upside down?—Earl's bathroom curtains! She stood staring down at them; they all stared down blankly; and still her mind had no room for amazement, it was so full of the thought of Earl—of Earl, whom one had known so well, Earl whom in a dazed way one had been so fond of, Earl who at least had always been kind—and now was a murderer. Charlesworth said again: "The Red Knight: the murderer—Earl Anderson!" and she lifted the covering fold of curtain material...

Dark hair. A leaden face. A horrible smear of blood, congealed and black... And Earl Anderson's witless blue eyes stared back into her own.

Chapter IX

A COURTING COUPLE, ARMS ENTWINED, HAD SAT DOWN upon the torso of Earl Anderson under a bush on the evening after Isabel's murder: and never felt quite the same towards one another again. It was lying in a patch of deep grass just off the main road to Maidenhead, and with it was a perfectly ordinary bread knife, the blade red and rusted, the handle so charred—doubtless deliberately—as to prevent any possible identification. There was no blood upon the scene nor any sign of a struggle; there were one or two footprints no longer very clear, and apparently made by the victim's own shoes, which lay chucked down beside the body; and what with one thing and another, the experts decided that the man had been dead not more than forty-eight hours, possibly a great deal less. "Rigor begins in the head and neck, you see, old boy... And in this case the neck..." It was all very unattractive.

Charlesworth shifted wretchedly about the chilly little mortuary. "Can't you give me anything more definite?"

"Have a heart, man, I've only just arrived from my breakfast, to be confronted with your assorted heads and bodies."

Charlesworth leaned over to look at the disembowelled torso on the slab. "No question of the wrong head on the wrong body, or anything like that?"

"My *dear* Mr. Chesterton—spare us your pretty fancies! We haven't got half a dozen headless bodies knocking around; not this week we haven't. You've found a head, and you've found a body—and by the oddest coincidence, they match."

"You don't know anything about pretty fancies till you've been in on the Isabel Drew case," said Charlesworth gloomily. "As if towers and knights in armour and Biblical analogies weren't sufficient, I've got a little imp of a man called Cockrill making my life hideous, forestalling my every thought, not to mention a few thoughts I don't have."

Littlejohn, the pathologist, suggested comfortably that Inspector Cockrill made something of a speciality in decapitations, didn't he? He flicked an enquiring finger at the slab. "Why this one? Do you know yet?"

"The murderer's trying to frighten and upset this poor girl: and you can't send whole bodies through the post—there's a fifteen pound limit or something. I presume the cause of death wasn't the beheading?"

"I haven't had enough time with him yet to be certain: but, no, I shouldn't think so. Off the record I should say that he was batted on the head first with the regulation blunt instrument—he's got a hell of a bruise on the back of his nut. Then strangled—throttled from the back, probably, same as the girl—these people always repeat themselves: and then the head was taken off quite soon after. Whoever it was just hacked away with a knife—nothing skilled about it. It would be frightfully difficult to do, actually—a horrible job. I should say he took quite a bit of time about it."

"He? Could a woman have done it?"

"Anyone *could* have done it, old boy: whether or not a woman *would* have—but I suppose that's just sentimentality. A good hard bonk on the back of the head—that's child's play. The throttling took a lot of strength, but if the man's unconscious it would just be a matter of finding the right grip and hanging on tight till he caved in. And then as I say, this business with the knife. I'll get it all nice and official for you by lunchtime."

Charlesworth met the infuriating Inspector Cockrill in a tea place opposite. "How the hell does one get hold of the waitress without calling her 'Miss'?"

Cockrill got hold of her at once, having no such inhibitions. They ordered coffee. "*I've* been on the mat this morning," said Charlesworth, ruefully. "My Chief is pretty unreasonable, I consider. He seems to think I ought to have somehow prevented this—this Salome act."

"Earl Anderson's head on a charger?"

"Only it was really more off the charger, wasn't it?" said Charlesworth, pleased by this flight of fancy. "Except that the charger was only an old circus pony, actually."

"Anyway, your Chief thinks you ought to have done something about it?"

"Well, apparently. Though how *I* could have prevented it, I don't quite see. I was looking for a man alive or dead: but not by the portion, I must admit. I suppose," said Charlesworth gloomily, spreading his toast with the pallid grape-fruit jelly striped with raw carrot which here, as in so many similar establishments, passed as marmalade, "that *you* knew all along that Anderson's head, wrapped up in his bathroom curtains, was on its way to Perpetua Kirk via the penny post?"

"No," said Cockie. "I didn't know about the head. I thought it probable that Anderson was dead."

"Because of the mystery Knight upon the Left?"

"As far as Isabel was concerned, the knight on her left was Earl Anderson," said Cockrill. "So why the Mystery?" He repeated the little verse again:

> *"Oh, Isabel, how beautiful thy face is!*
> *It brings out homage in unexpected places.*
> *And so the donor of this little gift*
> *Is who? The Mystery Knight upon the left."*

He said: "It told one such a lot: didn't it?"

"Good lord, yes," said Charlesworth, fervently. (Most illuminating!)

"The first thing that struck one was that Isabel Drew was not the person to carry around a bit of nonsense like that next to her heart—I mean, that she'd just shoved it down her front for somewhere to keep it. That argued that she had received the note some time since she had put on that particular dress, and even if she'd got it in her dressing room, she'd surely have just put it into her handbag. As I said at the time, the very wording of the note seemed to suggest that it was sent to her, or left somewhere for her—not handed to her by the writer. So all in all there was—well, a certain amount of reason to suggest that the note and the brooch had been left for her in the tower. No proof, of *course*."

"And no proof that the brooch was actually the 'gift'!"

"Well, no. But she wasn't wearing any other jewellery: and the fact that the pin of the brooch had gone through the paper did seem to suggest that she first stuffed the note down her bodice and then pinned the brooch into her frock over it. And it was a brand new piece of jewellery."

"She then marched up to the balcony and leaned well out…?"

"To see the "Mystery Knight"…"

"Who was *not* Earl Anderson," said Charlesworth. He added thoughtfully, however: "Except that there was this point about Isabel's beauty bringing out homage in unexpected places. Well, Earl Anderson was an unexpected place to find homage to Isabel's beauty. He'd been indifferent to it for years. Supposing he'd suddenly been struck all of a heap—he'd expect Isabel to be surprised at finding devotion coming from *him*."

"He'd also expect her to be surprised at diamond brooches coming from him: and rightly so. Earl Anderson was an out of work actor," said Cockie, with the simple scorn of those who if not actors, have at least never been out of work, "so far reduced that he had accepted a job riding around in phoney armour at four-pounds-ten a week. And this was a brooch of pretty considerable value."

"It might have been his Mum's old heirloom or Aunt Jemima's legacy: 'never part with this, Earl, my boy, except to the Woman you Make your Wife…'"

"It might if it had not been a 1948 model," said Cockie.

"Yes," said Charlesworth. *Mad*dening little man!

Inspector Cockrill reached for his shabby hat and thrust it on to his head, evidently only by way of keeping it out of the way while he unhitched his shabby mackintosh from the back of a neighbouring chair. He flung the coat over his shoulder, rose to his feet and called out simply: "Miss!"

"I'll do this," said Charlesworth hastily, shuddering a little at this bold frontal attack.

"No, no," said Cockie. He calculated the bill in his head and scrupulously contributed his share.

They walked off up the street together; a tall slim young man in a worn, but well-cut suit, and a little elderly man with stove-pipe trousers, a mackintosh trailing over one shoulder, and a battered felt hat at a rakish angle on a magnificent head. "And of course nobody ever did *see* Anderson at Elysian Hall that day," said Cockie, continuing the conversation as though it had not been interrupted by the paying of the bill. "Perpetua pointed out that his armour had been removed: but anybody might have removed it and at that very moment was probably putting it on. The best disguise in the world—a suit of armour."

"Except a diving suit," said Charlesworth.

Inspector Cockrill looked cross. "In this case, the introduction of a diving suit would have struck a very outré note: I think we can eliminate any such suggestion." He shifted his mackintosh on his shoulder and branched off abruptly across the street. "I'll leave you here. I'm supposed to be attending a conference!" You tried to knock sense into the young dunderhead and he started rambling off about diving suits! These modern boys…

George Exmouth had been to call on Perpetua Kirk: but Peppi was prostrate after last night's appalling shock, and receiving nobody: besides, added the garrulous charlady, there was a gentleman already with her. Ever so lovely, it seemed, the gentleman was; and foreign too. George handed in a large bunch of flowers and wandered miserably away. He felt very odd: he had not slept all night and his brain was going round and round in the most peculiar fashion. And when he got home, there was The Police, waiting for him. He sat down on the okapi-skin divan and put his poor, young, aching head in his hands.

Charlesworth explained his errand. Mr. Exmouth had heard that Earl Anderson...?

"*Too* horrible," said George, his fingers plunged deeply into his soft, rather spikey brown hair.

The police had come to Mr. Exmouth for help. Of course there was still the possibility that Earl Anderson had murdered Isabel Drew—by a method so far known only to Detective Inspector Charlesworth and a Chosen Few—and had himself been murdered afterwards, possibly by way of revenge. But he had not been seen since the evening before Isabel's murder; and that being so, the suggestion being that he was already dead when Isabel was killed, the question now was—who had taken his place in the pageant? George Exmouth had followed the Red Knight in their cavortings round the stage before Isabel's murder: had sat astride the horse facing him across the archway for perhaps a full minute just before she fell. Had Mr. Exmouth anything to suggest that might help in identification—might help to confirm identification...?

George stared open-mouthed. "You mean

somebody—somebody *else* was in Anderson's armour? Anderson wasn't in the pageant at all? Somebody had killed him so as to take his place…?"

"Somebody had killed him anyway: and taken his place."

"But that could have been anybody," said George wildly. "*Any*body!"

"Well, not exactly. It couldn't have been you, for example, because you were on your horse: and it couldn't have been Brian Bryan because he was on his horse, and it couldn't have been any of the other nine knights. On the other hand, it must have been someone familiar with the routine of the pageant; and someone who could go in and out of the Assembly room and not be particularly noted." Which left only Perpetua Kirk…

"It wasn't Perpetua," said George quickly. Since it was unlikely that they would take his simple word for it, he pointed out that all this time Perpetua was tied up and locked away in the little room.

Charlesworth obligingly disallowed Perpetua. "Which leaves Susan Betchley: and Mr. Port. And Miss Betchley was on the other side of a bolted door."

George Exmouth clutched his hair. His face was very white and his eyes very wild, and his pale lips trembled like the lips of a frightened child. He said in a terrified whisper: "You don't mean that Mr. *Port*…?"

"Came the dawn!" said Charlesworth to Sergeant Bedd.

But Mr. Port! "Why on earth should he want to kill Isabel Drew? He was in love with her: he was having an affair with her—or—or something, anyway," finished George uncertainly. Mr. Port was old, probably as old as fifty or even sixty:

did old men have "affairs" and if not what had there been between Mr. Port and Isabel Drew—who quite certainly did have affairs—anybody could tell that, just by looking at her: even anybody who was only seventeen and a half and had not as yet had any affairs.

"Mr. Port was very anxious that the news of the 'affair' such as it was, shouldn't get back to his wife; and Isabel Drew was probably not beyond exerting a little pressure in the way of blackmail."

"Even so—why kill Earl Anderson?"

Charlesworth moved restlessly in his chair, a tortured thing of plastic and twisted steel. Why should old Port kill Anderson? It was tricky, that. "You yourself suggested a reason," he said. "To take his place in the pageant."

"Would Mr. Port kill a man just for that? A man he had nothing against?"

"No," said Charlesworth. "I don't think he would. And if he did, he would hardly chop off his head and send it haring about the countryside in a nasty messy parcel. Unless of course Anderson was in cahoots with Isabel Drew over the blackmail business."

"But Anderson himself was being blackmailed by Isabel."

"Yes," said Charlesworth. "And there's still the business about Peppi Kirk—the notes and the adventure in the little dressing room, and the sending of the head. But there's only one thing that those three had in common, Isabel and Anderson and Perpetua Kirk—and that was that business about the boy, Johnny Wise."

"And of course Mr. Port knew Johnny Wise in Malaya."

Charlesworth picked up a pencil from Charity's nightmare desk and started idly to doodle on a sheet of paper.

"They *all* knew Johnny Wise in Malaya: Brian Bryan, Miss Betchley and Edgar Port. But just knowing a person is not sufficient reason for murdering on his account. People don't do murder for their casual friends—not long-calculated, long-planned, savage, cold-blooded murder."

"It depends how casual their friends were," said Sergeant Bedd, perched on the edge of his chair as though it would cry out if he put his full weight on to its atrophied legs.

"Well, they naturally all claim that Johnny Wise was quite a 'casual.' Miss Betchley played tennis with him, Brian Bryan met him at parties, Mr. Port thought he was a charming lad, and Mrs. Port was so fond of him—indeed Mr. Port says that Johnny reminded Mrs. Port of their lost son. But none of them knew him well. And we can't check anything. The records have gone up in the smoke of Japanese fires, friends and families are dead or dispersed: we've got to take their words for it."

"I never knew this Johnny Wise," said George carefully.

"You would have been about nine years old when he died."

George lost a shade more of his colour. He said rather quickly: "What about his family?"

"His family consisted of a father and a mother and two or three brothers as far as we know. A chap of that name was killed by the Japanese during the early days of the invasion: but just who he was, we aren't sure. Johnny had a twin that he was frightfully devoted to: and the classic thing would be that the murderer is his twin, come back to avenge his death. But there just is nobody in the cast who fits the role of the twin, so that's out." He had doodled a little row of people who might conceivably be taken to represent the "cast," and he now ticked them off lightly as he spoke. "Johnny was twenty-three or twenty-four when he died: he'd be about thirty now. And Mr. Port's in his middle fifties, and Earl Anderson is or was in his middle forties, and you're seventeen, and Brian Bryan's thirty-nine."

"*He* says," said George, significantly.

"No," said Charlesworth. "It's not just 'he says.' There's a difference between just over thirty and just under forty—and Brian Bryan is just under forty. It's in his walk and manner and his—his eye, and his hair and his teeth—he's not a *young* young man. If it's got to be the twin, it isn't Brian Bryan—and there's nobody else." He ticked off Brian Two-times with the rest of them—n.b.g.

So back to Mr. Port.

George had been, after all, trained to observation by a mother who made a fat living out of copying other people's ideas. He sat and thought for a long time, his thin fingers rumpling his little-boy hair, and said at last: "It's true that he—the Red Knight—did look rather *small* as he went off through the arch. Smaller than Anderson. One thought of it—if one thought of it at all—as the effect of—of pathos: one just thought how small and forlorn and rather pathetic he looked, staggering out of the place, away from all the dreadfulness: after all, he had known her for years—I mean, Earl Anderson had known her for years. And she did look terrible. I saw just a glimpse of her face when he lifted her up."

"Just a glimpse?"

"Yes, his cloak sort of hid her. I still don't see... I'm bewildered..."

Charlesworth could not be bothered clearing up matters for bewildered Master Exmouth. He got up abruptly off his chair, which let out a creak of relief; and began pacing the room. His fingers had twisted the paper he had been doodling on into a little scroll and he pointed it challengingly at George as he walked. "Never mind how he did it: suppose for the moment that the part of the Red Knight was taken—was definitely taken—by Mr. Port. Can't you remember anything, *any*thing that would confirm this? He didn't speak to you as you went round? He didn't make any sort of movement or gesture that you would recognize? There wasn't any—any distinguishing mark?" How a man in a full suit of armour could exhibit distinguishing marks he could not quite see: but dash it all... And the knights had worn their visors up so as to see which way they were going: surely, surely George Exmouth sitting his horse slap opposite the fellow for at least sixty seconds must have recognized something about his face? Well, the bridge of his nose, then? His forehead then? His *eyes?*

His eyes. George Exmouth said slowly: "Yes. I could see their eyes. I saw Brian Bryan look over at me with a sort of alarm and astonishment when his horse began to buck about: and then I looked across at the Red Knight, because I didn't know what on earth we ought to do. But Earl Anderson had blue eyes. And now that I think of it—now that I think of it—the eyes that looked back into mine that night—were brown."

Just precisely what Mr. Charlesworth had wanted to know.

Perpetua lay on her bed in a woolly jersey and dark slacks: and with rugs, and her eiderdown over her, for all the summer sunshine could not get warm. She looked very frail, her face pale and thin under the mop of queer, thick golden hair; her eyes were clouded and her mouth held its old look of pain and defeat. Brian sat quietly beside her, holding her hand. "Don't think of it, Peppi... Forget it, don't go on brooding over it... He is dead now, Peppi, what does it matter if somebody plays ugly tricks with—with him? He does not know, he does not care, he is peaceful. Forget all about it, go now to sleep, I am here, I look after you..." But now the telephone rang. He stretched out an arm for it. "Yes? Yes, I take it." After a moment, unobtrusively, he rang off, though he still held the receiver to his ear. "Sorry, I think you got the wrong number. This telegram is not for here." He held out his hand to her again and she took it in both her own and laid her cheek against it: and so at last went softly off to sleep. He sat looking down at her with pity and tenderness.

Inspector Cockrill was fated to attend not one full sitting of his conference. He was disturbed by a telephone call and went out grumpily to the little box in the hall outside the conference room. A high, clear voice said, out of the past: "Cockie, pet!—Is it really you?"

"Who is that?" said Cockie austerely.

But he knew. And even his grim old heart melted at that young voice. It said: "Do so many young women ring you up and call you 'Cockie, pet'?"

"No," he said. "Most of them haven't got the nerve. And only *one* that I know, has the nerve to track me down and ring me up at a police conference! That's Francesca Hart. What do you want, you naughty little girl?"

"Darling Cockie!" said Fran.

"Don't 'darling Cockie' me. What is it now?"

"You ought to be grateful," said the other end of the telephone. "I saw that you were interested in this case, Cockie, and by the most fantastic coincidence, I think I know something about it. Because I was in a telephone box in Piccadilly Circus underground the other evening—Tuesday evening—and I heard somebody talking to that man who's been found dead: Earl Anderson. I read about him in the papers this morning."

"You heard somebody talking to Anderson?"

"Yes. It was after ten and I couldn't get a taxi, and I was worried about not getting home because the baby wasn't very well… You know I've got a baby now, Cockie?"

"High time," said Cockie. "Well, so at ten o'clock you were in a call box at Piccadilly…?"

"And I couldn't get through. But, of course I knew there was someone at home, so I didn't ring off but simply hung on and waited. And I could just hear what the person in the next box to me was saying: you can sometimes, if you're not listening to anyone else. It was a man and he said: "Can I speak to Earl Anderson, please?" I noticed because it seemed such a funny way to put it: I mean, you'd call an Earl 'Lord' or something like that, wouldn't you? Or wouldn't you?"

"I've never called an Earl anything," said Cockie. "In this case it was a man's name: or the name he acted under."

"Well, yes, of course I realized that after a bit. Anyway, then I'm afraid I decided to press button B. and start all over again, so I missed what was said next; but still no answer from home, so I began idly to listen again, and this time it was a long story about a marvellous chance and something about Micky Balcon. So then I'm afraid I listened all the more, because it did seem nice for somebody to be having a marvellous chance and being talked about by Michael Balcon…"

"Why is it always Michael Balcon?" said Cockie.

"I must say it always is, isn't it?" said Francesca. "And they always call him 'Micky.' Do you mean to say that Earl Anderson was just a down-and-out, and Michael Balcon hadn't been talking about him at all?"

"I don't suppose Michael Balcon ever even heard of him."

"Well, this person said he had, he said that Micky Balcon simply adored Earl Anderson's work, and he mentioned a lot of other names. But I'm afraid I missed a bit here, because I got fed up and asked 'O' to try my number for me, and she did and I got through: but I did just hear the man say something about O.K. then, and they'd meet at half past eleven at the Golden Golliwog and he seemed to be giving directions and saying something about wearing a red carnation, as though perhaps Earl Anderson wouldn't recognize him. But then I got through and Nanny had been in her bath all that time, and the baby was perfectly all right; and in some peculiar way I'd got through without ever pushing button A., so I got my tuppence back and went away. Considering the time they'd taken getting me through, Cockie, I think that was fair, don't you?"

Cockie was not interested in the ethics of his girl-friends in swizzling the telephone company because their nannies took so long over their baths. "Where or what is the Golden Golliwog?"

"A very nasty pub, darling, out on the Maidenhead road. Pseudo-Tudor without, red leather and chromium within, and Dancing in what was the barn and still ought to be."

"Oh. Now, Francesca—any sort or kind of description of this man?"

But this was too much to hope. The man had seemed rather sort of slouched down in the call-box and he had a soft hat on and, as far as she remembered, a mackintosh; but he kept his back turned to her.

"You're certain sure it was a man?"

"He was dressed like a man," said Francesca, doubtfully. "But I couldn't possibly say that it wasn't a woman dressed up, if that's what you mean. I hardly really noticed what he looked like—we were sort of back-to-back in our little boxes, and as he wasn't even the Earl Anderson who was getting the Chance, I wasn't so much interested in *him*. All that I can say is that I have a vague impression that he wore a soft hat and a mac., but so did practically every other man in Piccadilly that night: it was a bit drizzly, if you remember? Most men would have worn a mac."

Inspector Cockrill knew of one man who *always* wore a mac. "What was his voice like? You can tell me that... Any— any peculiarities?"

But his voice had been—just a man's voice. Not a very old voice, not a particularly young voice, not high, not low, not squeaky, not apparently in any way disguised. And not "foreign."

Cockrill rang up the Yard and told Inspector Charlesworth. "A middling sized man," said Charlesworth, excitedly. "Ordinary English voice. On the night Earl Anderson disappeared—luring him away on this excuse—a chap like Anderson will hare off anywhere for the smell of a job!—down towards the Maidenhead road. He waited for him there, I suppose: stopped the car on some pretext, got him to go up the side-turning, perhaps, and there blipped him on the head, strangled him and lugged him out on to the grass and chopped off his head. A smallish man: ordinary English voice. And from nine o'clock onwards that evening Edgar Port was in his hotel room—he says. No alibi." He snapped his fingers and gave the desk a little bonk! with his clenched hand. "We've got him!" he said.

No use going back to the conference now. Cockie collected his hat, slapped it on to his head, and stumped out into the sunshine, his head thrust a little forward, his hands clasped loosely behind his back, very deep in thought. He stood himself an early lunch at the Maison Lyons and then walked on across the Park still thinking deeply: and came at last to the gate leading out into Bayswater Road. Miss Betchley was sitting on a bench near the gate. He changed direction and approached her without ceremony. "I was just coming along to see you."

Susan Betchley put down her newspaper; her eyes were red-rimmed as though she had been having a quiet cry behind its pages. She said ungraciously: "Oh! Were you?"

Cockie sat down beside her, crossing his short legs. "I wanted to have a talk to you, my dear girl. I think you're going to get yourself into a bit of a mess, if you're not very careful."

She folded the newspaper with inordinate care. She said again: "Oh," in that flat, uninterested voice. But she added: "In what way?"

Cockie rather liked Susan Betchley. She was a girl with "no nonsense about her" as downright and uncompromising as a man. He said: "What is there between you and this fellow Brian Twice, or whatever it is they call him?"

She opened her brown eyes wide. "Between Brian Bryan and me?—nothing whatsoever!"

"But—you're protecting him in some way: you're telling lies to protect him. Now, Scotland Yard is going to begin examining this young man's actions very carefully, shortly: and I'm a little afraid that you're going to get yourself into trouble."

"I thought you thought he was out of it? I thought you were encouraging all this—all this lovey-dovey with Perpetua Kirk?"

"Oh," he said. "So that's the way the wind blows?"

"The wind doesn't blow any way," she said, angrily. "There isn't any wind to blow."

Cockie took out the inevitable cigarette papers and tobacco and, sitting on the slatted wooden bench beside her, began to concentrate on making himself a cigarette. He said flatly: "My dear girl—you're in love with the fellow!"

He kept his eyes down: but he could see the big, brown hands clenched together between her knees, could see the short, unvarnished nails digging into the palms. She said at last: "What sort of a fool would I be, to be in love with Brian Bryan?"

"It's not always the most sensible thing in the world," said Cockie, "to fall in love."

She disregarded him. "At my age! Well over thirty—to fall in love, to wallow like any callow schoolgirl in a drama of unrequited passion!" She looked down at her hands, at her handsome unalluring legs and stubby, square feet. "As if any man could love me! Me—why, I'm like a man myself, heavy and ugly... He'd have to be a pansy!" She rattled the newspaper, holding it up fanwise before her face, as two tears tumbled over and raced one another down her swarthy cheeks. "Look at me! *Look* at me! Even—even in agony, I'm just rather—rather grotesque, a figure of fun, sitting here weeping into *The Times*, over a pair of blue eyes that have never even looked my way: trying to turn a silly schoolgirl *schwarm* into a *grande passion*..." She rubbed her cheeks with the back of her hands and pulled herself abruptly together. "Well—now I suppose I've given myself away, good and proper. But you can't despise me more than I despise myself."

He puffed at the completed cigarette. "I don't despise you, my dear child. He's a very attractive fellow, and when you come to *my* age, you'll look upon your own age as just about ripe for a nice schoolgirl pash! What I'm concerned about is, that you'll do yourself harm telling fibs on his behalf. The police are going to get very busy, very soon."

"I thought *you* were the police," she said sullenly.

"Well, I am, and I'm not. Anyway, in this matter I'm speaking only for your own good. You'll get yourself into a muddle, and not benefit him."

"I don't even see why you should think I'm going out of my way to defend him."

He looked at her from under his bushy eyebrows. "My dear Miss Betchley—I've been listening to witnesses giving evidence for something like forty years. I saw the way you looked across at Mr. Bryan when you said that you'd talked to him as he sat there on his horse; just before the pageant, you know, when Perpetua Kirk was being attacked outside. Now—that isn't true, is it?"

"What isn't true?" she said.

"That you spoke to Brian Bryan."

"Of course it's true," she said with an air of impatience.

"Honestly?"

"I give you my word of honour: there—will that do?"

"Yes," said Cockie. "It'll do very well." He flicked the long ash from his cigarette with a nicotined finger-nail.

"So if you're suggesting that Brian wasn't really sitting on his horse..."

"No, no," said Cockie. "We've gone through all that, he and I. But it's a funny thing: I could have sworn that you were hedging in your evidence about him..."

"You've just missed the bus a trifle, that's all," she said, with a faintly, just faintly, triumphant glance. "And anyway, there's nothing against Brian, is there? Whatever he might have done to Perpetua Kirk, he couldn't have killed Isabel Drew. That's flat."

"I know," said Cockie. "That's why I don't want you to complicate things for yourself and us by telling distorted truths."

A rider bucketed past them along the Row, sitting very upright and conscious on his tawny, varnished horse: bright-ringed hooves kicked up a chuff-chuff-chuff of soft earth. A car approached, ponderous in its shining black magnificence. "It's Mr. Port," said Susan Betchley. "We've all got to go down to Elysian Hall—the Detective Inspector wants us there."

"No doubt he's going to 'reconstruct the scene,'" said Cockie sourly.

Susan Betchley looked at him innocently. "Isn't that a good thing to do?"

"We don't do it in Kent," said Cockie, austerely. (They had done it in Kent once, it was true, but the less said about that the better.) "And anyway it usually comes at the end of a case. This case is about at the beginning, for all I can see." He graciously accepted a lift to Elysium, however, when Mr. Port stopped the car near the bench. Motherdear was in the front seat. Cockrill thought he looked dreadfully white and ill. He said: "Are you all right, boy? You don't look too good."

"Of course I'm not all right," said George, bursting out with it savagely, his miserable young eyes staring ahead of him, through Mr. Port's windscreen.

Mr. Port drove with nervous care along the broad road through the park. "The foolish lad has got it into his head that he's done me some harm. Something about the colour of my eyes or something." He turned his head with a brief, reassuring smile at George, but his face was haggard.

For George Exmouth, after an hour of agonizing examination of conscience, had gone to Mr. Port and told him everything: about the police visit, about his own final word of confirmation. Mr. Port said anxiously: "Young George seems to think, Inspector Cockrill, that they actually suspect *me*. Now, I'm sure that you can—can set his mind at rest..." Since Cockrill remained unresponsive, he outlined the case against himself. "Earl Anderson had blue eyes. He says that the Red Knight, when Isabel was killed, had brown eyes: and I have brown eyes. Now, Inspector—did you ever hear such nonsense?"

It seemed as though a weight had been lifted from Susan Betchley's heart. "Why should it be nonsense? You *were* in and out of the Assembly room, you *could* have taken Earl Anderson's armour: you *could* have rushed away off the stage and reappeared as yourself. And nobody'd seen you in the meantime. What's more, only you, of all of us, could have afforded to buy a diamond brooch."

"It's a lie," said Mr. Port, his lips trembling, his hands shaking on the driving wheel. "It's a lie. All lies!"

"And you had a good reason to get rid of Isabel Drew. She was going to tell your wife about your affair with her. She was blackmailing you."

"No," said Mr Port, trembling. "Not that. Not blackmail. She—she had a delicate conscience: sometimes she used to think that we should—should make a clean breast of the whole thing to my wife..." His face was the colour of clay, his little hands lay on the driving wheel like weighted gloves. "It's true that—I didn't want Isabel to say anything to my wife." He began suddenly to speak to them about his wife, hardly realizing perhaps that they were there, that he had an audience at all; that every word told against him like a nail in his prison coffin... About her sufferings, about her gentleness and courage and endurance, about her final breakdown when suffering was over, and endurance no longer the need it had been. About Charlesworth's visit, and the effect it had had: about his own sins against her and the weight upon his conscience because she was suffering anew... "What could Isabel Drew mean to me, in comparison with my wife's wellbeing...? And yet..." He burst out: "I made a fool of myself with that horrible girl, and now through my wickedness and folly..." He talked on and on. The car turned into Kensington High Street, and wound its way as though of its own volition, towards the Elysian Hall. "If anything happens to her—if she never recovers her true mind—I shall be guilty of her death: the death of her mind."

Miss Betchley said into the silence: "And yet you say you didn't murder Isabel?"

"How could I have murdered her?" he said, desperately. "Of course I wasn't dressed up in any silly armour. I was standing in the body of the hall, looking on."

"You haven't got any alibi, Mr. Port," said Motherdear, gloomily. "Not for the night before, when Earl Anderson was killed, and not for the whole day before the pageant either; except for the rehearsal in the morning."

"Nobody has any alibis for those times," said Cockrill, throwing a dash of cold water into the saucepan, lest it boil over before things became really interesting. He was fond of promoting discussion between the suspects: sooner or later something useful almost always emerged. He gazed blandly out of the window at the passing scene. London with her blind grey eyes gazed back.

"I had things to do all day," said Mr. Port stiffly. "I spent a lot of time with my wife. The night before, I went to bed early. Everybody did. I told them all to, so as to be fresh for the following evening: now didn't I? *You* can bear me out."

Miss Betchley and Motherdear acknowledged that they had obeyed orders and gone to bed early and so had no alibis either for the time of Earl Anderson's murder—always supposing it to have been committed during the night preceding the pageant. By this time, however, no one supposed anything else.

"I was in bed by ten," insisted Mr. Port; "soon afterwards, Isabel rang me. But of course I can't prove that now: because Isabel's dead."

"And so is Earl Anderson," said Susan Betchley. She leaned forward, one hand over the back of his seat, the other clenched on her knee, and there was nothing now in her face of the aching bitterness that Cockrill had seen there twenty minutes ago: only a sort of grim determination, terrible to see.

Mr. Port suddenly straightened his pudgy shoulders: his hands gripped the wheel, he put his foot down on the accelerator and the car shot neatly between two buses, rounded a corner, and overtook a taxi-cab. He said with a new initiative in his voice: "And there you are: Anderson is dead too. And I had no reason in the world to kill Anderson."

"Unless it was to borrow his armour," said Motherdear.

Mr. Port raised both hands into the air, and brought them down on the wheel with a little exasperated crash, "*I* kill Earl Anderson or any man for such a reason! Don't be ridiculous! And, anyway, why me? You two are very free with your accusations... Why me? Why not either of you?" He jerked his head back in the direction of Susan Betchley, sitting behind him in the car. "What about you, Miss Betchley: eh? What about you? You loathed Isabel Drew: you thought she was responsible for the death of poor Johnny Wise..."

"I've told you a thousand times, Johnny Wise was just a casual friend..."

"And she was thick with your precious Brian Bryan, that you're sick with love for..."

George slewed round to stare into the back of the car. Miss Betchley said savagely: "Shut up, you babbling old fool…"

"And you," said Mr. Port to Motherdear, lifting his hand and striking down upon the wheel again. "You're very free too with your accusations and your confirmations and all the rest of it… What about you, my lad? You and your mother had known Isabel a long time: long before any of us knew her… What was Isabel to you, eh? Just tell us that…"

George stared dumbfounded at Mr. Port's ashen face. "I? And Isabel Drew! I—I never—hardly ever even spoke to her. And anyway, if I had…" He began to gather courage from his very innocence of this monstrous, this ugly, this oddly disturbing charge. "Even if I had, what about it? At least I'm—*I'm* young, and I'm free, I'm not like you… If anybody's calling anybody names…"

They had reached Elysian Hall. The car stopped, Mr. Port leaned back in his seat. "How dare you, you young whippersnapper…?"

"Well, he has got something there," said Susan Betchley, teaming up with George against the base betrayer of her secret passion.

"Love is not confined to the very young," said Mr. Port, lifting an eyebrow. "You should be able to support me in that."

Inspector Cockrill leaned back quietly in his seat, and let the storm rage. Nothing like people having a good set-to: nothing like frayed nerves snapping and old wounds bursting out afresh, to bring out the truth among people too long under restraint. Now and again he contributed a word to bring the embers to a blaze again: but mostly it was unnecessary. Savagely and wantonly they struck out at each other; caring nothing for each other, they yet dragged out old injuries of the spirit, little old, long-forgotten grievances... Ashamed and bitter, they eased their souls of their own niggling secrets: Edgar Port, conscious of his own unworthy passion, jeered at Motherdear's impotent adoration for Perpetua, at Susan Betchley's unrequited infatuation: George struck back with ugly names for elderly men who doted on young women, Miss Betchley dragged forth the cause of the injured wife... United against a common foe, she and George Exmouth rallied together, together parried and struck. Mr. Port cried at last: "And as for killing Isabel—I no more killed her than you did. For all anyone knows you killed her: either of you or both of you..."

"Why in God's name should we kill Isabel Drew?"

"Heaven knows: but here's this affair between Perpetua Kirk and Brian Bryan, and after all one of you's in love with Perpetua, and the other's in love with Bryan..." He pushed open the door of the car and got out. "Either of you or both of you: there's nobody else. I don't care two hoots who killed Isabel Drew: I don't mind anybody knowing that I'm glad she's dead. But you've accused me; and now I accuse you back." He dashed round the car wrenching at the door handles, pulling open the doors. "Come on, come on, all get out. All come along to the tower. This thing could have been done: it was done, and it must have been done by one or both of you—and I'm going to prove it..." He slammed the doors shut after them, and marched before them into Elysium Hall.

The turnstiles at Elysium were clicking merrily away: they shouldered their way through the crowds, and salesmen and demonstrators paused in their exertions to point them out to goggling customers. From the throats of a dozen amplifiers, the tunes of the moment hurdy-gurdied across the air; the atmosphere was heavy with the press of people, urgent with their bustle and eagerness, with the concentrated effort of hundreds of sales demonstrators forcing their wares upon the indifferent or reluctant. But beyond the doors leading back-stage, the sound was subdued to a sort of high-pitched hum; in the Assembly room all was quiet, dusty and bare; only the twelve suits of armour hung from their gibbets, their helmets at dreadful angles on necks that seemed a foot long, on account of the gap between the lower pegs and those on which the helmets hung. Their shadowed eye-sockets stared hopelessly into space. In the centre of the room stood Inspector Charlesworth. He had Brian Bryan and Perpetua with him. He said: "I thought it would be convenient if we all met down here. I want to confirm something. One or two things." And he crooked a finger at George Exmouth who went over and stood beside him. He said: "You told me this morning that you saw the eyes of the Red Knight, just before Isabel fell. Now—do you see those eyes here?"

Such a very small thing to say: such an easy answer to give. And yet on his answer, a life might hang. George stammered, white and shaky: "They were brown eyes."

"I know. So you said. And who has brown eyes here?"

George looked wretchedly round the little group. Perpetua, Brian Two-Times, Miss Betchley, Mr. Port... Grey eyes, blue eyes: and two pairs of brown eyes. He gave a little defiant, obstinate shrug. The answer was obvious: why put the onus of saying the words on *him*.

Charlesworth turned slowly towards Mr. Port.

Inspector Cockrill said suddenly: "Inspector—Mr. Port has a theory. Perhaps, before you say anything…"

Edgar Port might not have managed the fire-walking stunts back home in the Malay, as Isabel had—how long ago!—suggested: but he had been a member of the local amateur dramatic society and frequently took such parts as that of the General in *French Leave* for the delight of the members of the Club. He now flung himself into a sort of Ruth Draper performance, dashing to and fro in vivid imitations of Miss Betchley and Motherdear, which would have made Charlesworth die of laughter had it not all been so deadly serious, and which brought a quizzical look to Inspector Cockrill's beady eye. "Miss Betchley and young Exmouth have—have made certain suggestions against me, Detective Inspector. Very well. I make counteraccusations!" It was all very dramatic, very "pompious" as Brian Two-Times would have said: and yet—the little man was very pale, his eyes were leaden; he was fighting for his life. "Half past five: Miss Betchley arrives. She looks through the arch to make sure that the stage is clear, she glances into the tower, she checks up the suits of armour…" He ran from suit to suit like a dog sniffing out a suitable lamp-post. "All O.K." His face took on a look of determined pleasure and relief. "Miss Betchley takes her place just outside the Assembly room door." He stood there for a moment, apparently to establish her squatter's rights. "The knights come in, in ones and twos and threes: they collect their armour and go off, some to the dressing rooms, some to the stalls; they fetch their horses…" He mercifully left ten of the knights to the imagination. "Meanwhile—Mr. George Exmouth arrives."

"I arrived at twenty to six," said George with tremulous defiance.

"He comes into the Assembly room," said Mr. Port ignoring him, throwing himself into the part of George coming into the Assembly room. "He takes his armour. He changes, here or in one of the dressing rooms or in his horse's stall..." He beckoned them all out into the corridor, and for a bad moment Charlesworth thought they were to be treated to a pantomime of George changing in dressing room or stall; Mr. Port, however, was content to walk along stiffly from this point, as though clad from head to toe in the phoney armour. "He secretes himself in one of the rooms. He calls, 'Miss Kirk—please come and help me out of my armour...'" To their acute discomfort, he called it, imitating George imitating Brian Two-Times' voice. "He ties Miss Kirk up..." He wrestled with an imaginary Perpetua, frightened and struggling. "He joins the other knights in the Assembly room, mounted on his horse."

Cockrill thought that they had lived through a good deal to learn what could have been said in half a dozen words. He stood patiently, however, while Mr. Port, having seen George safely on to his horse, and in the line of waiting knights, was metamorphosed without warning into Isabel Drew. "She comes out of her dressing room. She hurries through the crowded knights..." He wove his way in and out of thin air, like a fat little sailing ship, tacking before the wind. "She goes into the tower. She disappears from us." But she reappeared in the shape of Mr. Port hurrying back to become Miss Betchley, still waiting at the door. "*You* think I'm going to suggest that Miss Betchley waited until the knights had gone through, and then followed her and strangled her, while they were on the stage...!" He challenged them all triumphantly.

"No, I don't," said Charlesworth. "Mr. Bryan says that he let Miss Betchley into the Assembly room, after Isabel Drew fell, and that the door was bolted on this side. Whoever bolted it, it would be before the knights rode through to the stage—there was no one to do it after that."

Mr. Port looked slightly crestfallen. He said, however: "Exactly. I didn't forget that. So what I suggest is this: the knights are all in the Assembly room—they're packed tight, nobody notices that she moves through them to the tower..."

"Don't they?" said Charlesworth. "I thought she always stood at the door. Surely they'd have observed her, suddenly pushing her way through them... Surely someone would have mentioned it? After all, people don't become blind, deaf, and dumb because they're one of a crowd. She must have passed close to *some* of them."

"You suggested yourself that any of the knights could have moved about freely..."

"Because they were knights. Because they were in armour. Because the knights were accustomed to seeing people in armour moving about..."

Miss Betchley gave a snort of contemptuous laughter.

"You'll have Mr. Port suggesting that I dressed myself up in a suit of armour for this jaunt of mine! There was a spare one."

"It would have been a bright idea, wouldn't it?" said Charlesworth equably. "Then *no*body would have noticed you: in fact nobody would have recognized you, you might have been a man or a woman... After all, short of a diving suit, one can't imagine a better disguise: and if you happened to be caught sight of at the window or anything… Yes, it would have been a good idea. However—what now?"

"Now we have me creeping up the ladder to strangle Miss Drew," said Miss Betchley sarcastically.

"*I'll* be Miss Betchley strangling Miss Drew, Mr. Port," suggested Charlesworth, gaily. He moved over and stood in the little doorway of the tower. "Is that what you think happened?"

"Yes, I do," said Mr. Port firmly: but he was beginning to sweat a little, he was not so sure. "I think she strangled the girl and left her propped up against the window in the semi-darkness, before the lights moved up; and I think that she went back and out of the Assembly room door, and Mr. Exmouth bolted it behind her, so that we should all think what we *have* all thought: and then the knights rode through." He shepherded his flock on to the stage, where they stood like a party of sightseers, staring obediently up at the window of the tower. Charlesworth appeared there, and leaned towards them over the balcony. "And Mr. Exmouth had the noose arranged and he pulled the body down? Eh, Mr. Port?"

"I was the knight on her *right*," protested George, uneasily. "The poem said the knight upon the left."

Inspector Cockrill glanced at Charlesworth with a gleam in his eye. "As I said at the time—an *e* or a *y* makes such a difference."

Mr. Port's eye shifted to him. He declaimed the last couplet of the poem: "'And so the donor of this little gift, Is who?— the Mystery Knight upon the left.'"

Cockie stood facing the tower. "The left might mean either side of the archway—according, as I said earlier, to the point of view. *Thy* left would have meant Isabel's left; then we should have been certain that the Red Knight was the Mystery Knight and not..."

But Charlesworth was staring at Mr. Port's little round face. He said: "How do you know the words of the poem?"

There was a moment of absolute silence. You could see Mr. Port's heart go cold within him. He stammered at last: "We all knew a poem had been found..."

"The wording of it has not been made public. Well, never mind," said Charlesworth, waving it to one side, "carry on with the reconstruction. We'll come to that later."

But the reconstruction had fallen flat. "I merely suggested that the girl might be already dead," said Mr. Port, sullenly. "And young Exmouth had the ropes arranged and pulled her down."

"Why?" said Cockrill.

"To create just the sort of mystery that was created: to prove that Miss Betchley couldn't have done it, when in fact she could."

"Except," said Miss Betchley, coldly, "that I happened to be on the other side of the door all this time: the door being bolted on the inside."

It shook Mr. Port for a minute: but he waved a pudgy hand at Brian Bryan. "So *he* says!"

Brian's eyes shone with the light of battle. "Ha! Am I now also having collusions? With Miss Betchley and with—him?" He looked George over from head to foot, as though Mr. Port had dragged in and laid at his feet a small, furry rabbit, infinitely harmless, really rather sweet. Charlesworth said hurriedly: "There is not the slightest suggestion that either

Miss Betchley or Mr. Bryan had ever set eyes on Mr. Exmouth before the rehearsals for the pageant started: and moreover, whatever their individual reasons may be for wishing Isabel Drew dead, he and they have absolutely nothing in common. I think we must keep this thing within the bounds of common sense. If Miss Betchley and Mr. Exmouth are in collusion, Mr. Port, then Mr. Bryan's testimony is reliable. And he says that the door was bolted."

The rain of the previous evening had been a last effort before the sun took over and a heat wave set in. It was very hot in the hall. All about them, the noise of the exhibition drummed, the chatter of a thousand voices merged into a continuous high-pitched drone, the fatuous sentiment of the songs of the day blared out from loudspeakers in a tinny torrent of treacle. Beneath their feet the stale air beat up from the dirty boards of the stage. Perpetua stood at Brian's shoulder in her narrow flowered summer frock. Life was very strange. A week ago—three days ago—it had been but a dusty dream: a dream that she had endured because she had not the courage nor the interest left to put an end to it, a dream in which she had lived in the company of Johnny, dead, and Earl Anderson rather earthily alive. But now Earl was gone: and—strange, half-terrible, half-happy realization—Johnny was going too. The memory of Johnny and of the sin against Johnny was fading into a gentle regret: remorse always, regret always—but no longer the death in life that remorse and regret had been. She thought: "I am beginning to find peace again." Peace. Not happiness—not yet. But in the last terrible days there had been a gleam, through the stark terror of the scene in the dressing room, through the shock of Isabel's death and the fantastic horror of Earl's dead face staring up at her from the depths of a cardboard box—through the personal fear that had dogged her ever since the first of the threatening notes had come—still something forced its way which could not be mistaken: the glimmerings of happiness once more. She knew that she was in deadly danger. She knew without telling, that the telegram which Brian had pretended not to accept in her room that morning, had been a new threat to her. But, nevertheless—there it was. Somewhere in the nightmare of mystery and fear was the first faint gleam of the dawn of happiness. She stood at Brian's side and from him seemed to flow security and strength. She did not love him, she loved nobody, she would never love again... And yet...

Brian Two-Times was unconscious of her presence beside him. He fought Miss Betchley's battle, blue eyes blazing. "Here is nonsense! First, Miss Betchley kills Isabel and afterwards Mr. Exmouth pulls her down: but Isabel died at the time she fell or was thrown—not ten minutes before! No need, therefore, for collusions. Very well, then, Miss Betchley killed her and *threw* her down. But she could not have got out of the Assembly room, bolting the door behind her. So! Idyotic!" He stood with the black felt hat pushed on to the back of his head, the inevitable mackintosh hanging loosely about him, his hands thrown out, his shoulders almost up to his ears in a shrug of despair at the folly of Mr. Port. Susan Betchley fixed on him a gaze of passionate gratitude. Inspector Cockrill twiddled his thumbs.

Mr. Port fired his final shot. "It all depends upon that door being bolted. Nothing to prevent Miss Betchley and *Mr. Bryan* from being in collusion."

Brian took off his black hat with one hand and with the

other solemnly tore his bright hair. "We keep asking ourselves why the body was thrown down," said Mr. Port, disregarding this exhibition, as the idea grew and took fire in his brain. "Supposing it was thrown down for this very reason: to give Mr. Bryan the chance to urge his horse through to the Assembly room and to give Miss Betchley an alibi about that bolt." The colour had come back into his face, he was alight with excitement and relief at his own escape. And yet... He knew what it was to be terribly near to—discovery... He said, apologetically: "I'm sorry, but there it is."

Brian Two-Times replaced his hat and gave it a sharp slap down upon his head. He said sharply: "You do not flatter me, Mr. Port. We plan this murder: and I confine myself to a few raw lies, and allow my partner to do the killing. And that partner—a woman!" He made Miss Betchley a comic little, foreign little bow.

George Exmouth said thoughtfully, almost to himself: "A woman!"

Inspector Charlesworth turned away from them and walked a few steps, deep in thought, and returned. He shook off Brian Bryan's protestations. "No, no, of course I don't believe such nonsense. I know you wouldn't let any woman do a job like that. But—you were rather dazed by your fall, Mr. Bryan, *weren't* you? Can you be absolutely certain that that door was bolted?"

"Certainly I can be certain," said Brian, immediately.

"Because if it wasn't..." He was suddenly galvanized into action. "Let's try it." He ran off through the arch and reappeared at the window in the tower, leaning perilously over the fragile balcony to call down to them. "The knights have all ridden through on to the stage. Miss Betchley has waited till the Assembly room was empty, and then come through and into the tower. I'll be Miss Betchley. What I propose to do is to wait till Isabel's big moment, and then creep up on her from behind, and throttle her—I've got rather strong hands. Then I'm going to scoot back to my post outside the door and when the fuss subsides a bit, I shall come out on to the stage and be ever so surprised at what has happened to poor dear Isabel…"

Inspector Cockrill stood with his hat on the back of his head as he stared up at the tower, his hands loosely clasped behind the swinging tails of his shabby old mackintosh. He listened only vaguely to what Charlesworth was saying. For now the first piece of the puzzle had suddenly settled itself into its place on the board. Something that had been said— something that had been said in the past half hour, had placed the piece there: and oddly enough the first piece was the most important piece of all—was a figure in armour—the figure of a murderer! Usually, one filled in the background, settled the other figures into their proper places: came at last, by elimination to the final piece. But in this case, the last piece came first: because the clue given could point to only one person. There were a hundred pieces still to be fitted in, and until they all found their places nothing could be done, nothing should be said: the ropes, the bolt, the brooch and the note, the brown eyes of the Red Knight, the head of Earl Anderson wrapped up in a pair of bathroom curtains in a box: the voice that had said to Perpetua, "I com back!", the voice that had promised Earl Anderson a meeting with "Micky Balcon" at the Golden Golliwog… In his mind, Inspector Cockrill picked up a piece of the puzzle, and turned it over in his fingers, and after a little while replaced it where he had taken it from. Mr. Port had brown eyes, and Mr. Port would have had access to the Red Knight's armour, and Mr. Port might have been closer to Johnny Wise than he now revealed... But at the time that the voice in the telephone box was speaking to Earl Anderson, Mr. Port had been at home in his hotel: for Isabel Drew had put through a call to him there... Perpetua said that Isabel had told her she would ring up Sugar-Daddy and get some comfort from *him*—and now the hotel confirmed putting through a call...

Charlesworth broke in upon his reflections, gaily declaiming from the balcony above their heads. "Now—I'm Miss Betchley. I wait till the lights are concentrated on the knights down below, and then I take two hands to Isabel's throat. And I pitch her dead body over the balcony, so that the knights will stand frozen with horror and astonishment long enough for me to make my getaway out through the Assembly room..."

Cockie decided it was time to stop all this nonsense. He called up crossly: "It couldn't have been done."

"Why not?" said Charlesworth, slightly taken aback.

"The knights *didn't* stand still frozen with horror and astonishment. The body fell almost on top of the white horse, which reared and bucked and then bolted through into the Assembly room. There wouldn't have been time for Miss Betchley to have got across and out of the door. The White Knight would have seen her."

Charlesworth was slightly dashed. He said, hopefully, however: "Of course he was rather dazed."

But Brian Two-Times was not timing his stupors for the benefit of Mr. Charlesworth. "He was dazed by the fall from the horse," said Cockie firmly. "He was well into the Assembly room before he fell—I was watching the whole thing, remember, and he didn't actually tumble off until he was right through the arch. In that bare room he must have seen anybody trying to make their way across."

"Oh," said Charlesworth. He stood with one foot on the rail of the balcony, leaning forward to look down at them, his elbow across his knee. They stared back up at him, with craning necks. Now and again Motherdear glanced uneasily at Miss Betchley, and then gazed up at the balcony again. Perpetua stood close to Brian: he seemed to have forgotten her, but there was something about his very presence that gave her comfort; it was like standing in the glow of a fire. The back of Mr. Port's neck was creased into a little fat roll; he avoided looking at Miss Betchley's set mouth and resentful eyes. They were all silent.

Charlesworth straightened himself at last. "Well—let's try it anyway. Let's just prove that it couldn't have been done. Let's see, at any rate, how far she could have got... How long would you say, Inspector, was Mr. Bryan's horse bucking about?"

Cockrill considered. He said, his eyes consulting Brian's, "Half a minute?"

"Half a minute. Right. Well, now, I'm Miss Betchley. Inspector, perhaps you'd be Mr. Bryan, would you? And cut out Mr. Port with a nice equine impersonation, bucking about for half a minute and then galloping through into the Assembly room. O.K.? Good. Right, now—one, two, three..." He disappeared from view.

Inspector Cockrill did no bucking about, but he stood stoutly in the archway for thirty seconds by his watch and then let the rabble through. Charlesworth was legging it half-way

across the Assembly room. He threw up the sponge immediately. "It's getting down the ladder that takes the time. I
don't think you *were* more than half a minute bucking about,
Horse, were you?"

"On the night, you mean?" said Cockie. "No. Half a minute. And even that's generous."

Around them the twelve suits of armour grinned down,
their visors gaping above the long necks that were not really
there. "It couldn't have been done," said Cockrill, with an air of
finality. "She couldn't have got down those steps and across this
room in the time, and closed the door behind her. He would
have seen her." He put his hands behind his back and stumped
off through the archway on to the stage again. Waste of time!

Charlesworth followed him, irresolutely. "Let's just try it
once again. It's so frightfully important. Because if it could
have been done..." He left the air filled with unspoken menace, and went back through the arch. After a little while, his
voice called from the window: "O.K. Half a minute from
now." As Cockie stood grumpily counting they heard his feet
clattering down the ladder within the tower. Twenty seconds.
Twenty-five seconds. Half a minute... They pushed aside the
bead curtain, and looked through into the Assembly room.

There was nobody there.

Cockrill went to the tower doorway: there was nobody in the
tower. George Exmouth said in a half whisper: "He's done it! It
could have been done." He confronted Susan Betchley, his white
young face staring with frightened eyes into hers. "He's proved
that it could have been done. You could have killed her and flung
her down, and got across the room: and just pretended to rattle
at the door so that Mr. Bryan thought that it was bolted..."

George Exmouth with his young, white, peering face: Edgar Port, little and round, dapper hands beaded with nervous sweat: Perpetua, cool and gentle, with anxious grey eyes: Brian—Brian standing beside Perpetua with his hand on her arm, comforting and strong—as if it were she, Perpetua, who needed strength… Susan Betchley closed her aching eyes against the pain and fear and bewilderment of it all. She said: "Supposing that I could have done it—for God's sake why should you *think* that I would do such a thing. I—I didn't care two hoots about Isabel Drew. I thought she was bad, I thought she was cruel and selfish and immoral, but all that was nothing whatever to do with me. I hardly knew the woman. I met her because Johnny Wise had written to me about her: when I got here, I found that it was true that she had—well, caused his death. I think she did. And I think she deserved to die for that. But it wasn't for me to kill her. Johnny was nothing to me: nothing but a nice, good, charming—casual friend. And one doesn't commit murder for one's casual friends."

Mr. Port said: "He may have been a greater friend than you say. He may have been your lover, for all we know… He was just your age, after all." He repeated it more slowly, staring… "He was just—your—age…"

"And Johnny Wise had a twin," said George. His frightened eyes looked into the steady brown eyes, looked at the strong square jaw and strong hands, at the swarthy skin. His voice went high. He said: "I knew it! She's a man!" And he put out his hand and caught at the fastening of her blouse.

A suit of armour detached itself from the wall against which it dangled; and came forward in two strides and knocked away his hand.

Chapter X

ANOTHER PIECE OF THE PUZZLE CLICKED INTO ITS place, dovetailing neatly with the figure in armour already in the centre there. Charlesworth through the raised visor cast at Inspector Cockrill one glance of exquisite, unalloyed triumph. He held George Exmouth by the wrist, and after a moment, flung back the hand with a vicious force that almost knocked the owner backwards. He said. "These dramatic disguises—they don't work in real life. A man who has been a normal man for years can't suddenly look and talk and walk and behave like a woman." He put the backs of his knuckles for a moment against Miss Betchley's brown cheek. "This skin has never been shaved."

Motherdear stood scarlet with mortification. He mumbled wretchedly: "I'm sorry."

Perpetua supposed that it would be "womanly" to go and stand beside Miss Betchley, to rally to her own sex in some way; but it seemed rather dramatic and self-conscious. She looked uncertainly at Brian for guidance. Brian had no inhibitions about drama. He left her side and strode forward and you could see immediately that idyotic was simply not the word for it. "So! She is not a man. Everybody can know that—except this foolish boy. And also I may tell you—she is not a murderer. The door was bolted. Even if she could have got across the room she could not have bolted that door behind her. When I went to the door, I woss not dazed. The door was bolted. So!" He challenged Charlesworth with his bright blue eyes.

"She is not a man," said Charlesworth. "But that doesn't mean that she is not a murderer." He unfastened the latches of his helmet and wriggled his head free; it was made in one piece and hinged down the back, so that, closed, it formed a sort of metal pot. "You say that the door was not bolted: but after all, though I don't believe in your collusion with Miss Betchley, there's such a thing as accessory after the fact. You'd have protected anyone who killed Isabel Drew by way of revenge for the death of Johnny Wise. Wouldn't you?"

"Certainly, I would," said Brian coolly. "But if this is so—why then the nonsense with the armour? My horse comes bolting through the arch, I see Miss Betchley running across the room, making for the door. I say: 'What you are doing here?' She says: 'I have just killed this Jessabel who killed poor Johnny.' I say: 'You have my help. Go now through the door and I lock it on this side.'" He smiled at her. "*I* would not give her away."

"She wasn't to know that," said Charlesworth. "She couldn't foresee that your horse would bolt and you'd come through." He thought out carefully why Miss Betchley should have put on the armour. "That bead curtain—it dangled and swung in the draught through the arch. Just possible that the audience might have seen her as she passed across the room from the door to the doorway of the tower. And then, Isabel herself—better, just in case anything went wrong, just in case she didn't die outright, that she shouldn't recognize her assailant. And the murder itself: suppose Isabel were to struggle, suppose for a moment they were to appear at the window of the tower and be seen—suppose that anything unforeseen turned up—then the armour, an impenetrable disguise, would have been a Good Thing."

Click, click, went little bits of the puzzle, fitting themselves neatly together. Only bits of the outside background though. Cockie pushed them to one side of the frame. Charlesworth went on. "And something unforeseen did happen. The White Knight came hurtling through the arch when she was less than half-way across the room. She stood still, petrified with the shock: and he looked at her blankly, interested only in keeping his seat on his horse. A piece of armour, against the wall—there was nothing much out of the way about that."

"Except that when I came back through the room after letting Miss Betchley in," said Brian, "this armour was against the wall, true, but the helmet was on the peg eighteen inches above it. Was I not perhaps surprised that suddenly the neck had become so long?"

"You needn't have noticed it. And after all, I did the same thing just now, and none of you realized that one of the suits of armour was actually wearing its helmet."

"Just now you were one of twelve suits of armour," said Cockie. "Then there was only one suit, in an otherwise empty room."

"Well, say he was busy with his horse: he just didn't notice it, that's all. And he had no time to be observant: the weight of the armour and the unexpectedness of the whole thing was too much for him and he toppled off and gave his head a frightful bonk and lay, flat out for a minute, on the floor. She saw what had happened: she scrambled out of the armour, left it propped against the wall and hooked up the helmet over it, and dashed across to the door. Once on the other side, she began to hammer and yell as though she couldn't get in. He staggered up and went and opened it, fumbling at the bolt in his half-dazed condition: probably she held the door from the other side and he had a job to pull it open. He was still very muzzy. Maybe he genuinely thinks the bolt was shot. Maybe he doesn't. But either way—it was not. Miss Betchley had been in the Assembly room since the knights had ridden through and had murdered Isabel and thrown her down, and come back and let herself through that door." He looked like a tortoise, very earnest and concentrating fiercely, his head sticking out over the circular metal rim of the armour's neck.

"But then," said Perpetua in her sweet, vague, just faintly stupid way, "who was it that I heard whistling?"

He turned on her sharply. "Whistling?"

"But I *told* you, Mr. Charlesworth: 'Sur le pont d'Avignon.' All the time I was lying bundled up in the cloak in that horrible little room."

Charlesworth relaxed the tenseness of his position at Miss Betchley's side. "Ye Gods, Miss Kirk—has it just entered your head to point this out?"

She eyed him limpidly. "Well, no. I've been thinking of it all along. I was waiting for you to work it all out and show that Miss Betchley *could* have done it, and then show how she couldn't after all because all the time Isabel was being killed, she was sitting there whistling." She added gently: "As I told you."

Inspector Cockrill was far too busy to repay Mr. Charlesworth's earlier glance of triumph. Click, click, click went the pieces of the puzzle, sorting themselves out, arranging themselves into little groups to be fitted later into their proper places. Miss Betchley had an alibi, then, for the time of Isabel's murder. So had Perpetua who had been locked up in the little room. So had Brian Bryan, to which alibi several thousand people could testify. And Mr. Port had an alibi for the time when Earl Anderson's murderer had been in a telephone booth in Piccadilly, luring him out to his assignation with death. And Motherdear...

Charlesworth was passing the whole thing off, ever so careless and all-for-the-fun-of-finding-out. He offered cigarettes all round, and fumbled in his pocket for his lighter. There was a twist of paper there. He could not think where he had got it from.

He had got it from George Exmouth's home and on it was written: Here, in unconsecrated ground, lies George Exmouth who for the honour of the woman he loved...

Perpetua could not get to sleep that night. Brian Two-Times had seen her to her door and there had kissed her hand and said good-night and gone off down the road, with his odd, rather bouncing stride, the black felt hat on the back of his golden head and the mackintosh flapping half-way down his calves. There was something just faintly comic about him, once the compelling charm of his nearness was removed: something just bordering upon the pathetic, because he was so cool and gay and certain of himself, so serenely unaware of the utter unsuitability of an Anthony Eden hat and a long flapping mac. on a midsummer day in town. Perpetua, lying awake in the hot night, wondered to herself whether this really was something to be welcomed—this metamorphosis of her strength and stay into a sort of grown-up little boy, that nobody but his mother could love because he was boastful and self-confident and a bit of a show-off, and had big, knobbly knees. She smiled to herself tenderly in the half dark of her room. Brian Two-Times might have knobbly knees, but he had nice hands: hands that made your heart turn over with a little bonk, when they took your own. All foreigners kissed people's hands of course: but nevertheless it was nice to have your hand kissed by Brian Two-Times, standing in your doorway, looking up at you as he bowed over your finger-tips with friendly, smiling, shining heavenly blue, blue eyes...

She could not sleep. She got up at last and put on a pair of slacks and a jersey. The room seemed incredibly small and stuffy: she must get air. Quietly, so as not to wake the sleeping house, she let herself out of the big front door. The clock of a Bayswater church struck one—two—three.

The streets seemed very strange. Perpetua's nights out for the past seven years had ended at closing-time. Earl had been a great one for sitting about in pubs chattering away impersonally to a vast circle of acquaintances whose names he did not know, whose concerns were of no interest to him, whom he never saw or thought of outside "the local." At half past ten or eleven, they had wandered back to his flat or to Perpetua's room, and there made tea or coffee. When Earl was in town, it was more or less a routine. But now the streets were not like the streets she knew. They were so silent: and so empty. On the doorsteps, little groups of milk bottles huddled with their dirty white collars, waiting for the roundsman to collect them next morning and take them off to be washed and spruced up and sent out on duty again… In the areas, the dustbins spilled forth unsightly contents, relentless reminders of man's mortality: now and again the still air gave a tiny sigh, and a whiff of decay was borne away upon the breeze. The plane trees rustled, whispering a message from the dustbins: "All is rottenness: all is death…", the high street lamps cast shadows in angled walls that seemed as black and bottomless as eternity. A couple reeling home late from a party were swallowed up by a dark doorway: already the glow and the rapture were fading—tomorrow there would be sick headaches and queasy tummies… Beauty vanishes—beauty passes… Only the cats were heedless and unafraid, darting across the patchwork shadows of the streets on plush-cushioned, soundless paws. What threat had death and decay and nothingness?—to a sleek, suave gentleman with nine lives before him and every one packed with adventure that had nothing to do with death—on the contrary!

Perpetua wished that she had not come out. The air was refreshing but a new sense of danger pressed on her as stiflingly as though she had been back in her little room. If I were a cat, and each of the threats a life, she thought, I should have only six lives left. And then there had been the attack in the dressing room, and the—the head… I must have died a death each of those times. So that's only four more. And if a threat is a death—four lives isn't very much between me and eternity. Between the *threat* of murder and—murder. She swung round suddenly and began to retrace her steps as fast as she could go:

and then the very fact that she was hurrying seemed in itself a frightening thing, and she slowed down her footsteps. Clop, clop, clop went her heels on the pavements in the quiet night.

Somebody was following her.

All of a sudden she knew it: knew that the sense of danger had not been born only of the night and the breeze and the shadows—knew that an inner ear had heard first what her ears now too clearly, too terrifyingly clearly, heard. The pad, pad, pad of feet on the pavement: following her.

If she stopped for a moment—would the following feet stop too? But she did not dare to stop. Her footsteps quickened, she broke into a little, shambling, terrified trot, jerking her head over her shoulder now and again, to stare back into the secret shadows through which the footsteps padded relentlessly. On a thin, high note a voice cried suddenly: "Perpetua!"

"Perpetua, stop! I am the murderer!"

She began to pray, running along, stumbling along, her feet like lead dragging themselves at what seemed a snail's pace over the mile-long pavements. "Oh, God! Not this—not all alone out here in the dark, don't let me be killed, don't let me be strangled all alone out here in the dark... Don't let me see his face staring at me, waiting to watch me die... Don't let me see his hands, coming at my throat..." To have lived so long, to have thought and dreamed and planned and suffered so much, and now to come so swiftly and suddenly to this—to be cut off in a brief moment of horror, alone out here in the dark... She thought of Isabel, turning to see the murderer standing there balefully in the shadows of the tower: of Earl, frozen in a moment of cold terror by the change in a pair of friendly eyes... "Oh, God, save me! Save me! Don't let me die…" Behind all these doors people lay sleeping, kind people, friendly people, sane, safe, protecting people—all unaware that a few yards from them a girl ran past their doors, too terrified even to scream out for their aid. She came at last to her own little street and as she turned into it, it seemed to her that suddenly the following footsteps ceased. Sick with relief, sick with reaction, she moved on her faltering legs towards her door: and gasping and sobbing turned in at the little porch and fumbled in her pocket for the key.

Two hands came out of the darkness and grasped at her and pulled her down. The shadows closed in.

Chapter XI

In his modest hotel, Inspector Cockrill moved uneasily on his unfamiliar bed. London! Not content with waking you up at the hour to tell you the time, a hundred noisy clocks reminded you of it every quarter: and now it was half past three and he tossed and turned in the stifling heat and cudgelled his weary brain with his jigsaw puzzle... But would even the completed puzzle—with nobody getting any credit for it outside Scotland Yard—compensate his colleagues in Kent for his non-attendance at the conference? He moved his head from side to side on the hard pillow. In an attic room across the park, Brian Two-Times muttered a name in his sleep: and at their hotel near by, Miss Betchley sat, a substantial, pyjama'ed ghost and scribble-scribble-scribbled on a little pad, and Mr. Port lay like a pudgy corpse in his narrow bed, very still, staring up at the invisible ceiling, sick to the heart with fear of all that had been discovered, of all that must surely soon be discovered, all that would happen when the truth was known... Isabel was dead; and Earl was dead; and Brian Bryan slept, and Edgar Port watched and Susan Betchley scribble-scribble-scribbled through the night: and George Exmouth stood shivering in the shadows of a Bayswater door with a fainting girl clasped in his reedy arms.

He found the key of her door in her pocket and opened it silently, and, half dragging, half carrying her, took her to her room. He had been there once or twice, and every detail of the house was printed like a photograph on his brain. A second key opened her door. He lugged her in and heaved her on to her bed. When she came to, she found him sitting over her, and her hands and temples cold and wet with the water he had splashed there to bring her back to life. He was dreadfully white: his thin hands trembled sickeningly. He said, in a whisper: "It was I who killed Earl Anderson and Isabel. I couldn't sleep. So I came to find you."

She looked about her wildly for help, for some sort of weapon with which to defend herself. It was only George Exmouth after all: hardly more than a child, poor, thin, shivering, white-faced boy, and yet—one had heard that lunatics were cunning and strong... And if Earl had not been able to defend himself—nor Isabel... She pulled her drifting wits together and decided upon conciliation. She put out her hand to him, nervously. "But—you wouldn't hurt *me*, George?"

He took her hand; and tumbled forward, half across the bed and burst into a torrent of tears.

She sat quietly, letting him hold her hand. "Don't cry, George! Don't be so unhappy, George. Tell me everything and we'll see what can be done about it..." Broadmoor, she supposed, was what would be done about it: poor mad, terrified, terrifying boy...

He raised his head at last. His face was all slobbered with tears and she took the damp cloth with which he had brought her back to her senses, and gently wiped it clean as though he were a child. "There now—tell me."

"I was going to the police," he said, trembling. "I couldn't bear it any longer, and I was going to the police to confess. I thought I would come past your house, Perpetua, and—and say good-bye to it. I've been here often in the night. I've seen the light in your window and I've walked about staring up at it: and when the light's been out, too, Peppi, I've walked and walked and at least felt that I was near you." He put his poor, tired, hot head in his hands and said miserably: "I love you so *much*."

"Oh, George!" she protested.

"You must have known, Perpetua? You couldn't not have known? Why, every thought I ever have is for you or about you. When I go to bed I resent going to sleep because I shan't be able to think of you… Sometimes I dream, but the dreams are always terrible. I suppose I've—sort of reversed things: during the day I've been living in exquisite dreams; in my sleep I've known the miserable truth. You don't love me, Peppi, do you, and you never could? I'm just a gangling schoolboy to you, I'm just a mother's darling without any experience or any poise or any grown-up sense… You can't believe in your heart, that I've got a real mind that works and thinks and puts two-and-two together and—suffers: you can't believe that although my heart's only a boy's heart it's as capable of agony as any man's. Calf love's just a joke, isn't it? And this is only calf love—*I* know that. To you I'm just a great, lumping, lumbering hobbledehoy with big hands and feet and clumsy manners, incapable of understanding or feeling or heartbreak, incapable of anything delicate or sensitive... Just that poor kid George, tied to his mother's apron strings, a lout of an adolescent schoolboy, with a bit of a pash on Perpetua..." He broke off at last and was quiet, sitting on the edge of the bed with his face turned away from her, and his hands hanging dejectedly between his bony knees.

Perpetua was appalled at the bitterness and pain in his voice. She said: "Nobody ever seems to know anything about other people's suffering. But perhaps you and I can understand each other a little bit because we've both of us had such a bad time. I've touched rock bottom, George, you know. They say that remorse is the worst hell of all: and my suffering has been remorse. It's true that I haven't taken any notice of you, it's true that if you've loved me all this time I haven't bothered about it, I haven't even troubled to realize it... But I've never bothered about anything, or realized anything: I've been too much wrapped up in my own suffering to care. So you see that it wasn't because you're young; and goodness knows it wasn't because you were a hobbledehoy as you call yourself: it was because there was something wrong with me—not because there was anything wrong with *you*."

He raised his head: something of the stark misery left his red-rimmed eyes. "I see," he said.

She was alone in here, shut up in this little room with a murderer: and if he was a murderer it could only be that he was mad. I must calm him down as much as I can, she thought, and then get him to follow up his idea of confessing to the police... She went on talking to him, quietly and kindly, holding his thin hand in her own. "But now things are different for me, George, and if you're patient and battle through this, perhaps they'll be better for you too, soon. You'll forget me—because after all, I *am* a lot older than you—and you'll meet someone too that you can love, instead of me."

He withdrew his hand sharply. "Do you mean that you're in love with someone?"

"No, no," she said quickly. "It isn't that. I only mean…" But he cut her short. "You are! You *are*! You're in love with that fellow Bryan. I *hate* him, I hate him, but you, you're in love with him…! It wasn't because of Johnny Wise that you didn't care about me: it was because of *him*." He grasped at the light counterpane of the bed and tore at it ruthlessly with crooked fingers. "You love him, and I'm nobody—I'm nobody to you, because you're in love with that horrible fellow… I *hate* him. He stood there today, sneering at me, contemptuous of me because I made a mistake and said that that woman was a man… Well, she *might* have been a man. She looks like a man, her voice is deep like a man's—it was a perfectly sensible idea. And I—it's true that I clutched at her dress but I didn't tear it, I didn't do anything, there was nothing to sneer and mock at me about."

"Brian didn't mock at you," she said patiently.

"He did, he stood there sneering and making me look a fool… Well, all right, I may be a fool, I may be just a gauche boy, but I've done something that he would never do! I've killed a man: yes, and a woman too. He was going to marry you, Perpetua, that vile creature Anderson, and he had a wife already… And Isabel was agreeing to it, only then she'd have blackmailed both of you for the rest of your days…"

"Oh, George," she said, horrified: "you killed them—you murdered them—because of that?"

"I did it to save you, Perpetua. And I don't mind, I'm proud of it. I'm not frightened, I wasn't frightened when I did it and I'm not frightened now—I'm proud of it. I'm going to confess to the police…"

She put out her hand for the telephone but she was afraid to bring about a change of resolution. "The police will— they'll think you were extraordinarily—sort of daring and clever, George. To fool us all like that…"

"Perhaps it might be a good thing to go on fooling them," he suggested, flattered and pleased.

"Well, tell *me* about it, George: and then you can go on fooling *them*."

He looked at her suspiciously. "You think I'm mad, Perpetua. You're trying to sort of baby me along to tell the police."

"It was you who said you were going to tell the police."

"That's what I came out for," he agreed.

"Well, do what you like about it, George," she said, striving to appear indifferent. "You say that you did this for me—*I'm* not likely to split on you, am I? Just have it your own way."

"Yes," he said slowly. He got up off the bed. "I'll think about it. I'll think what to do."

Was it safe to let him go off out of the room: mad and dangerous as he was? But the moment the door was closed on him, she could telephone the police: they would pick him up before he was off the doorstep. "Perhaps either way you'd better go along now. It's four o'clock in the morn- ing, and you don't want to involve me in a scandal, do you?—after you've—after you've done so much to protect my honour."

"No," he said seriously. She stood before him, straightening his rumpled coat, brushing back his tangled hair as though he were a child. "Well—go along now, then, George, dear: and—and make up your mind what you're going to do."

"Yes," he said again: like a child. And went off quite docile and gentle, into the night.

She locked her door behind him and three seconds later was gabbling frantically into the telephone.

Charlesworth rang up Inspector Cockrill next morning. "I thought I'd get you before you started out. The Exmouth boy has confessed to both murders."

"Good," said Cockie. "Then I can get on with my conference." He slammed down the receiver, slammed his hat anyhow on to his head, slammed the door behind him and stumped off down the street. "Grand slam!" he thought to himself, having thus relieved his feelings. It was not often that he made a joke, and he chuckled over it with the greatest satisfaction as he marched through St. James's Park.

Susan Betchley was waiting for him there, loitering about the path, guessing that he would come that way to Scotland Yard. She was a pasty white under her sunburnt brown, her bright eyes were heavy with worry and sleeplessness, her hands were clasped nervously over her handbag. She came forward with a sort of darting movement. "Inspector Cockrill—I was waiting for you, I've been hanging about here, I didn't know whether you'd come this way but I know you're staying at the Shirland, Miss Kirk told me so, so I thought you might walk across to Scotland Yard…"

"Stop dithering," said Cockie. "And tell me what you want."

She clasped and unclasped the fastening of her bag. "I—I want to confess."

His eye gleamed. He said quickly: "What do you want to confess to?"

It was desperately hot. The satiny blades of the grass caught the rays of the sun and shone back like diamonds: here and there in the park a couple of deck-chairs could stand it no longer and leaned limply together for support, the children walked listlessly beside their nurses dragging reluctant dogs that wanted only to lie in the shade under the trees with their thin, pink, quivering tongues hanging out for coolness. They faced each other, a little alert sparrow of a man, and a young woman with steady eyes and shaking hands. She said at last: "I want to confess to murder."

"Good," said Cockie briskly. "You're in just the right place for it." He took her brown arm above the elbow and swivelled her round to face Scotland Yard. "Over there," he said.

"I want to confess to *you.*"

"This is nothing to do with me: it's not my case. Go over there, ask for Detective Inspector Charlesworth and say what you have to say."

"I can't talk to *him,*" she said. "He's too young. It's like going to a doctor that you know personally. He's too young and—and attractive..."

"So you come to me," said Cockrill. He was much amused. She moved her head wearily. "I don't mean *that...*"

"Well, never mind what you mean," he said brusquely. "I'm not a doctor and I'm not a priest and I don't want any part of any confessions. Besides, I've got a conference to attend."

He waved his stick in the general direction of a green bench sitting with grim determination out in the sun. "Park yourself for ten minutes by your watch and think the whole thing out carefully: and then go down to the Yard and tell your story to the oldest and most repulsive sergeant on duty that you can find and he will take it down in shorthand and pass it to Inspector Charlesworth, who will doubtless throw it into the wastepaper basket and ask you to tell him all over again: but by then the ice will be broken." Women are wonderful, he thought, marching off again down the hot, dry paths. Even confessing to murder they can't keep sex out of it. Glancing back he saw her sitting herself down obediently, a solid round mushroom in her white dress on the green bench. Let her sit for a bit; he wanted to take this morning walk in peace and giggle to himself over the famous joke. On an impulse he turned into a telephone booth in Whitehall and dialled a number. "Francesca?"

"Cockie, *pet!*"

"I thought you would be interested to know that your evidence about the man in Piccadilly ringing up Earl Anderson has been very useful indeed. Very useful."

"Well, I hope it doesn't mean that anybody will get sort of hanged or anything, Cockie, does it? Because I wouldn't like to think that it was me that caused anybody to—to die."

In the past Francesca had caused three people to—to die: but not through her own fault, not by any carelessness or cruelty of hers. "No, no. On the contrary, you provide an alibi for the innocent. Er—I thought of something this morning, Francesca, this might amuse you… I was sort of slamming my way out of the house and I said to myself…"

"Oh, Cockie, half a second, pet, I can hear the baby crying." He could hear her calling, her head turned away from the mouthpiece: "Nanny! What's the matter with baby?" An answer echoed faintly and the receiver was put down with a crackle and he could hear her voice receding as she moved away. "But it's lovely, *lovely* Milk of Magnesia, pet… A lucky, lucky baby to have such lovely Milk of Magnesia…" He hung up crossly and slammed his way out of the booth. *Hon*estly! Women!!

And there was Edgar Port, white and shaking as a milk jelly, standing at the entrance to Scotland Yard. Cockie admitted defeat. "Don't tell me, don't tell me! You want to confess!"

"Yes," said Mr. Port.

"Well, all right, confess to Inspector Charlesworth."

"He's not here," said Mr. Port. "He's gone round to George Exmouth's."

"You don't say?" said Cockie. He looked round with exaggerated curiosity. "Any sign of Mr. Brian Twice wishing to confess?" And click, click, click went the pieces of the puzzle.

The figure in the centre was getting packed round with detail: it was enthralling to have got to this stage, to watch it all grow. He took Mr. Port by the arm. "Well, all right. Come along with me."

Inspector Charlesworth having been called to George Exmouth when at nine o'clock that young man finally made up his mind to go through with his resolution, was summoned by telephone back to Scotland Yard by the news of Miss Betchley's arrival. Not knowing of Mr. Port's presence there, he did not yet appreciate that confession had become an epidemic. He left Sergeant Bedd to cope with George, and himself departed to deal with the Betchley. Far removed from all this riot of self-revelation, Perpetua and Brian Two-Times sat under the trees in the park, and only because it was so hot, did not hold hands. The mackintosh lay neatly folded on the bench beside them, under the black felt hat; from the paraphernalia of an English gentleman, Mr. Bryan was inseparable.

Left alone with Motherdear, Sergeant Bedd perched himself on a whitewood chair which had every appearance of a severe attack of lumbago, and got out his notebook and pencil. "Now, Mr. Exmouth, sir—you was saying?"

"Have I got to just tell *you*," said George.

"If you'd be so good, sir. Of course you'll have to come along to the station later and make a proper statement: but if you'd tell me, then Mr. Charlesworth could be quite sure that it was…" Mr. Charlesworth wanted to be sure that George's journey would be really necessary: but this sad lack of impressment Sergeant Bedd did not reveal. "I'll just make a few notes, sir, to remind me. Doesn't bind you in any way." He made a few meaningless squiggles on the clean page, just by way of demonstration.

Motherdear passionately wanted to be bound by this confession. And he wanted to make it dramatically to a detective inspector, preferably two or three or a dozen detective inspectors, and at Scotland Yard: not to mumble out to a stolid police sergeant with kindly—and just faintly mocking?—eyes that—that he had killed Earl Anderson because Earl was wrecking a—a certain lady's life: the name of which lady should not pass his lips… And that he had killed Isabel Drew because she was aiding and abetting Earl, and between them they would ruin Perpetua—er—the Lady's life.

"Couldn't you just have told the young lady, sir?" suggested Sergeant Bedd, respectfully.

George was indignant. "How could I tell her? Tell her that the man she loved was a villain and a bigamist, was— was plotting this ghastly thing against her: as though *I* were trying to gain her affections by such a revelation. A man of honour can't do that kind of thing." He thumped his narrow chest and looked the sergeant in the eye. Terrific!

"So you killed Miss Drew, sir. How did you manage that?" The pencil hovered over the page.

"I'm not going to tell you," said George with simple dignity.

Sergeant Bedd tucked the pencil away in the breast pocket of his tunic and leaned back in his chair, though it seemed like cruelty to the poor twisted thing to do it. He held his hands loosely clasped in his lap, softly tapping together the cushions of his thumbs. He said: "You don't know, son: do you?"

"I do know," said George angrily. "But why should I tell you? Find out for yourselves."

"All right," said Bedd, comfortably. "That's what we shall have to do. What about Anderson?"

"I lured him out by a phone call on the Maidenhead road and killed him there: and then cut off his head and sent it to Peppi in a cardboard box."

"Why?" said Bedd.

"Well, I mean, it was like Salome. Herod wanted John the Baptist's head, so she got it for him. Perpetua—the lady, that is—wanted Anderson's."

"You've got your facts a little mixed," said Bedd, who

himself read a verse or two of the Bible every night, though nowadays he could hardly have told you why, except that Mrs. Bedd fancied it. He had not resumed his note-making. He said: "What did you wrap up the head in, in that box?"

George eyed him warily. "You know that: why should I tell you?"

You can't, said Sergeant Bedd again. He continued to lean back in the chair, tapping his thumbs together. "Now, look here! You could have killed Anderson. You have no alibi for the time of his death, you knew he'd go off with you readily enough on the smell of a job and your mother does theatrical decor, you may know everybody in The Profession for all I know, you could easily fool him that you had influence. And you could have gone back to the flat as somebody did and gone in with his keys and packed his stuff and taken it away. You could have: but you didn't. Because one of the things taken away was Earl Anderson's bathroom curtains: and that was what the head was wrapped up in, to keep it from—er—leaking. And you didn't know that, son, did you?"

George sat silent, his hands dangling between his knees.

"We get this kind of thing with murder, you know," said Bedd gently, watching the downcast face. "Some chaps—it's upsetting, having such ghastly things happen: it puts them off their balance just a bit. Take you for example. You're a young gentleman who has a hard time: your mother's a masterful lady, all respect to her, and your father's gone, and she doesn't like to let you go too free. So when a bad thing like this happens, it's tough on you. She's away in Scotland and can't get back to be with you because she has work there: and you take to brooding. There's a lady in the case," said Sergeant Bedd, waggishly, but his eyes were very kind, "and everybody's fussing over the lady, and the lady perhaps is fussing a bit over somebody else, and nobody seems to be fussing over you. The police suspect everybody but you. That's because they've got nothing against you; but *you* don't think about that, you just imagine it's because you're young and not important and they suppose you're not capable of the sort of courage and the sort of—of passion and suffering and rage and determination that must lead up to calculated murder. You'd like to show them that you *are* capable of acting like a man, and a very strong and daring man at that: and then the young lady, you'd like perhaps to be more important in *her* eyes, you'd like to have her pitying you and worrying about you and thinking what a chap you'd been, killing off people like that, and all for her sake. Even if it was to be proved nonsense in the end—she'd at least have noticed you, at least you'd be on her map for the rest of your days. All that's very natural, son: many people have made phoney confessions of murder before *you*, in many different ways—but almost always for the same sorts of reasons. Perhaps you'd never have got around to it, really: but then something happened that simply drove you to action. You made that mistake about Miss Betchley, yesterday. You accused her of something that sounded silly when it was proved to be untrue: and you put your hand out to tear away her blouse, and the Inspector hit it aside, as though you had been a silly kid. And Mr. Bryan, your rival in the affections of the young lady, standing there so companionable beside her, looked at you with contempt and called you a 'foolish boy.' It galled you: it sent you nearly mad, and you thought of it and resented it, and the hot night went to your head.

And so you cooked up this confession. Well—you could have murdered Anderson; but you couldn't have killed Miss Drew, my boy, and that's flat. She died at just about the same time as she fell: no question of her being killed any time before she was thrown over. You could have pulled her down, the ropes might just as well have been on your side of the arch as on the Red Knight's. But you didn't go near her. You sat there on your horse: you never knelt down and touched her, like the Red Knight did. The Red Knight could have killed her: we've proved that. But you couldn't. Your whole confession's untrue." He got up out of his chair and walked to the window and turned and faced the boy. "It's untrue!"

George got up also; and confronted him. He said: "*But I was the Red Knight.*"

Chapter XII

Down on the Embankment opposite the Yard, Edgar Port sat on a bench with Inspector Cockrill and watched the Thames go by. The sun threw a shiver of sequins across the grey water; on the bank opposite, barges lay moored up alongside each other like crocodiles basking in the heat on the mud, and a boy was asleep on the wall before them, one brown leg dangling in its grubby sandshoe. Exquisite to be a child, innocent and carefree, sleeping in the sun! Mr. Port said miserably: "So this is my confession, Inspector. I thought I would rather tell you than young Charlesworth."

"You were wasting your time," said Cockie, his short legs stretched out before him in their wrinkled stove-pipe grey flannels. "I don't think *he's* got all this worked out. But I have. I *know*."

"You know about Isabel?"

"We all know now that Isabel was threatening you—oh, in a delicate way, of course. She might get a fit of conscience, she might go writing and "confessing all" to your wife. You had to stop that at any price. You paid and paid—in presents, in treats, so that Isabel would not dream of killing the goose that laid the eggs: even for the sake of that searing conscience! But she tightened the screw, she picked a silly quarrel with you, it all looked more and more menacing… You were thankful when she rang you up the night before the pageant. But she rang off abruptly, evidently she wasn't in the mood even to receive presents. It frightened you more than ever. You went off and bought her something that she would not be able to resist—diamonds! You got a diamond brooch and you took it down to the hall that evening. But still Isabel wouldn't talk to you—when you knocked on her dressing room door she sent you away. So…"

"You've left something out," said Sugar Daddy. "When I arrived there was a telegram from Earl. He had got some job or other and he was ditching me: he was not coming down to the pageant. I couldn't think who should take his place; and then I realized that I should have to. It didn't matter: I was used enough to riding, out in "the Malay" as poor Isabel would have called it, and heaven knows, I knew all the movements of the pageant. And then I thought, I would have—have a bit of fun with Isabel: give her the brooch in some amusing way so that she wouldn't refuse it. I wrote that silly verse, all in two seconds, and left it with the brooch in the tower where she would find it at the last minute. Then I collected the Red Knight's armour, and went on and did his part in the pageant."

"I see," said Cockrill, slowly. He prompted: "And then she fell."

"And then she fell," said Mr. Port. His pudgy cheeks shook like jellies at the thought of it. "I was petrified, I sat there on my horse, staring: nobody moved, nobody did a thing, it seemed like hours. I didn't realize that she was dead, of course: God knows I never dreamed that she'd been murdered. I thought she'd just fallen over the balcony: fainted perhaps, I don't know what I thought… At last I came to a bit, somebody had to do something and I got down and went to her and turned her over. Till that moment, I swear no thought of myself had come into my head."

"But you saw at once that she was dead?"

He looked like a poor little mole sitting there in his brown summer suiting, with his little hands clasped before his rounded breast. "Her face was so terrible! Yes—I realized that she was dead. I was pretty sure she was dead. I turned her over, very carefully and then I saw my brooch in her dress, and sticking up out of the neck of her silver gown, a piece of white paper. I realized at once what she had done: she had picked them both up in the tower, and having nothing else to do with it, she had thrust the note down the front of her dress. All of a sudden it came to me that it would be found there and if there was an enquiry into the accident—as I thought it—everything would come out. So I tried to take the note. My cloak was all round me, nobody could see what my hands were doing. I tried to pull the paper out; but the pin of the brooch was through it, I couldn't get it free. I was frightened. I got up, and stood back looking down at her: and I realized how serious it was all going to be. The papers would get hold of the silly little verse, and my poor wife—" He broke off, wretchedly. "It came to me that nobody knew I was there: nobody could recognize me. I staggered away as though I were too upset to bear it, and out in the stalls I scrambled out of the armour and I came back pretending that I had been in the audience." He looked at Cockrill anxiously. "You do believe me?"

"The question is," said Cockie, "will Inspector Charlesworth believe you?"

"You don't think—you don't imagine he'll still think that I pulled her down and—and killed her?"

"There's no saying what he'll believe," said Cockie, sourly.

Mr. Port clasped his little paws. "But you'll tell him for me, Inspector: you'll convince him that there was nothing criminal, you'll explain everything—he can't but see how well it all hangs together, he can't but realize that every word I say is true?" He beat with his folded hands against his own breast. "You'll tell him, Inspector, won't you? You'll tell him for me?"

"What exactly do you want me to say?" said Cockie, cautiously.

"Why—that *I was the Red Knight*," said Mr. Port.

And at the Yard itself Miss Betchley, having sat the prescribed ten minutes on the green bench, wilting in the sun, now poured forth her soul to Inspector Charlesworth. "I want to tell you the truth, I want to confess the truth, that *I* killed Earl Anderson and *I* killed Isabel..." She sat on the edge of the wooden chair in the little office and clasped her hands before her on the clip of her bag. She had a strange white look about the eye-sockets, and the bones of the knuckles were pearly against her brown hands. She said: "I know that you don't think I could have done it, Mr. Charlesworth: but the simple truth is this—that I was the Red Knight."

Mr. Charlesworth did not know as yet of the rush for the position of the Red Knight. He listened attentively, his eyes on her troubled face. "I killed Anderson, Inspector. It was all just as you worked it out: of course I have no alibi for that time. Next day it was Isabel's turn. I knew of course that Anderson was dead: I took his place. That was what I had planned. I joined the knights when they rode through the arch and took his part in the pageant. I was out on the stage all the way through. I pulled Isabel down with the ropes and strangled her: and then I blundered away through the Assembly room. It would all have been terribly simple: I should have gone through to the Assembly room, slipped out of the armour while they were all bewildered and doing nothing, and gone to my post on the other side of the door. Then I'd have appeared, saying that the Red Knight had come blundering out and—what on earth had happened? But there was a mishap. The body fell on the tail of the white horse and it came bolting through. I stood, as you worked it out, huddled against the wall, in my astonishment: and if Mr. Bryan saw me before he tumbled off his horse, he thought I was a suit of armour, propped up there. It wasn't a question of the spare suit being used: it was me in Earl Anderson's armour. But Mr. Bryan got knocked out by his fall: and when I saw that, I went on and got rid of the armour out in the horses' stalls and hurried back and began hammering at the door. It was easy to convince him that it was bolted on his side: he was dazed, and he believed what I said—he still thinks that it was bolted, he thinks that it came from him that the door was bolted—but *I* put the idea into his head when he was too stupid to understand. Everything else was just as you've worked it out. I'd taken the ropes off when I strangled Isabel, and pushed them under her skirt. That's all."

Perpetua had said that she heard whistling all through the earlier part of the pageant: had heard Miss Betchley whistling "Sur le pont d'Avignon." But Peppi had been through a bad experience just before, she had been found in a fainting condition: was it necessary that she had been conscious at all, was it not possible that she had been knocked-out and dreaming during the first ten minutes? It now seemed possible that it might be so. Charlesworth said: "Why do you come to me now, with this confession?"

She shrugged. "My job's done. I wanted to kill them both, and I *have* killed them. I thought I might get away with it and maybe I could have. But having done it, Inspector, I find I don't want to get away with it. I don't care any more, I have nothing to live for or bother about any more." She gave him a lop-sided little smile. "You protected me yesterday: you said I wasn't a man—and I'm not. But, Inspector—why does everybody assume that Johnny Wise's twin was a boy?"

"You are Johnny Wise's twin?" said Charlesworth.

She raised her head. "I'm Johnny Wise's twin sister: and *I was the Red Knight!*"

On their bench in the park Brian Two-Times and Perpetua sat idly in the shade—not holding hands because it was so hot. Perpetua told Brian about the night's adventure. "Now, in the broad daylight, I see of course, Brian, that it must have been all nonsense. The poor kid wanted to make himself important. But last night—one hasn't much sense of proportion in the early hours of the morning, has one? and I felt so helpless and frightened and all alone..."

"I am your protector, Peppi: you are not frightened if I look after you?"

"But you can't look after me in the *night*, Brian, can you?" said Perpetua plaintively: not really thinking.

Brian Two-Times looked as if that were just too bad.

They decided to go and get some lunch and got up off the bench and Brian collected his mackintosh and the black hat and was with difficulty restrained from putting them on, because an English gentleman surely would not walk about in Town without a hat and coat? He consented, however, to hang the mac over his arm and walk along twirling the hat on the bunched fingers of one hand. An envelope was jerked out of a pocket by this vigorous twiddling and he stopped and picked it up. "Oh, lord—a letter comes for me today to my digs and I put it in my pocket and forgot all about it. Such a hurry to see *you*, Perpetua, eh? He turned it over in his fingers. 'Express Messenger too! Oh dear! Who then is this letter from?"

"Open it and see," said Peppi. (*Rather* sweet of Brian Two-Times to forget his morning's post in his hurry to come and see her!)

Brian tore it open with a hooked finger. "Susan Betchley? Why then she writes to *me*?" As he hastily scanned the close lines, he said now and again: "My God! My *God!* Oh, this woman!" And when he was finished, folded the note and thrust it into his pocket: and his blue eyes were a million million miles away. He came back with a start to the London park and Perpetua. "Peppi—sorry, I must leave you. I must go now to Scotland Yard. I must tell that Charlesworth…"

"To Scotland Yard?" said Perpetua, astounded. "To tell

Mr. Charlesworth something? But Brian—all of a sudden like this—*what?*"

"That I woss the Red Knight," said Brian, and left her abruptly, striding away through the park with his bounding step.

Charlesworth gathered them all together in his office at the Yard: four contestants for the enviable position of Red Knight in a game of murder. Inspector Cockrill stood by to see fair play. Brian Two-Times cast his black hat upon Charlesworth's desk and his mackintosh over the back of a chair and confronted them, blue eyes ablaze. "Well—now—I confess to these silly murders! This good lady—she has upset my apple cart with her fine confessions." But at sight of her stricken face, he went over to her, and took her brown hand in his. "You meant for the best: but do you think I would let you confess to a murder to let me go free?" He addressed them all, and while he spoke he kept her hand in his. "This morning she sent me a letter: but I am in a hurry, I think nothing much of it and put it in my pocket. Just now I read the note. She has been thinking all night: sitting up writing all night. The heat has gone to her head—I think it has gone to all our heads. She tells me. 'I loff you!'" He raised her hand for a half-second to his lips. "For this—thank you, mad'moiselle: it is something for any man to be proud of. But, she says, she thinks I love somebody else: to love this lady also would be something to be proud of." He bowed in homage to an absent Perpetua. Cockie thought that if he would cut the cackle and come to the hosses he would really have something to be proud of after all. But the pieces of the puzzle were clicking like magic into their places: and the central figure stood firm.

Brian Two-Times came to the hosses. "She says that she knows that I am the murderer: she has known it from the first. She says that she realizes now that I am the brother of Johnny Wise. Johnny Wise had two brothers and a sister and a father and a mother. One brother was his twin: and the other brother was older than the twins—and I am that brother. My name was Bryant—not Brian: but I changed it when I came over here to murder Isabel Drew and Earl Anderson, and called myself Brian Bryan—Brian Two-Times as Isabel used to say. All this Miss Betchley did not know: she only guessed. What she knew was this…." He swung round upon her. "Tell them!" he said.

"It is all lies," she protested. "He's doing this to protect *me*."

Inspector Cockrill thought he had never seen so many people protecting each other in all his born days: but this was the real McCoy. He leaned forward, keenly interested; and a huge piece of the puzzle was settled in, once and for all. He waved the interruption aside. "Go on, go on!" Once they started on another exchange of compliments heaven knew when it would end.

Brian went on. "What she knew was this. She told you all that when the White Knight sat on his horse in his armour ten minutes before the pageant, she went up and spoke to him. That was true. But what she did not say was that he did not *answer* her. What she said called for no answer: she wished the White Knight luck or some such thing, and moved on about her work. When she said this, I seized upon it: I used it later, I said that she had talked with me. That was not true. To speak to a person and to talk with a person are two different things. Miss Betchley spoke to the White Knight seated on his white horse: but nobody answered her. And for a very simple reason—there was nobody there."

Sensation. But Cockie had had it all worked out long ago. "You had trained the horse to go round with the empty armour on his back?"

"I am used to horses," said Brian. "Yes, I trained him. I tried him several times: several times he has done that pageant alone: after all, he is a circus horse. If anything went wrong—if anyone had found out at the "rehearsals"—what harm? I am having a joke with everybody, I am pulling the leg of our good Mr. Port." He was obviously about to bow to Mr. Port. "Go on, go *on*," said Cockie.

"So the night comes. Anderson is dead—and now Isabel must die: Isabel or Jessabel which ever you like to call her. For me, she is Jessabel. I saw it all when first she introduced me to the pageant. The Tower! It was a pretty piece of justice: it was the finishing touch, an exquisite coincidence. As Jezebel she had lived: as Jezebel died, so she should die." His blue eyes blazed with a desperate sincerity: and for the first time, Cockrill thought: I believe the fellow's a little mad.

He seemed to have forgotten them all. He spoke staring straight ahead of him with the heaven-blue eyes. "I killed Anderson. This also was to avenge my brother, but it served a useful purpose: it left free the Red Knight's place in the pageant. I saddled my horse and placed my armour on it and gave the horse a whack: and in it went, and took up its position and patiently waited there. Meanwhile I changed into the Red Knight's armour and waited until the last minute so that nobody could question me: but Miss Kirk was wandering about hurrying up the knights, and I was afraid she would spot something. I turned my cloak inside out, so that only the white lining showed, and I pushed her into the little room and locked her there. I did not mean to hurt her and I did not: but murder was on my mind, and she was dangerous to my plans." He stopped. Cockie thought: Two minutes silence now, in respect for Miss Kirk!

"So I rode through," he went on, "and took my place as the Red Knight. The white horse took an empty suit of armour through the routine. And when the time came, I jerked the rope and down she came, and I dismounted and bent over her—and strangled her. But to my horror—things went wrong. The white horse bolted into the Assembly room. I decided I must follow it. I registered deep grief and got myself off the stage. Once in the Assembly room, I ran to the outer door and bolted it. Then I took off the red cloak and put on the white one that the empty armour had worn. Miss Betchley hammered at the door and I ran to open it: I think I put up a good imitation of a man dazed by a fall from his horse. We went through to the stage."

Charlesworth digested it all in silence. He said, at last: "But there was a second man. What about the knight in armour that passed you and Miss Betchley on his way out?—whom you both called up to now, the Red Knight?"

Brian held tightly to Miss Betchley's hand. "There was no second man. Miss Betchley was astounded and bewildered by all that was happening so fast. We hurry through the room to the stage: she does not know what horror she will find there. We pass, it is true, a suit of armour by the wall: when I suggest into her mind that a knight has passed us, she does not think, she takes what I say for the fact. Later, perhaps, she doubts: but by then she has observed something which she did not mention at the time—that the knight on the white horse did not answer her. And..." He paused. He said: "She is so kind as to say that she—likes me a little. She realizes: she knew my poor Johnny—she knows what a boy he was—this golden boy!—she knows these people in their own way have murdered him. She sees me not as a murderer but as an executioner. She keeps silence." He bowed to her again.

And with the bow, the last piece clicked into place. The figure of the murderer in the centre—the figure that had been there all along: the Knight in the red cloak or in the white cloak, which ever way you cared to regard him—Brian Bryan, a little mad, a little unbalanced by events under the régime of the Japanese, brooding for years in his concentration camp over the wrongs of his brother, "this golden boy." There were details here and there, in the background, little inconsistencies in the shapes of the supporting pieces of the puzzle—but here was the pattern of the whole thing clearly in shape—a flower-banked stage, a castellated wall, a cardboard tower, a foolish little balcony: glare of floodlights, upward shifting, ten knights in shining armour and flowing coloured cloaks, one suit of armour empty on a white horse with a white cloak... Cockrill remembered the tiny mounting of the heart one had felt at their first entry: jingling, jangling through the arch, right out of a fairy-book picture in childhood days—jingling, jangling through the arch, standards astream, cloaks flying, armour gleaming... Through the arch and straight down the stage towards him as he stood there in the audience: bright light focused on the leading knight, so bright that... So bright that...

The puzzle scattered into a hundred pieces: the central figure was flung from its place and lay uncertainly on the heap. The sky caved in, the scene collapsed, the pattern was a kaleidoscope of colour without form. Cockrill got up slowly out of his chair. He pointed at Brian Bryan a thin finger stained mahogany brown by the smoke of countless cigarettes. He said: "The whole thing's a fabrication from start to finish. You were no more the Red Knight than I was. You were the White Knight: and if you were the White Knight, you couldn't have killed Isabel Drew. You are not a murderer. I can prove it myself." And he turned to Charlesworth and said: "He rode down towards me on the white horse, wearing the silver armour, holding the white standard, with the white cloak flying. The light flooded full upon him. His visor was up." And he looked into those twin pools of blue and dragged it out of himself reluctantly: the central piece of the wonderful pattern of the puzzle. "I saw his eyes," he said.

Chapter XIII

AND SO SUSAN BETCHLEY HAD MADE HER HEROIC GESture: and Motherdear had made his heroic gesture, and Mr. Port had made his heroic gesture and Brian Bryan had made his. And inspectors Cockrill and Charlesworth, propping up a shiny bar in a shiny pub chosen by Charlesworth were for once in complete agreement—they could have slain the lot of them.

"I thought we had him," said Charlesworth, putting back a pint and asking the dazzling barmaid for the same again. "But of course if you say he definitely was on that white horse…"

"The whole thing is a lot of nonsense," said Cockie, not using the word nonsense. "He made it up as he went along. The white horse was not carrying an empty armour: I saw his eyes as he rode towards me. And he was not the Red Knight. Remember what young Exmouth said…"

Charlesworth turned back the pages of his memory for what George Exmouth had said: "I saw Brian Bryan look at me with a sort of alarm and astonishment when his horse began to buck about: and then I looked across at the Red Knight and—the eyes that looked back into mine were brown." He said: "Of course George Exmouth now says that he was the Red Knight."

"That's all nonsense," said Cockie, again not saying nonsense. "Because if he was—who was the Blue Knight?" They replaced their tankards at the same time, and he made a twiddle over them with the hand holding the inevitable cigarette, for the same again. "And then," said Charlesworth slowly, "there was the matter of the cloak."

"The cloak?" said Cockie.

"The Red Knight's cloak. Bryan says he was wearing it on the stage. But it was found lying out in the stalls somewhere: and he now says that he never went beyond the Assembly room—the Betchley met him at the door and they both turned back and came through the arch again. All right, how did the cloak get out?"

"Oh, yes, the *cloak*," said Cockie. (He had somehow allowed that matter of the cloak to slip by.)

And so it was all done: smashed to smithereens, the neat puzzle built in round the central figure of Brian Two-Times in the armour of the Red Knight. Charlesworth said: "It was like a jig-saw: I had it all fitted together as neat and nice as you please..."

"Oh, yes," said Cockie, politely, trying to attract the attention of the young lady behind the bar for the same again.

"I seemed to get a few clues, and then suddenly the central figure just dropped into place. That was the odd part—that I got the murderer first, and everything seemed to be working in round *that*."

"Always fatal," said Cockie, severely.

At home in Kent the pubs were little and low-ceilinged and many of them dark with the uneventful history of a couple of centuries: with scrubbed wooden counters and patches on the walls where the old gas brackets had very recently hung: not neon and bakelite with a bright, clean duster polishing away every friendly, familiar sign of a ring of beer. At home in Kent, the people behind the bars were friends of getting on for half a century: Bill and George and Joe, and Mrs. Bill and Mrs. George and Joe's nice friendly lump of a young daughter… And when Inspector Cockrill appeared, there also appeared like magic a pint of his usual, and another pint appeared when that pint was gone… None of your little bits of skirts-and-blouses sidling up opposite you and asking: "What was it you was having?" "Bass," he said crossly. "B-a-double-s, Bass: perhaps you've heard of it?"

"Sarky," said the barmaid, reproachfully indulgent of the impatient customer.

Charlesworth was, as usual, blissfully unaware of under-currents. He chattered on ruefully about the fearful errors into which he had fallen, and what his Chief was going to say. Cockrill thought of another session of the conference missed, and wondered what *his* Chief was going to say. "The way I had it," said Charlesworth, "he came home bent on revenge just as he made out, with all the trimmings: fixed up the noose round the window—they were always clambering about the tower and fooling round, it needn't have been impossible—using two bits of rope to 'make it more difficult': got the brooch and wrote the poem…"

"No, no," said Cockrill. "Port got the brooch: and probably

wrote the poem too. He knew it off by heart. I think Port's story is probably true. He put the brooch in the tower for her to find, and..."

"Well, all right, so it was just a bit of luck that that had happened: it caused Isabel to lean out and look down at the Mystery Knight upon the left, and so it was easier to get her neck in the noose. He'd relied upon doing it when she bowed to the audience, or some time like that. So he yanked her down and all went as he said. Only now it wasn't that at all!" He could not help grinning at his own discomfiture.

It was almost exactly Cockrill's own discomfiture. He acquired an increased respect for this young man who had all this time been quietly coming to approximately his own conclusions—even though they might be wrong. He said, however; "My dear boy—you got the whole *thing* wrong way round! Take one small point—Port knew the words of the rhyme, therefore Port wrote the rhyme, but if Port wasn't the murderer how could he have known that the Knight upon the Left wouldn't be Earl Anderson? Unless his whole confession's true, and the Knight upon the Left has nothing to do with the murder at all." His tankard was empty. Charlesworth twiddled a finger in the general direction of the two tankards and the barmaid immediately refilled them with the same again. "They know me here," he said to Cockrill, with simple pride. "Good lord, that girl's probably known me for three months. It's nice to get an established pub and stick to it, I think, don't you?"

Under the influence of the third pint they became more genuinely friendly: and under the influence of the sixth decided that the only thing to do was to charter the horses for the evening, recall the knights, and lay on the whole pageant again, after hours tonight, and go through it inch by inch with a toothcomb; and by comparing and checking and questioning and timing surely, surely sift out some discrepancy. "And if this were a detective novel," said Charlesworth, buoyantly, "probably confront the criminal at the moment critique!"

"This is not a detective novel," said Cockrill. "In real life the police don't 'reconstruct the crime' so as to confront the criminal. These writer people never get their police procedure right."

"It would be so deadly dull if they did," said Charlesworth. "I suppose they reckon that their job is to entertain and not to worry too much about what could or would or couldn't or wouldn't have happened... After all, their books are just fun to read—not treatises on the law. However, the idea of putting our lot through their paces tonight is not so much to unearth the criminal as to eliminate the impossible..."

"They're *all* impossible," said Cockrill, shaking his head, staring down at the upturned end of his burning cigarette. "Let's face it. Susan Betchley was sitting on a stool outside a bolted door, whistling: Peppi Kirk heard her whistling, and it's wishful thinking to pretend that she didn't, to suit our own theories—*your* theories," he corrected hurriedly.

"And old Port had definitely an alibi for the time of Anderson's decoyment to his death, so his story about playing a jolly trick on darling Isabel may be quite true."

"And Brian Twice was on the white horse in full sight of the audience and never touched the girl at all."

"And Motherdear was on a *black* horse in full view of the audience and ditto," said Charlesworth.

"And Peppi Kirk was lying trussed up in a locked room, and Earl Anderson was lying under some bushes minus his head, and if Port's story is true there are two nooses to account for, and a spare suit of armour to be taken into consideration..."

And click, click, click, click, the pieces of the puzzle were tumbling over themselves to settle into place again... Cockrill turned to Charlesworth and his beady eyes were bright with excitement. "I've got it! The central figure—your central figure and my central figure—that wasn't this Brian Twice (Brian Twice indeed!)—that was—"

A bunch of Charlesworth's police pals were elbowing their way over to them in a state of friendly jollity. As far as Inspector Cockrill could make out, they were all called George. "This is old George, Inspector. And here, Inspector, this is dear old George. Oh, I seem to have left out George, Inspector. And this," said Charlesworth to his friends, "is Cockrill, Kent police. You remember he made a bit of a nonsense over that military hospital case down at Heron's Park..."

Click, click, click went the pieces of the puzzle, neatly dovetailing themselves until every space was filled and the picture laid out clearly in every detail before him. But when Charlesworth dismissed his jolly pals and turned to him, politely asking what he had been saying just before they turned up—Detective Inspector Cockrill, who had made such a nonsense of that case down at Heron's Park—simply couldn't remember.

The crowds had melted away. At ten o'clock, not relying upon the Clock of Flowers, the loudspeakers blared forth *God Save*

the King, and on the stands the languid figures of the demonstrators tensed themselves into an attitude all ready to spring
at the split second that the last note sounded: hooking down
canvas covers, lugging great shutters from the narrow cup-
boards, packing away merchandise into drawers and boxes,
spreading dust sheets, sweeping and polishing in readiness
for opening time tomorrow. The lights died one by one, and
footsore men and women in their resuscitated tropical kit,
and their cheap cotton dresses, crept with their last ounce
of energy down the stifling aisles for the final battle for the
bus and home: there to argue feebly over their wilting salad
and a glass of water with Eno's in it to counteract its sluggish
tepidity, the merits of Flee-flea Insect Powder and Bowels-
work Barley Sugar and the very last word in can-openers and
screwdrivers combined. "My order book…" "Commission
on two pounds ten…" "Walked right over and chipped in
with my customer, my dear, and I'd been working on him
for half an hour…"

Soon the stage was an island of light in the dim hall.
Nobody remained but Charlesworth with his men, and
Cockrill, and the five poor suspects and the nine supporting knights. Bill Clever, the groom, was minding the horses
out in the stalls. One or two caretakers and commissionaires
hung about—and that was all.

Charlesworth made them a speech. "This all looks very
sensational and what-not, but I assure you it isn't. I just want
to run through that pageant again, a couple of times and see
that we haven't missed anything: I don't propose to expose
anybody or arrest anybody or any nonsense like that. And I'd
rather, if you wouldn't mind, that you didn't talk about it to

the press boys. They go making a Thing of it and the public get excited and begin expecting results, and we all look silly." He looked very nice, standing up there, tall and slim, with his young face smiling rather deprecatingly and the caretakers and commissionaires felt quite fatherly towards him and vowed in their hearts to say not a word about it, not even to their old mothers, not even to their missuses in bed that night. Not so the nine knights, who said to each other in well aspirated Oxford accents that they might sneak a nice little puff out of this, and each secretly determined to rush *straight* to the telephone the *minute* they were set free, and ring up Associated Press and try if they couldn't make a couple of guineas. They had no wives: and if any of them had mothers they had long ago forgotten them in the bitter glory of being On the Stage and having had rather too little to eat for so long a time.

Though it was long after sundown, the air was stifling still. It seemed as if soon there must be a storm. So it was in the brightly lit centre of the vast hall. The knights waited listlessly about, the horses stamped bored hooves with a tinny jangling of harness, the cloaks and standards hung their heads, a flowerbed of colour, wilting in the sun. Outside it was hot, it was dusty, it was leaden and dull: within it was dusty and hot and dull as well. Inside and outside, they awaited the storm.

There was a crash of thunder: a rumbling cannon crash of thunder that jolted them all to alertness once again. And Charlesworth said, briskly: "Let's just run through the whole thing..."

Too tarsome, said the knights. Several of them had missed important meetings with Micky Balcon, to be here. Charlesworth took George Exmouth by the wrist. "You claim to have been the Red Knight. All right—this time you are: let's see how it goes."

He wrenched his hand away. "I take it all back now. I was just—making it up. I wanted to be—well, all right, I wanted to be important. I was just the Blue Knight on the other side of the archway: I sat there, I never moved…"

"So you say now."

He looked a little desperate. "But, look—I tell you, I saw their eyes. I couldn't have done that if I hadn't been there, if I hadn't been the Blue Knight. I saw their eyes, just before she fell. The White Knight had blue eyes. I saw them turn to me in alarm when the horse bolted, and I saw the Red Knight's eyes across the arch—brown eyes…"

"It's easy to say that now," said Charlesworth. He took the red cloak and chucked it to the boy. "Here, put that on: for this run through, you're the Red Knight. I'll be the Blue." He had had the horses brought down for the occasion, and now marshalled the knights into their old formation. Sergeant Bedd played the part of Isabel, the blue chiffon veil flowing from the tall hat, perched on his grizzled head. He ran skittishly through the crowd to the tower, and disappeared within. Brian Bryan on his white horse rode through the arch, and led his line through the evolutions of the pageant. They ended up in their tableau beneath the tower. Sergeant Bedd threw over a pillow to represent the departed Jezebel. The white horse trotted through the arch into the Assembly room: the knights were still. Charlesworth said to the Red Knight: "Dismount: and go to the body."

Motherdear sat his horse defiantly. "I never went near the body."

"Well, go near it now." The boy dismounted reluctantly and went and knelt over the pillow. The red cloak spread itself about him like a velvet tent. "Now get up and walk away through the arch."

Miss Betchley and Brian Bryan came through the arch on to the stage, George Exmouth crept back after them. He had taken off his helmet and he looked deathly white. Charlesworth said: "Well?"

"I've told you, I—I made it all up. I wanted to be important. I..." He broke off and then said passionately: "I just didn't seem to be anybody. I wasn't even suspected. I was only a kid that couldn't possibly murder anybody, let alone be in love, properly in love, enough to do murder... And then I—I made a fool of myself, yesterday, I accused Miss Betchley of being a man, and—well, I know I made a fool of myself... So I thought—I wanted Perpetua to think..." He stared wretchedly at the ground. "But I didn't do it. When I saw that I might really be accused I—I—changed my mind." To Perpetua, watching in her sort of vague pity, he said: "I thought I was in love with you: but I know now that even that wasn't true. I—it was just stupid calf love. And now—I can't even keep up the lies I told. I'm just a coward, I suppose, that's all..."

Perpetua put out her thin hand to him. She said: "I always think it's so brave of people to admit to not being brave," and looked about her, with a little smile, as though for applause. Brian Two-Times said: "I also." Blah, blah, blah, thought Inspector Cockrill to himself.

"It suits you to say all this now," said Charlesworth, coldly.

George looked about him desperately, all his new-found courage burned to ashes in this new flame of terror rising up out of a past that already seemed not his own. "All right, then—if I was the Red Knight: who was the Blue?"

Outside a thunder-clap shook the cardboard tower and swayed the cardboard wall and made the dusty floorboards tremble: and Charlesworth walked over to the black horse which still stood wonderingly with its forefeet poised on the wooden block, and said: "Well—tell us who you are!"

There was no answer: out of the blank shadows of the empty helmet, nothingness stared balefully out at them. There was no Blue Knight at all.

George took to his heels and ran.

Inspector Cockrill met him at the Assembly room door. "I thought you'd do that, my boy. Come along back with me." He led him, already spent and unprotesting, back to the stage. "You're a man now: you said so yourself. You must act like a man just a bit more consistently. The whole thing's hooey: nothing to be afraid of. Come on back." As they crossed the room he said: "The Inspector's only testing things: and he's tested this. *You* didn't walk off the stage that night: you were there when I climbed up. And if you'd gone off and somehow unobtrusively crept back, trusting that nobody would notice one more knight more or less—well, what about that empty armour? That wasn't on the stage when I arrived, and it didn't get taken away *after* I arrived, because the place was guarded. Come along now, and put a good face upon it. And be a man." He dropped his arm and strolled through the arch with the boy at his elbow and said off-handedly to Charlesworth: "Well—that wouldn't have worked, would it?"

"No getting rid of the armour," agreed Charlesworth at once. He gave George's shoulder a pat. "Hope I didn't put the wind up you?"

"Good *lord*, no," said George. He admitted: "Well—it did actually. I'm afraid I lost my head and behaved like a kid." But honestly, *hon*estly, it would be the last time!

A crackle of lightening lit for a moment the glass in the roof of the hall: thunder crashed overhead. Charlesworth said: "So it wasn't our George!" and he looked at the others, at Mr. Port and Brian Bryan and Susan Betchley and said: "Which of you?"

Charlesworth might not be expecting to make an arrest, but there were policemen posted all round the circle of light. And at something in his tone, they began to close in: imperceptibly, cautiously, with an unconscious menace tightening the ring round the bag. Charlesworth said: "One of *you!*"

Mr. Port looked back at him steadily. He said: "You have been over and over and over all this. Not me because I couldn't have killed Anderson. Not Bryan because he could not have killed Isabel. Not Miss Betchley because... because..."

"Because she had just failed to kill Perpetua," suggested Charlesworth pleasantly. And the ring closed in.

Cockrill took Perpetua's arm, gently, and stood beside her, holding her. As though for comfort, George Exmouth moved closer to them. It left Mr. Port and Brian and Miss Betchley alone together. Brown eyes and blue eyes and brown eyes again looked steadily at Charlesworth. He said: "All for one: and one for all!"

"And all for Johnny," said Brian softly.

The lightning flashed again: thunder rumbled away into

nothingness. In the bright light the nine knights stood staring, in the shadows the police stood close. Charlesworth repeated: "And all for Johnny!" He started to speak, very quietly. He said:

"Johnny Wise had a father and a mother and two brothers and a sister. He had a twin. Whether the twin was a brother or sister, we don't know. But he left them all to come to England; and in England he died. The Japanese net closed in about his family and they could not come home to avenge him. But they waited the day. When at last they were free, their plans were all made. Johnny's father: and Johnny's brother: and Johnny's sister. Johnny's mother was broken in her mind by all that she had been through—and by the death of her 'golden boy' and this also was to be revenged. Her illness delayed matters, perhaps: but finally they got her home, a poor sick creature with no memory of the past—and the day came.

"Three victims. Three murderers. A man and two women, who had been responsible for Johnny's death: a man and an old man and a woman to exact the penalty. They apportioned the work out accordingly. Johnny's brother to kill the man, Johnny's father to kill one of the women: Johnny's sister to kill the other. But first they must suffer. The threatening notes began.

"The young, the strong, the daring one must set the pace. So Earl Anderson was lured out to a quiet spot and there Johnny's brother murdered him and took a large kitchen knife and cut off his head…" He paused. Out of the shadows where he stood with Perpetua and George Exmouth, Cockrill repeated softly: "*And cut off his head!*" Charlesworth did not notice the interruption. He went on.

"Mr. Port could have killed Isabel Drew: but he couldn't have killed Earl Anderson. Well, that was all right—Earl Anderson had been attended to. The next evening, as the Red Knight, Johnny's father dealt with the lady whom Mr. Bryan refers to as Jessabel..."

"Not always," said Inspector Cockrill.

"... and she also paid the price. The white horse bolted through and it was a ticklish moment while they wondered if it would upset their plans—but it didn't. They were all conspirators together, out there in the Assembly room. Johnny's brother and sister met at the door and cooked up a nonsense about the door being bolted, because it must be impossible for *her* to have killed Isabel: and Johnny's father crossed with them as they came out to the stage. Perhaps as they met they made the Victory sign."

Inspector Cockrill thought that Charlesworth might well spare them the frills. "All right, all right, all right," he said. "And then?"

"And then the last of them, the worst of them, the girl whom Johnny had loved and who had betrayed him and sent him to his death—then her turn came. But first she must suffer, she must be afraid, she must be played with like a mouse is played with and tortured by a cat... She must be threatened, she must have that vile obscene filthy, terrifying parcel sent to her; and all the time Johnny's brother must prove once again that she was faithless, that a few blue glances would cast the last of Johnny's memory out of her heart for ever. Any time would do for killing her. Johnny's sister had that matter in hand. They were all a little mad by now. Johnny himself—how delicately balanced between madness and sanity, that at the sight of his girl in another man's arms, he goes out and kills himself without waiting for explanation or regrets!—Johnny's mother, tipped over the edge of normality because her son is dead. It was 'in the family' as they say to be just a little mad—delicately balanced, on the border line between the normal and the abnormal. Johnny's sister could take her time over her vengeance. Till Perpetua's turn came, everything must go according to plan: nothing must interfere before all three were wiped out and off the face of the earth. But now—the others were accounted for, she could take her time... The right moment has not so far shown itself. That's all. That's the only reason that Perpetua Kirk is alive today."

Silence. On the glass roof a patter of raindrops scampered like the feet of little mice, but otherwise there was silence. The outer ring of the police, the inner ring of the nine knights, gaping, the seven in the centre, Charlesworth facing Mr. Port and Brian Bryan and Susan Betchley, Cockrill standing to one side of them, his hand on Perpetua's arm. And suddenly Perpetua spoke. She said: "Brian—tell me that this isn't true!" and broke from Cockrill's restraining hand and ran to him and caught his hands in hers.

He bent down and swiftly kissed her. He said: "This is good-bye, Peppi." To Cockrill he said: "You know—don't you?"

"Yes," said Cockrill: and he took three paces forward and caught Perpetua by her narrow wrist.

Chapter XIV

AND SO ONCE MORE INTO THE ROUTINE OF THE PAGEANT:
and for the last time. Once more, and for the last time, the
lights blazed down on the shining armour and the flying cloaks
and standards and the jingle-jangle of the knights. "Take it
from the beginning," said Cockrill. "Get out of the armour.
Start all over again." He said to Charlesworth, perfunctorily:
"Is this O.K.?"

"I suppose you know what you're doing?" said
Charlesworth, not very hopefully.

"You and your family parties!" said Cockrill.

"Well, it could be. We still can't find a thing out about any
of them—not a sausage. Records have all gone to blazes, in
the Far East, of course: practically everybody new on the job,
and you cable out a lot of questions about a chap and they
cable back, 'Never 'eard of 'im.' So I thought…"

"It was ingenious," said Cockie, kindly. He dragged
Perpetua with him by the wrist, and she went unprotesting, her face deadly calm among the protests of the rest.

He ignored them all. "Let's reconstruct it just once more. The knights rode through into the Assembly room. She left them gathering there, and took with her the spare suit of armour—nobody would notice it if Perpetua Kirk was seen moving armour about—it was for just that kind of job that she was there. Nobody pushed her into any room: she went into the room herself, and there climbed into the armour. In the armour she rejoined the knights in the crowded Assembly room. They rode off through the arch caving her there—propped against the wall, probably, to look like an empty suit of armour…"

"But she heard me whistling," said Miss Betchley, faintly protesting.

"Of course she heard you whistling: of course she could tell us the tune. She heard you through the door of the Assembly room."

For the last time, the knights filed through the archway to the stage. Charlesworth followed them. He stood to one side, watching their evolutions, Sergeant Bedd at his side. A figure in armour appeared for an instant at the window far above them: the pillow came hurtling through the air and fell at the hind legs of the horse, the horse duly bucked, and a moment later dashed through the arch. Charlesworth followed. Rider and horse were standing in the centre of the room with Cockrill at the bridle: and half-way across the room, leaning against the wall, was a figure in armour. Cockrill said: "The White Knight came riding through: he fell, he was dazed: he noticed nothing odd about the suit of armour propped against the wall. She had bolted the door on the inside: he heard Miss Betchley hammering at it and he got up and staggered over to it, and let her in." He left the White Knight and went over himself and opened the door to her. The archway filled with knights, curiously looking on. Cockrill did not move them back. He had finished with demonstrations. He said: "Mr. Port, as the Red Knight, came through the room and passed out: and Miss Betchley and Mr. Bryan went through and on to the stage. For quite a long while, the Assembly room was empty: and in that time she was out of her armour and into the little room and had locked the door on herself and thrown the key under it to slide into the corridor." And he turned to her, still grasping her wrist. He did not go into any histrionics, not Cockrill: but he said to her quietly, and reasonably, yet somehow savagely: "What was anybody's desire for vengeance compared with yours? Johnny Wise might have a mother and father and brothers and sisters to grieve for him: but for you he was the lover, he was your future, he was everything in life that you had. I remember you then, Peppi, in those old days." He waved a hand towards Brian on the white horse. He said: "I was saying to Mr. Bryan the other day—you were a merry little grig, happy and confident and very much in love. And suddenly all this is swept away from you. They get you tight, you don't know what you're doing and—the light goes out of your life. And without light you blunder through your world for years, too apathetic with grief and remorse even to cut yourself free from the two people who extinguished your light for you. Until one day—until one day you find that they're plotting against you again: are conspiring together so that Earl Anderson can go through the form of marriage with you, having already a wife; and Isabel Drew suck you both dry from that day forward by blackmailing him on the strength of the truth she knows. That woke you, Perpetua didn't it? Mad! Talk about Johnny's people being mad—who was more mad than this poor Ophelia of a girl, drooling round with the memory of her sorrows and her remorse and her growing desire for vengeance…" And suddenly he stood back from her, and made a sign to Charlesworth. And Charlesworth went up and stood before her and said: "Perpetua Kirk, I am arresting you for the murder of Isabel Drew and of Earl Anderson and it is my duty to warn you…"

A voice said, quite pleasantly: "Oi!" And Brian Bryan stood in the doorway of the Assembly room, with a revolver in his hand.

Chapter XV

AT SIGHT OF THE REVOLVER, A TRIUMPHANT GLEAM DIED out of Charlesworth's eye. He glanced for a moment at Inspector Cockrill and was mollified by the stricken look on the old man's face. Cockie moved over to Perpetua. He said. "I'm sorry, child," in a voice that humbly kissed her hand. Peppi did not look at him: her glance never left Brian Two-Times' face. Brian moved a little and with the swing of his body, the revolver moved also, pointing directly towards her. He said: "You see—it was true that when I kissed her it was 'good-bye.'"

There was no trace now in his voice, of a foreign accent.

Charlesworth repeated the warning. Brian flung back his head and laughed delightedly. "As for arresting me—come and get it!" His blue eyes shone with mocking laughter, but all the time the single black eye of the revolver watched every move for him. Behind him the doorway yawned: he sidled into the room until his back was against the wall—no getting taken in the rear for Brian Two-Times!

They stood watching him: glancing now and again at

Charlesworth to see what move he could make. Charlesworth looked about him, saw in the edge of the shadow his men at the ready. But ready for what? They were unarmed: and he knew that Brian was going to shoot his way out. He played for time.

Brian swung to Miss Betchley: the black eye of the gun fixed itself upon her—a wary eye, ready at a second's warning to swivel away upon the danger point. He said: "You knew—didn't you?"

"I knew it was true that you were Johnny's brother," she said. "Twin or not."

"Johnny's twin is mad," said Bryan: and Cockrill saw there again the light that had blazed in his eyes when he had said, in the office at Scotland Yard when he had pretended to be the Red Knight—that Jezebel had deserved to die; when in his passion of pain and sincerity he had forgotten for a moment to call her "Jessabel." "He was always delicate: he never could go about with Johnny very much. Then when Johnny came to England without him to join up—that broke his heart. But he was proud of Johnny: he saw him as a shining hero, going forth to battle, and if Johnny had died 'with the sword in his hand' he would have accepted it. Well, Johnny died; but you all know how. And so Johnny's twin is mad: a drooling, blubbering, witless creature that lived through the Japanese occupation when sane men died, and now is cooped up in a madhouse, capering like an ape about his little room, and all running to flabby white fat..." He paused. He said: "It was not only on Johnny's account that Earl Anderson and Isabel Drew were to die. This is what they paid for: and this is what Perpetua Kirk would have paid for, only..."

"Only that I explained to you that she, at least, was innocent in that matter," said Cockie. "She was as much injured as Johnny: she was to be pitied—not blamed."

The eye of the revolver glanced his way. "*You're* a clever little man," said Brian, admiringly. "You knew that after that, whether I was a murderer or not, she would be safe with me. And I wasn't a murderer: I meant it when I told you that. These creatures killed my brother: the law couldn't deal with them, but out in the East, we've learned in the past few years to constitute ourselves executioners, when necessary." He said to Perpetua: "It was too late then—I'd already sent off the head. But I did what I could to prevent your receiving it—mark that up in my favour. I came in the morning, but it hadn't arrived by that post: another threatening letter was there, but I couldn't get it—the cleaner hung about. And anyway—I had to go on doing these things a bit—it would have looked funny if all threat to Perpetua Kirk had stopped the moment I was made to realize that she had been innocent. I saw to it that they didn't frighten her. I took the telegram I myself had sent her when they phoned it through, and didn't say a word to her about it: only told the police."

Click, click, click went the pieces of the puzzle: leaping in their places, settling down again. The revolver focused its eye on Charlesworth: "When did *you* finally guess?"

"This morning when you confessed all that nonsense about being the Red Knight," said Charlesworth. "It was a brilliant stroke that—confessing to a method that was almost watertight—with all the time a loophole for wriggling out of! You made the story sound good: you explained a lot of things that in fact were true. But it was gilding the lily to tell us gratuitously that your name was really Bryant, with a 't.' For heaven's sake!"

Brian Two-Times burst out laughing again. "Gosh, I had fun over that!—and some bad moments too, before I could afford to have fun, before the first part of the job was safely done. As if it weren't enough to have Jezebel christening me Brian Two-Times, this old image here"—he waved the revolver at Cockrill, "has to innocently up and call me Brian Twice. Brian Bryan. Brian Twice, Bryant Wise!" He went off into his pleasant, easy, genuine laughter again. "I thought any moment you'd tumble to it," he said.

Charlesworth could not help grinning a little. He wondered how Inspector Cockrill liked being called an old image. Poor little man—building up this wonderful fairy story about poor Peppi Kirk! Perpetua had had an alibi for the Anderson-luring that long ago had counted her out: for while the man in Piccadilly had been phoning Anderson, Isabel Drew had put through a call to Peppi, in her own room. But these old boys oop from t' country, they doddered on and on and never seemed to know when they were beat. He glanced at the little inspector with a commiserating air. Cockie followed every movement of his thought, and his blood boiled. Charlesworth said kindly: "I suppose you see *now* how it was done?"

"I saw all along how it was done," said Cockie coldly.

Nothing but the assembled company gazing respectfully upon Britain's wonderful police, prevented Charlesworth from saying, Oh yeah? He asked instead, sweetly: "And Miss Kirk?"

"Miss Kirk was a Ruse," said Cockie firmly.

"To bring about what?"

"To bring about the confession of Mr. Bryan. Or I suppose," amended Cockie, "we should now call him Mr. Wise."

"Wise after the event, Inspector, eh?" said Brian. They grinned at one another, pleased with this pun.

Charlesworth was not amused. "Well—so you did bring about a confession! It's a pity you didn't calculate on a revolver as well!"

Cockie's face fell. He said, however, not daunted: "Yes—we ought to have thought of the revolver! It was so much—so much part of the whole trappings: to carry a gun." And to Brian he said: "I believe everything you've told us. You came over to murder and revenge: but because murder is a nasty, sordid business, involving other innocent, ignorant people, and because you're not a nasty, sordid person, you—you relieved the ugliness and meanness with a—a sort of cloak of fantasy: your own white cloak, as it were… You clutched at the suggestion of Biblical symbolism, you took unnecessary risks, you made a sort of violent game of it all… You grew gradually wilder. Careful at first: you didn't want to get caught before you'd carried out the whole job. The murder of Anderson was simple, and cautious. You knew his telephone was out of order, but you sent him a note, perhaps or something, to ask him to be in a certain call-box at such and such a time: then you put through a call from Piccadilly to that box—talking of course in your ordinary voice, because you no more had a Dutch mother than I did. And—that was Earl Anderson. On the second night, you locked Peppi Kirk up in cold storage while you turned your attention to Isabel. The white horse went through the pageant alone—you'd trained him to do it: and meanwhile you bolted the door of the Assembly room so that you shouldn't be disturbed, and waited in the shadows at the foot of the tower stair. And at the moment you'd chosen, you went up quietly and—that was Isabel!" He stood with his brown fingers rolling an unlit cigarette, and looked up at Brian from under his bushy eyebrows. "One always wondered—*why throw the body down? But of course you had to get the empty armour back to you. You knew that the horse would be shocked by the fall—but wouldn't step backwards on to the body...*"

"One's always heard that they don't," said Brian chattily. "It was interesting—and a considerable relief—to find that it's true."

"...so you threw her down. The horse bolted forward through the arch. You caught his bridle, hauled off the empty armour and propped it in the place of the spare armour against the wall: and took the white cloak, and there you were—the White Knight again, just a bit dazed by a nasty fall from his horse! Miss Betchley hammered at the door and you opened it. You went with her through to the stage and stood beside the dead body of Isabel: and after a moment you reverently covered her with your white cloak. A charming gesture: to you a particularly charming gesture in its irony—especially as with the white cloak went the new white ropes that had tied the armour on to the horse. The empty armour on the white horse." And he went to the white horse standing patiently, nodding, a little away from them all: and put up his hand and tugged at the armour, and the armour dragged a bit and at last came down. A rope passed through one empty sleeve and up to the standard, rigidly fixed to the saddle; and another round the waist of the armour, under the white cloak down to the crupper at the horse's tail. Two lengths of white cord—each tied into a noose.

After the tinny crash of the armour—silence: silence but for the throbbing of the rain on the roof. The thunder and lightning had ceased: no sound now but the beat, beat, beat of the rain. And into the silence, suddenly, shrilling, the young voice of George Exmouth cried: "But I saw his eyes! There *was* someone on the white horse! *You* saw his eyes, his blue eyes, you said so yourself; and *I* saw them, just before the horse bolted; turned to me with a look of—sort of alarm and astonishment…"

"Well—not *his* blue eyes," said Cockrill.

"Not his eyes? Then…?"

And so the central figure of Cockie's jigsaw puzzle was established finally in its place—the figure that had turned out not to be Brian Two-Times after all: not exactly. Cockrill said: "How do you think Earl Anderson looked that night— when his kind friend, carrying him gaily off to the Golden Golliwog suddenly turned out to be—not so kind? I should think alarm and astonishment would be putting it mildly."

"You mean…?"

"I mean that there was nobody—no body—on the horse," said Cockrill. To Brian he said: "It was somehow out of character that you should have cut off the man's head for no reason: or just for the ugly pleasure of sending it to the girl."

"That was a red herring," agreed Brian, pleasantly. "I had to carry attention away from my real reason for possessing myself of the head. I wanted the late Earl to be my alibi on the horse: but you can't lug around an eleven stone body. A habit of carrying a black hat in one hand, however, and draping a mackintosh over one's arm, whatever the weather—so foreign!—covers a multitude of—heads. And for the rest…" He paused. And there rose up in all their minds, a vision of the hour after murder had been done: of the empty armour hanging in the Assembly room with the empty helmet on the peg above it: of Brian Bryan fretting and fuming in Mr. Port's little office, the golden hair, the blue eyes shining, the pillar of the throat rising out of the round rigid neck of the armour— the helmet tucked away nonchalantly, under one arm…

Silence again. Under the bright lights, they made three almost concentric circles—the police on the fringes of the shadow, the knights in their silly tin armour, rather hurriedly shifting their helmets from under their arms: the little central ring of the principals, gathered here together for the very last time—Cockrill and Charlesworth and Mr. Port and Miss Betchley and Perpetua and Motherdear… Two dozen people in three concentric rings—held at bay and helpless by the little black ring of the muzzle of a revolver: twenty-four pairs of eyes looking desperately into the single roving round black eye, the "evil eye" whose glance was death. Charlesworth did not quite see what was to happen next: and he was afraid. He was responsible for what happened to twenty-four people—and to a murderer—and he was afraid. He said to Brian Bryan: "What now?"

"Now 'good-bye,'" said Brian, pleasantly. "In a moment I shall be outside this door and down this corridor and if anybody tries to stop me, I shall shoot. I'm not afraid to die for this—I think that perhaps it's true that I am mad—that there is in my whole family a tendency to madness—that Johnny and I, as well as my poor brother, had all the seed of madness in us—because I don't care about dying: I'd hang by the neck till I was dead, and I wouldn't care a jot—now that the job is done. But I'm not going to ask for it. I've got everything laid on, for escape out of England—I've had it laid on from the beginning. I only waited to see justice done to this girl." He waved the gun towards Perpetua. "I thought Inspector Cockrill had spotted me when he said so significantly earlier this evening that I had cut off Earl Anderson's head: and soon after when he said that I did not *always* pronounce the name 'Jessabel.' So I sent on the empty armour in the last "run-through" and I was going to slip away then—only then he accused the girl." He grinned at Cockrill. "So your mistake has had some good effect, Inspector—for here I still am and with my confession all set."

"And with your revolver all set," said Charlesworth sourly.

"Yes," said Brian. And he pointed it slowly, with a sort of gay menace, all round the inner circle of them, and said: "And so—good-bye." He began to sidle back towards the door.

Charlesworth stood irresolute. He said to Cockie savagely: "I had the men all ready for him to bolt: they'd have caught him up outside. And now this. A pretty muck you've made of it for me!"

"Yes," said Cockie humbly. And he raised his grey head and said with a quiet determination: "We shall have to do something about it," and with quiet determination and as steadily began to move forward. To Brian he said in his grumbling old voice: "It's all up, son. You may as well give me the gun."

Brian steadied the revolver. "One more movement and I'll shoot. Have no illusions: I like you, Inspector, I always have, all along—but this is my life. Don't think I shall have any beautiful inhibitions about your charms or your inoffensiveness or your grey hairs—because I shan't! One step more and I give you my word—I shoot." He pointed the revolver at the little man's heart at blank range: and Cockrill continued quietly on his course: and Brian Two-Times fired.

Click, click, click went the chambers of the revolver, turning round upon nothingness: and in the brief interlude, Charlesworth and George Exmouth were at Brian's throat and pulling him down. The golden head submerged in a sea of knights in armour, of uniformed police: the blue eyes drowned beneath the battering of fists and elbows. He emerged from the melee and there were hand-cuffs upon his wrists—but his eyes were bright as stars. Charlesworth gave an order: and without a backward glance he allowed himself to be dragged away down the long, dark corridor—blue eyes shining, golden head held high, an executioner going to his own execution. And they who watched him knew that he would be hanged by the neck till he was dead, as he had said: and that, as he had said, he would not care a jot!

And in the middle of the Assembly room, Inspector Cockrill sat quietly on the floor where the scrimmage had landed him, and broke open Brian Bryan's revolver for the second time that day. "Wise *before* the event, you see," he said with ineffable sweetness to Inspector Charlesworth: and scrambled to his feet and slung his old mackintosh over his shoulder and slammed his shabby hat on his head. "Got to get home to bed now," he said. "Early start tomorrow. I'm going home to Kent." He added: "I'm afraid they're going to think I made rather a muck of that conference."

And with a satisfied twinkle in his eye, he stumped off into the night.

THE END

If you've enjoyed *The Death of Jezebel*,
you won't want to miss

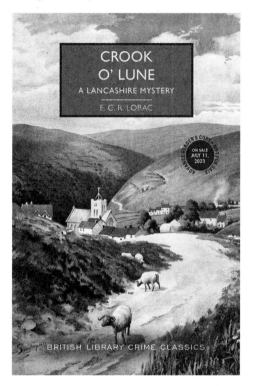

the most recent BRITISH LIBRARY CRIME CLASSIC
published by Poisoned Pen Press,
an imprint of Sourcebooks.

Praise for the
British Library Crime Classics

"Carr is at the top of his game in this taut whodunit... The British Library Crime Classics series has unearthed another worthy golden age puzzle."

—*Publishers Weekly*, STARRED Review,
for *The Lost Gallows*

"A wonderful rediscovery."
—*Booklist*, STARRED Review, for *The Sussex Downs Murder*

"First-rate mystery and an engrossing view into a vanished world."

—*Booklist*, STARRED Review, for *Death of an Airman*

"A cunningly concocted locked-room mystery, a staple of Golden Age detective fiction."

—*Booklist*, STARRED Review, for *Murder of a Lady*

"The book is both utterly of its time and utterly ahead of it."
—*New York Times Book Review* for *The Notting Hill Mystery*

"As with the best of such compilations, readers of classic mysteries will relish discovering unfamiliar authors, along with old favorites such as Arthur Conan Doyle and G.K. Chesterton."

—*Publishers Weekly*, STARRED Review, for *Continental Crimes*

"In this imaginative anthology, Edwards—president of Britain's Detection Club—has gathered together overlooked criminous gems."

—*Washington Post* for *Crimson Snow*

"The degree of suspense Crofts achieves by showing the growing obsession and planning is worthy of Hitchcock. Another first-rate reissue from the British Library Crime Classics series."
　　　　—*Booklist*, STARRED Review, for *The 12.30 from Croydon*

"Not only is this a first-rate puzzler, but Crofts's outrage over the financial firm's betrayal of the public trust should resonate with today's readers."
　　　　—*Booklist*, STARRED Review, for *Mystery in the Channel*

"This reissue exemplifies the mission of the British Library Crime Classics series in making an outstanding and original mystery accessible to a modern audience."
　　　　—*Publishers Weekly*, STARRED Review, for *Excellent Intentions*

"A book to delight every puzzle-suspense enthusiast."
　　　　—*New York Times* for *The Colour of Murder*

"Edwards's outstanding third winter-themed anthology showcases 11 uniformly clever and entertaining stories, mostly from lesser known authors, providing further evidence of the editor's expertise...This entry in the British Library Crime Classics series will be a welcome holiday gift for fans of the golden age of detection."
　　　　—*Publishers Weekly*, STARRED Review, for
　　　　The Christmas Card Crime and Other Stories

Poisoned Pen
PRESS

poisonedpenpress.com